All the Way Home

Nancy Ann Healy

Edited by Holly Schneider
Cover Design by Nancy Ann Healy

ISBN-13: 978-0692148723
ISBN-10: 0692148728

Chapter One: Wedding Day
Saturday, May 19, 2007

"What are you doing? We're going to be late!"

Sarah looked in the floor length mirror across the room and groaned. "I look ridiculous. Orange? Who picks orange as a wedding color?"

"It's not orange. It's Autumn Leaf."

Sarah turned to the sound of a familiar voice. In the doorway stood her best friend. For the next hour, that is who Katelyn Summers would be—for one more hour she would be Sarah's Kit Kat. After that, she would become Mrs. Masters. Sarah allowed her eyes to sweep over the woman who had traveled beside her during every major event for the last fifteen years. Katelyn Summers took Sarah's breath away. It wasn't the wedding dress she wore. It wasn't the way Kat's hair wound tightly in a twist, leaving light wisps of auburn to fall down the sides of her face that stole the breath from Sarah's lungs. Granted, the way Kat's dress hugged her hips, just enough to give a hint of the curves beneath was intoxicating. The way Kat's hair gently framed her face, a hint of gold and light brown adorning her eyes seemed to accentuate the mirthful brown that Sarah had helplessly lost herself in since the sixth grade. Everything about the woman standing in the doorway was alluring. Kat had captured Sarah's attention the first day Sarah had seen her nursing a skinned knee on the sidewalk. Katelyn Summers may have been the one that fell off her bike that day, but it had been Sarah falling every day since. Catching Kat's gaze, Sarah had to remind herself that the vision making her pulse quicken was not meant for her. Kat was on her way down the aisle to marry the second most important person in Sarah's life, her brother, Neil.

Sarah took a deep breath as her eyes met Kat's. "Jesus," she muttered.

"What about him? Bet he liked Autumn Leaf," Kat playfully bantered.

"You are gorgeous," Sarah commented without hesitation.

"Yeah? You look pretty spiffy yourself."

Sarah laughed and looked down at herself. "You think? What did you dress Neil as, a tree?"

Kat laughed. "You're nuts." She moved to embrace Sarah. "I love you, you know?"

"Yeah, only because it's required now that we'll be family," Sarah replied.

Kat pulled away and looked at her best friend thoughtfully. Sarah had been by Kat's side since her family moved into the neighborhood. That had been the day before her twelfth birthday. Sometimes, it felt strange to Kat, the reality that she was marrying Sarah's little brother. He hated that term, "little brother." He might have been a year and a half younger than his sister, but Neil was quick to remind them that he towered above them both.

Kat smiled at Sarah. Sarah resembled Neil in more ways than either Neil or Sarah cared to admit. The most notable difference between the two, was that Neil hovered a solid foot over his sister. Kat had always puzzled over how one sibling got the tall gene and the other seemed to have inherited a recessive short-stop chromosome. That's what she called it. The comparison horrified Sarah, which delighted Kat endlessly.

Neil and Sarah shared a head of wavy, dirty-blonde hair and blue eyes that often sparkled with a hint of green or gray. Kat had always marveled at the mischief that twinkled in Sarah's irises. Sarah's eyes seemed to whisper hints of a mischievous scheme. Kat admired her best friend. To most people, Sarah Masters possessed the girl next door look, unassuming and approachable. Her outward appearance caused strangers to underestimate Sarah at times.

Kat often mused that Sarah was the most complicated and the most genuine person she had ever known. It was an odd combination when Kat thought about it. Sarah's interests were endless, and when she set her mind to something, Sarah was undaunted in her pursuit to master it. It didn't matter if that thing was playing the guitar, becoming a lifeguard, receiving acceptance letters from every college she had applied to, or learning how to make baskets. Basket making—that one had intrigued Kat. Why, she had asked Sarah, did a law student want to learn how to make baskets? Sarah had shrugged. "Never know when you might need one," she said.

Kat sometimes teased Sarah that Sarah took her last name a bit too seriously. But if Sarah was determined, she was equally loyal and genuine. Kat found it amusing that Sarah's academic and athletic successes seemed to overshadow the prankster, the comedienne, the comforter, and the adventurer. Those were the pieces of Sarah that moved Kat beyond words. In some ways, Kat was glad that other people failed to see all of Sarah's layers. It seemed to solidify their bond, and Kat never wanted to imagine her life without Sarah in it.

"Hey," Sarah grabbed hold of Kat's arm. "Where'd you go? I lost you there for a minute."

"Oh, sorry," Kat apologized. "I was just thinking."

"I'm not sure you're allowed to do that on your wedding day," Sarah joked. "Not particularly if my brother hopes you show up."

"Cute," Kat replied.

Sarah grinned.

Kat leaned in and kissed Sarah on the cheek. "Thank you," she whispered.

"You should—thank me, I mean. You are most definitely the only person I would dress up as a pumpkin for."

Kat rolled her eyes. "It's Autumn Leaf, you fool, not pumpkin. And, besides no pumpkin I know looks that good in a dress. I'll be lucky if anyone sees me once they get an eyeful of you."

"Trust me, Kit Kat, everyone in there will be looking at you." Kat's eyes began to fill with tears. Sarah cleared her throat, hoping it might somehow banish her emotions. Her feelings were riding dangerously close to the surface, and they seemed determined to find a pathway to her mouth. She had no intention of letting Kat see how painful this day was for her. All eyes would be on Kat, including Sarah's. That was the truth.

Sarah was sure that once she saw Kat walking down the aisle, everyone in the world would disappear. For Sarah, that had happened years ago. Today would serve as another reminder that while Sarah only had eyes, ears, and a heart to love Katelyn Summers, Kat's heart belonged to someone else. The only person Kat would see once they left this room was Neil. That was Sarah's stark reality, driven home again like a knife through the heart. She needed to change the tenor of the conversation quickly. Kat's compliments had made Sarah more vulnerable than she was willing to allow.

"Well, look at it this way—at least, you don't have to worry about me stealing your man. I think they outlawed inbreeding like a century ago."

Kat giggled. "I'm sure Beth will be relieved," she said. "I know I am."

Sarah smiled. "Neil is a lucky guy," she told Kat.

"Yeah, well, Beth is a lucky lady. When are you going to make an honest woman out of her?" Kat teased.

Sarah nearly choked. She'd been with Beth Greer for three years. They met during law school. Beth had pursued the standoffish Sarah Masters relentlessly. She'd tried every tactic from romantic gestures to a period of showing complete disinterest to get Sarah's attention. Sarah didn't take the bait—not once. Not until the night that Sarah found herself stuck on campus with a dead car battery and a somewhat suggestive offer from Beth for a jumpstart. That night, Beth caught Sarah's attention. But hook, line, and sinker was not a scenario that Sarah planned to fall into. She'd grabbed the line, and every so often Sarah had to admit she felt the urge to let Beth reel her completely in, but she'd never succumb to the temptation. She let Beth cast the line while she continued to tug away at the other end. They shared a life together. They even shared a home. Still, Sarah was determined not to be "caught."

Kat had made more than a few casual comments since Sarah and Beth had arrived home for the wedding, suggesting that perhaps Sarah was next in line for the altar. Sarah couldn't blame her. After all, Kat had no idea that Sarah was in love with her. To Sarah, Kat was the ocean, an all-encompassing sea that surrounded her, washed over her, moved her, and served as the breath in her lungs. She needed the freedom to swim in that freely—the ocean that was Kat. Sarah loved Beth. Who wouldn't love Beth? Kat had pointed that out on numerous occasions as well, and Sarah had no argument against the sentiment.

Beth Greer was attractive, charming, intelligent, and one of the funniest people Sarah had ever met. She did love Beth. She loved being with Beth. She even loved being intimate with Beth. But, one thing remained missing. Sarah had never fallen *in love* with Beth. It sounded insane, even to her own ears, so much so that Sarah had made a deliberate effort to make herself jump, hoping she would fall freely into Beth's waiting arms. She tried to force herself to hold onto the line Beth cast and let Beth reel her in. She'd gotten close a few times. Each time, something held her back.

Sarah didn't need to examine the reasons why she held back. The reason was always clear to her, as clear as the ocean when the waves abated, and the sun illuminated the water—Katelyn Summers. Sarah tried to convince herself that she could fall in love again. But, as the years passed, she began to believe that she would either be forced to settle for a string of meaningless affairs or accept contentment in a comfortable friendship.

She had found that with Beth. They had a comfortable, amicable, and passionate relationship. Eventually, the truth always seemed to smack Sarah in the face like an unexpected surge in the tide. Contentment for Sarah equated to complacency. She had never settled for anything less than what she believed in or desired in life. Maybe that was selfish. Sarah knew what it felt like to be in love. Even if she could never express that to the object of her affection, she could also never betray the truth. Kat had been the love of her life for the last fifteen years. She'd never doubted it. She'd never questioned it. She'd also never spoken to a soul about it and she never intended to. Nevertheless, if she couldn't spend the rest of her life with Kat, Sarah could not imagine spending it with any other person either. At some point, it would become hollow. She knew that. Looking at Kat right now, she was reminded of that reality in the most painful way imaginable.

"Beth is more honest than you and me put together." Sarah turned back to the mirror, effectively dismissing the idea. "Really, Kit Kat? Orange?"

Kat sighed inwardly. Sarah never wanted to talk about commitment, not Kat's to Neil, and certainly never about Sarah making a commitment to Beth. "I just want you to be happy," Kat muttered.

Sarah closed her eyes, gathered her emotions, and turned around. She took Kat's hands and looked in her eyes. "Are you happy, Kat? Today? Are you happy?"

Kat smiled and nodded.

"Good. That makes me happy," Sarah said. "Now, come on. You are inheriting a lot more than The Iron Giant down there."

"Yeah? Like a sister, huh?"

"Or like a mother-in-law," Sarah jibed.

"I love your mom."

"Me too, but she is my mom," Sarah reminded her friend. She took Kat's hand and started to lead her away.

"Sarah?" Kat stopped abruptly.

"What?"

Kat shook her head. "Nothing. Save me a dance, huh?"

Sarah winked. *Why does she always insist on dancing with me?* It never failed that Kat would grab Sarah's hand and want to twirl around the floor like a couple of fools, just like they had when they were kids. "You supply the beer. I promise you a nice dip."

"Oh, no," Kat said as she accepted Sarah's hand. "There will be no dipping after beer."

"Why not?" Sarah asked.

"Dipping after beer is called dropping Kat. No way. This dress cost a fortune."

Sarah laughed. "And, you call me nuts?"

"Because you are, you fool."

"Ah, who is more foolish—the fool or the fool who lets her do the dip?" Sarah asked.

"Geek."

"Diva."

"Am not!"

"So are."

"What on earth are you two bickering about now?" Deborah wondered.

"We're not bickering, Mom. I'm just pointing out to your daughter-in-law here that she is a diva," Sarah told her mother.

Kat stuck out her tongue at Sarah.

Deborah Masters laughed raucously. Little had changed between the pair descending the stairs since they had first met. Had it not been for the wedding dress Kat was wearing, Deborah could have flashed back ten years. "Do me a favor, Sarah?"

"Yeah, Mom?" Sarah asked as she offered Kat a hand down from the last stair.

"Don't interrupt her vows with any suggestions," Deborah deadpanned.

"Me?"

Deborah rolled her eyes and turned her attention to Kat. "You look stunning. He'll be lucky if he stays on his feet."

"Wouldn't be the first time he fell on top of her," Sarah mumbled.

Kat was oblivious to Sarah's muttering. Deborah, however, had caught the sentiment behind her daughter's mumbling and jabbed Sarah lightly in the ribs. Sarah flinched and fell silent.

"Your mother is in the den," Deborah told Kat. "Go on. Sarah will be right there."

Kat looked at Sarah skeptically. Sarah flashed her a winning smile. "Contrary to popular belief, I can walk in these heels. I promise."

"It's not your heels I am worried about," Kat replied.

Sarah sighed. She knew exactly why Kat did not want to move from her spot at the bottom of the stairs—Jean Summers. While Kat's mother had never said anything in front of Sarah, everyone was aware that she had reservations about Kat's engagement to Neil. Sarah guessed that was because Neil was a working stiff. He could have gone off to college. Neil had been a decent student. Neil loved cars. He had no interest in college. For as long as Sarah could remember, all her brother had ever wanted to do was play with cars. Over the years, Matchbox and Hot Wheels had given way to tinkering under the hood of their parents' cars. Eventually, Neil had graduated to rebuilding classics in the garage.

Sarah's parents had always supported both their children's choices. Sarah had opted for college followed by law school. Neil had chosen a career as an auto mechanic. That was not what Jean Summers had envisioned for her only child. Sarah was positive that Neil's profession was the driving force in the woman's objections to a marriage between Kat and

Neil. Sarah shrugged them off whenever Neil or Kat would express frustration. She asked them one simple question: do you have to live with Mrs. Summers? When Kat and Neil would answer in the negative, Sarah would shrug. "Then who the hell cares what she thinks? She'll get over it when you have a kid." And, that is precisely what Sarah believed.

"Kat," Sarah stepped forward and smiled at her best friend. "Don't let her ruin this day for you, okay? Nothing she can say changes anything."

"She won't say anything if you are there."

"I'll be right behind you. She won't have a chance to say hello and you will see me standing in the doorway."

Kat nodded nervously. "Don't trip on your way," she called back as lightly as she could manage.

"I don't trip unless I've had beer! And, that's only when I dip!"

"Eighth grade, Mrs. Noyes. You so do!"

Sarah chuckled and turned back to her mother. "What?"

"Have you seen Beth yet?" Deborah asked.

"No. I talked to her a while ago. Why?"

Deborah smiled knowingly. "She looks amazing. I think she's anxious to see you."

Sarah's smile did little to light her eyes. "Well, we'll see how smitten she is when she sees I am dressed as a pumpkin."

Deborah grabbed her daughter's hand. "She does love you, Sarah."

"Good thing since she lives with me."

Deborah nodded, and kissed Sarah on the cheek. "Not Beth," she whispered. "She does. I know you wish…"

Sarah pulled back. She needed to put space between them and she needed to end her mother's musing. "I need to catch up to the bride," she said as she broke away. Deborah sighed and let Sarah go.

"You about ready?" Jack Masters put his hands on his wife's shoulders. Deborah stood watching Sarah's figure disappear in the distance. "You can't make it okay for her," he observed.

Deborah took hold of his hands and held them tenderly. "No, I know. I'd give anything if I could. Today is going to break her heart," she said.

Jack pulled her closer and she willingly let him support her weight. "I think that happened a while ago," he said.

She turned in his embrace and closed her eyes. "I wish she could let it go."

He kissed her on the forehead. "You know, she will never say a word."

"That's what makes it so hard to watch," Deborah replied.

"Deb, I don't think it would have mattered…"

"No, that's not what I mean. I mean that she will pretend she's over the moon for Kat and Neil."

"That's a bad thing?" he was puzzled.

"For them? No. For her? I don't know, Jack. I can feel it. She hides it pretty well. I know she's lonely. I just wish she could find someone."

"Once she steps away again things will even out. Seems like she and Beth are on that track," he observed. Deborah smiled unconvincingly. "You don't think so?" he wondered.

"I hope so," she said. Deborah took Jack's hand and led him toward the backyard. "Give it a chance, Sarah," she mumbled.

"What?"

"Nothing," she replied. "Let's go see how the groom is holding up."

———— • • ————

Sarah's eyes closed as two arms encompassed her waist.

"You look amazing."

Beth. Sarah sucked in a ragged breath. *What is wrong with me?* Sarah had been asking that question for years. What was wrong with her? She took a deep breath and turned to face the woman holding her.

"So do you," Sarah complimented her girlfriend. It was the truth. Beth's eyes flickered with bursts of desire, awe, and love whenever she looked at Sarah. It made Sarah's heart ache. She leaned in and placed a gentle kiss on Beth's lips.

"Thank you," Beth whispered.

"For?"

Beth smiled.

Sarah sighed inwardly. Beth Greer wasn't only intelligent, she was intuitive. Sarah was sure that any half-witted fool could see the way she looked at Kat. Everyone it seemed except Kat. Beth's smile was laced with sorrow. Sarah set out immediately to quell it. She cupped Beth's cheek and smiled genuinely. "Dance with me?" Sarah requested.

"I thought you'd never ask."

Kat's eyes fell on Sarah in the distance.

"Beth seems lovely," Jean Summers commented.

Kat's eyes remained riveted to the sight of Sarah holding Beth close on the dance floor. "She is," Kat said.

Jean studied her daughter silently. She'd long suspected that Sarah's feelings for Kat were much deeper than Kat realized. She had suggested that to Kat a few times. Each time, Kat had dismissed the notion with a chuckle. "Just because Sarah is a lesbian doesn't mean she is attracted to me, Mom," was always her reply.

Something in Kat's eyes as she watched Sarah in the distance made Jean wonder if Kat had realized the truth all along.

"Why the sad face?" Jean wondered.

"I'm not sad."

"No?"

Kat turned to her mother. "No. I just wish I knew why she holds herself back."

"Sarah?"

Kat nodded.

Jean looked over at Sarah and Beth. Beth was laughing, and Sarah was smiling. "What do you think she's holding herself back from?"

"Commitment," Kat answered.

"She seems happy."

Kat barely managed a smile. Sarah could seem many things to most people. She was a master at outward appearances. Kat could sense that something was bothering her friend. She wasn't sure what was driving the anxiety she felt pouring off Sarah. Beth was clearly head over heels for Sarah, and Kat could tell that Sarah loved Beth. She couldn't understand why every time the subject of making a commitment arose, Sarah would balk.

"I guess."

Jean put her arm around Kat's shoulder. "Where is your husband?"

Kat grinned. It sounded strange to hear Neil referred to as her husband. It made everything suddenly real. Kat glanced down at the ring on her finger before searching the room for Neil. She laughed. Neil was surrounded by three of his friends. She was surprised when he turned to meet her gaze and lifted his beer. Kat offered him a smile and a wink.

"Maybe you should go steal him," Jean suggested.

Kat was surprised at her mother's overture. Jean had never been Neil's greatest fan. Kat sometimes wondered if her mother would ever be happy about her marriage. Maybe she'd finally given up the ghost.

"Maybe I should," Kat agreed. She set off to take her mother's advice.

Sarah captured a glimpse of Kat looking up at Neil. Her eyes closed in resignation. Let her go, Sarah. Let her go.

"What do you say we skip out of here?" Sarah whispered in Beth's ear.

"Now?"

Sarah pulled back and held Beth's face in her hands. "Now."

Beth's grateful smile might have stopped Sarah's heart had it not already plummeted into a deep abyss earlier that day. She took Beth's hand, determined to escape before anyone had the chance to stop her.

"Let's go."

"Where's Sarah?" Kat asked her mother-in-law.

Deborah offered Kat a warm smile. Kat did love Sarah. There was no question about that. It might not have been what Sarah desired, but anyone with eyes could see the bond that the two young women shared. She had little doubt that Sarah's disappearing act would hurt Kat's feelings. Deborah also understood Sarah's need to flee. She had to give her daughter credit. Sarah had painted on a smile the entire day. Deborah wasn't sure how many people could detect the sorrow beneath the cheerful façade her daughter painted on. She could see it as clearly as the sun in the sky. It blazed through Sarah. Deborah had learned that sometimes people saw what they needed to see. She was confident that Sarah understood that as well.

"She and Beth escaped out the back a while ago," Deborah explained gently.

Kat's smiled faded immediately. "She left?"

Deborah smiled.

"Without saying goodbye?" Kat was stunned.

Oh, Kat. That's exactly why she left. It's her way of saying goodbye.

"I can't believe she left." Kat looked at her feet.

"You know Sarah," Deborah said. "She puts on a good show, but crowds are not her favorite thing."

"She knows everyone here."

Yes, she does, and that makes it worse.

"She could have said goodbye."

Deborah nodded. "I think you were with Neil. You'll see her tomorrow at brunch before you two leave."

Kat's forced grin tugged at Deborah's heart. Sarah was Kat's best friend. She remembered her dreams of a wedding day. To be sure, the center had been Sarah's father. But there was another component to the dream—sharing it with friends and family. Deborah understood. Kat had imagined laughing and celebrating with Sarah. Sarah had played that part the best that she could. Deborah had willed her tears into submission when she listened to Sarah offer a toast to Kat and Neil. It had been witty and heartfelt. It had also lacked honesty. Honesty was not a luxury that Sarah had. Deborah had watched Sarah and Kat over the years. She had thought that in time Sarah's fascination with Kat would fade. That time had never come to pass. Sarah had accepted her role in Kat's life, and she did her best to play it to perfection. Some things were just too much to bear.

Deborah put her hand over Kat's. "This is your day," she said. "I suspect she just wanted to give you that."

It was the truth. Deborah was confident that Sarah's need to distance herself was as much for Kat and Beth's benefit as it was for self-preservation. No one could wear a mask forever. Watching the person that you loved more than anyone marry your brother had to push every limit in Sarah's life. Kat couldn't see that. Sarah tended to command attention in a room without trying. She had always possessed that ability. Deborah hoped her explanation might make sense to Kat.

Kat nodded. "I'm going to go find Neil."

Deborah let out a heavy sigh as Kat walked way.

"Is she okay?" Jack Masters inquired.

"She was looking for Sarah."

Jack nodded. "I think Sarah needed to get away."

"I know. I also know that is something Kat doesn't understand."

"Maybe that's for the best."

"Maybe. Things have a way of coming out, Jack. I've never known any secret to stay buried forever no matter how deep the hole it's placed in."

Jack pulled Deborah into his arms. "Well, that may be. Things tend to work out, though. Sarah looked happy when she waved to me in the parking lot earlier."

Deborah smiled. *And, sometimes, looks can be deceiving.*

———•◆•———

"Are you really leaving tomorrow?" Kat asked Sarah.

"Bright and early. Why?"

"I don't know. I guess I figured you'd want to spend some time with your folks."

Sarah folded a few shirts and placed them in her bag. "Beth has a big interview on Wednesday. It will be good for her to have a day to relax before that. It's not much of a time difference, but it does make a difference."

"Do you still like it there?"

"In California?" Sarah sought clarification.

Kat nodded.

"I guess."

"You guess?"

Sarah shrugged and zipped up her suitcase. "It's got its good points and its drawbacks like every place else."

"Like here?"

Sarah's heart dropped in her chest. *Like here.* "Like every place, I'd imagine."

"Do you think you ever might?" Kat asked.

"Ever might?"

"Come home."

Sarah took a second and looked around her childhood bedroom. She raised a playful eyebrow at Kat. "Umm… Did I miss something?"

"You know what I mean."

"I do. I don't know," Sarah answered honestly.

"Because Beth is from California?" Kat asked.

"No," Sarah replied. *Well, Sarah, at least you can be honest with her about that much.*

"You don't miss home?" Kat asked.

Sarah sat down on the edge of the bed. "I miss home. But home isn't the same anymore."

"I don't think it's changed all that much," Kat offered.

Sarah smiled. It hadn't changed all that much for Kat. Kat's parents lived in the same house. Sarah's parents lived down the street. Neil was a permanent fixture in Kat's world as he always had been. Kat was about to start teaching at the school where she and Sarah had tormented teachers together with their laughter. Sarah's world had changed completely. That had begun the day that Sarah happened upon Kat and Neil in the back of Neil's truck. That day had determined the direction Sarah's life would take. Sarah chose to attend law school on the opposite coast. Home would never be quite the same for Sarah after that day. She missed her family. She missed Kat. Kat wasn't her Kit Kat any longer. For Sarah, Kat had come to define home. She needed to create a new reality. California had provided a place to begin.

"Kat," Sarah lifted Kat's chin with a finger. "It's not like you can't come visit me too."

"I know. We all miss you, though."

"I'll be home for Christmas."

Kat found it impossible to summon a smile. Life was not the same without Sarah. Christmas was months away. She missed Sarah. She was sure that Neil did too, even if he would never admit it. She decided to change the topic.

"So?" Kat urged.

"So?"

"What about you and Beth?"

"Good Lord. Are you on my mother's payroll or something?" Sarah teased.

"I just want you to be happy."

"And, that means I need to be married?"

"I don't know. Don't you want to be? I mean, you and Beth have been together a while."

"I'm not sure I'm the marrying kind."

"There's a kind?" Kat teased.

"Usually is."

Kat groaned with frustration. "I get it. Let it go."

Sarah winked. "Not everyone needs to be married and have 2.5 kids to be happy, Kat." The words escaped more harshly than Sarah had intended.

"I know that."

"That didn't come out the way I meant it."

"Yes, it did," Kat disagreed. "You've always thought that my dreams were lame."

That's not true. "No," Sarah said.

"Yes," Kat argued. "You've always wanted to conquer the world. Maybe some of us just want to live in it, Sarah."

Sarah had no desire to argue with Kat. She was exhausted. Kat would never understand. All Sarah had ever desired was to live in the world with Kat by her side. All her dreams centered on that one thing. She would have sailed the world or stayed right beside the lake if Kat had asked her too. Kat's life centered on someone else. That left Sarah with the need to create a new narrative.

"I don't think your dreams are lame, Kit Kat. Maybe there just isn't a whole lot of room for me in them now."

Sarah leaned in and kissed Kat's cheek. She stood, placed her suitcase in the corner, and walked out of the room leaving a stunned Kat to stare at the space she had just occupied. Sarah walked a few steps down the hallway and into the bathroom. She shut the door and fell back against it as her tears spilled over. *Time to go home, Sarah, whatever that means.*

Chapter Two: Collisions

Fourteen Years Earlier: Wednesday. June 13, 1993

"Come on, Sarah, let me ride it!" Neil begged his older sister.

"No way," Sarah replied.

"Why not?"

"Because you have your own bike—one with a bar."

"So, what? I'll let you ride my bike," Neil whined.

"Why do you want to ride a girl's bike anyway?" she challenged him.

"'Cause yours has speeds."

Sarah rolled her eyes. Neil always seemed to want to do everything Sarah did. Most of the time she was amused by her little brother. Occasionally, he annoyed her to the point that she wanted to throttle him. This was one of those times. It wasn't that Sarah minded sharing with Neil, she didn't. But, sometimes a twelve-year-old needed a little space. Twelve was older than ten after all. Neil had asked his parents for a BMX bike for his tenth birthday, and a super soaker. He got both.

"Why did you ask Mom and Dad for that thing?" she pointed to the shiny new racing bike that stood at the end of the driveway.

Neil shrugged. "All the guys want one."

"So, what? You're not all the guys," Sarah pointed out.

"Come on, Sarah. Please?" he begged. "Yours goes faster."

Sarah's lips curled into an evil grin. "What would the guys say if they saw you riding down the street on my ten-speed?"

Neil shrugged. "Nobody's gonna see, it's Wednesday."

Sarah shook her head, groaned, and swung her leg over to dismount her bicycle.

Neil's eyes brightened. "We'll trade!" he said.

"What makes you think I want to ride that thing?"

Neil grinned. "Bet I can beat you to the end of the street and back," he mounted a challenge.

Sarah's eyes narrowed. Dare her, bet her, challenge her—Sarah Masters suddenly became the most determined person on earth. A few times, her mother had gently suggested that Sarah take it easy on Neil. That idea was more horrifying to Sarah than the creepy My Buddy doll Neil insisted on sleeping with until a couple of years ago. It reminded Sarah of Chucky. Just the sight of it lying in bed with Neil gave her nightmares. Many nights, Sarah had plotted Buddy's demise. Any scheme to 'off' Buddy would have to be covert. Parents were not optional allies in this scenario, and for some reason Neil was attached to the thing. Sarah envisioned it lurking behind curtains and under furniture. She knew a thing or two about hiding in corners. Buddy would never put one over on her. Sarah had—by her own standards—achieved the level of expert when it came to skulking.

She frequently camped out underneath the large reclining sofa in their family room when she was supposed to be in bed. That would have been enough on its own to get her grounded. The fact that she had seen nearly every horror movie ever made would likely have gotten her banished from the television forever. Still, the risk of getting caught was half the fun. The truth was, Sarah cared very little about watching movies after bedtime, particularly not the films her parents seemed to enjoy. She sometimes wondered if her parents were pod people from another planet or maybe zombies on the loose. She imagined that one day they would turn on their children and eat their brains. No wonder she had nightmares! Why would anyone want to watch dolls with knives or boogey men in masks? It wasn't just creepy, it was downright alarming. Buddy's presence added to the horror. Suddenly, the perfect plan came into view.

"Tell you what," Sarah addressed her younger brother. Neil folded his arms and waited for her proposition. "If you beat me, I'll do your chores for the next two weeks—all of them." Neil hated chores, it was the perfect proposition.

"What if you beat me?" Neil asked.

Sarah shrugged. "You surrender Buddy to me—forever."

Neil swallowed hard. Surrender Buddy? There were limits to what even he would do for Sarah.

Sarah stood still, patiently awaiting his reply.

Neil sucked in a deep breath for courage and straightened his shoulders. "Deal," he said.

Sarah's lips curled into a devious smile. Goodbye, Buddy. Sarah hurled her leg over the seat of Neil's BMX bike. She giggled as Neil attempted to climb onto her ten-speed. "End of the street and back," Sarah said. "First one back to the end of the driveway wins."

"I'll call it off," Neil said.

Sarah shrugged. "Go ahead. Do you need a head start too?" she teased.

"No," he replied. "Ready?"

"Oh, I'm more than ready," she replied.

"Okay—on your mark, get set, go!" he yelled.

With the final word, Sarah and Neil were off. Within seconds Sarah had passed her little brother. She concentrated on the stop sign at the end of the street, determined to be victorious in her quest to rid the house of Buddy. She pedaled as fast as her legs would allow until she reached the stop sign at the end of the street. Sarah let herself coast slightly past the red sign and turned her bike around before starting to pedal for all she was worth again. Neil was closing in. She had to admit she was moderately impressed with his handling of her ten-speed.

"No way," Sarah muttered, standing her full weight on the BMX pedals and hovering over its handlebar slightly. She glanced back over her shoulder for a second to gauge her brother's progress. That's when it happened. With a crash, Sarah came to an abrupt halt. "Ow," she groaned. It wasn't until Sarah looked down that she saw the obstacle that had stopped her. She immediately forgot about the pain in her leg at the sight on the sidewalk less than a foot away. Sarah tossed Neil's bike aside and made her way to the dark-haired girl lying beneath a blue and white bicycle. "Hey," she called. "Are you okay?"

Katelyn Summers looked up at a pair of concerned blue eyes.

Sarah smiled at the girl. "Looks like you banged up your knee pretty good," she said.

Katelyn looked down at her knee and winced. Sarah moved Katelyn's bike aside and offered her hand to the girl. "Sarah," she introduced herself.

"You were going really fast," Katelyn said.

Sarah shrugged. "I was racing with him." She pointed to her brother as Neil rode up on her bicycle.

Katelyn grinned. "Is that his bike?"

Sarah laughed. "No." She looked back at her new friend. "Did you just move in to the Breer's old house?" she asked.

"Yeah. Sorry, I'm Katelyn Summers."

"Sorry about the collision," Sarah apologized. "You probably should clean that up," she pointed to Katelyn's knee.

"Um, you might want to do the same thing."

Sarah was puzzled. She followed Katelyn's gaze downward to a trail of blood running down her left leg. "I wondered why that hurt," Sarah commented. "Must've hit it on the pedal." She smiled back at Katelyn and then looked at Neil. "Take our bikes home," she instructed him.

"Why me?"

"Because I need to take Kat home," Sarah said.

"She said her name was Katelyn," he rebuffed his sister.

Sarah was ready to tell Neil that she would rid the world of Buddy herself if he didn't shut his mouth. Katelyn's voice startled her. "It's okay."

Sarah turned to Neil and gloated. "Just take the bikes home."

"Yeah, well—I won," he grumbled.

"No one won," Sarah disagreed. "And, if you want to keep that little companion of yours safe, you'll take the bikes back to the garage."

Neil swallowed hard and took hold of his sister's bike. Sarah snickered as the two bikes wobbled in his grasp. She picked up Kat's bike and smiled at her new friend.

"Thanks," Kat said. "You don't have to do that."

"Well, it was my fault."

"Not really. I sort of hit you."

Sarah shrugged. "I wasn't looking where I was going," she said. She pushed Kat's bike along as they walked. "So, you just moved in?"

"Yeah."

"You don't sound happy about that," Sarah observed.

"It's a long way from home."

"Where's home?" Sarah inquired.

"Virginia."

"Yeah, kind of a long way," Sarah agreed. "So? How come you are here now?"

"My grandma's been sick. My mom wanted to come home, I guess."

Sarah nodded. She looked up at Kat's house. "Mrs. Breer was a nice lady."

"She died?" Kat asked.

"Yeah. I guess her kids didn't want the house," Sarah explained. "Where do you want me to put your bike?"

Kat grabbed the handlebar of her bike. "I'll put it away," she said. "Do you want to come in?"

"Are you sure that's okay?"

Kat smiled. She found herself studying the girl before her. Kat had been dreading the move to Massachusetts. Her life had always been in Virginia. That is where her friends were. The only person she knew in this new place was her grandmother. Her father assured her that she would make new friends quickly. Kat had her doubts. Something about Sarah seemed to ease her fears. She was sure that she had never met anyone like Sarah before.

The lingering silence unnerved Sarah. "Um, Kat?" Sarah waved a hand in front of her new friend's face. "You didn't hit your head too, did you?"

Kat giggled and grabbed Sarah's hand. "Let's go inside."

Sarah let Kat lead her in through the front door of the house. A smile crept onto her lips. Twelve was not an age generally equated with wisdom. Somehow, Sarah Masters understood that with the clasp of Katelyn Summer's hand, her life had changed instantly and forever.

One Year Later

"Sarah, you can't," Kat whispered.

Sarah grinned. "Why not?"

"Steal Buddy?" Kat laughed. "I know you hate that thing, but it's just a doll."

"It is not just a doll. It's a creepy, evil, little dummy. Do you know about those things?"

"Sarah," Kat giggled.

"You saw the movie."

Kat shook her head. Sarah was the smartest and funniest person she'd ever met. Kat had never had a best friend. Now, she had Sarah. Most Friday nights, Kat slept over at the Masters' house. Sarah's favorite game was sneaking into the family room and watching horror movies without her parents knowing. Even at a sleepover, Sarah needed to create an adventure. School was no different. Sarah was seldom content to play a game the way it had been created. She enjoyed making as much of a challenge as she could out of the simplest things. Kat admired her. Being with Sarah made her feel important and special.

"Sarah, you can't," Kat implored her friend. "Neil will be crushed."

Sarah sighed. Kat never let her get too carried away with her plots. Kat was sensitive. Many of their schoolmates viewed Kat as quiet. Sarah laughed inwardly at the idea of Kat being shy or reserved. No one could make Sarah laugh the way Kat could. Sarah knew that Kat chose her friends carefully. That made being Katelyn Summer's best friend special to Sarah.

"That thing is dangerous," Sarah said.

Kat grinned. "Are you scared of a doll?"

"I'm not scared. I'm aware. Be aware, Kat."

Kat burst out laughing.

"It's not funny! Have you ever heard of the Warrens?"

"Who?"

"That couple that goes around getting rid of possessed items—you know—like dolls?"

Kat rolled her eyes. "You can't do it."

Sarah groaned. One way or another she was going to find a way to rid the world of Beelzebub Buddy. "Better hope he doesn't crawl into your sleeping bag tonight," she mumbled.

Kat lost all hope of taking Sarah seriously. Her laughter filled the room.

"What?" Sarah asked.

Kat looked at Sarah's stricken expression and fell back into a fit of laughter. Every time she thought she might catch her breath, she'd look up and glimpse Sarah's pout, and it would begin all over again.

"I'm glad you find this so funny," Sarah said.

Kat pulled Sarah down next to her on the floor. "I'll protect you."

Sarah's heart skipped several beats. She swallowed the lump that had suddenly formed in her throat. She'd been trying to understand the effect that Kat had on her. Sarah had loads of friends. Not one of her friends had ever made Sarah feel the way Kat could. She hated being apart from Kat. Sarah found herself checking the clock all day long at school, waiting for the final bell so that she could walk home with Kat. She lived for weekends when Kat would sleep over and they could stay up all night talking. As much as she longed to spend time with her best friend, Sarah had made a point of keeping her distance physically. For some reason, any time Kat touched Sarah, Sarah's pulse would quicken, and her mouth would go dry. When that happened, Sarah would find any distraction she could.

Kat giggled at Sarah's constant shifting. "I thought you needed protection?"

Sarah searched her brain for a response—any response. Kat was so close to her that she could feel Kat's breath on her cheek. Nothing—she had nothing. Her body seemed to be humming with energy and her mind had gone blank.

Kat kept giggling. She pulled Sarah closer and held her. "No more scary movies for you," she said.

Sarah's heart hammered so forcefully in her chest she feared Kat would feel it. *What is wrong with me?*

"Come on," Kat took a deep breath and let it out in contentment. "Tell me a story."

A story? "Umm… uh…" Sarah began to stammer.

"You always have a story," Kat said. She closed her eyes. "Come on. Tell me where we're going."

Sarah sucked in a full breath. She settled in next to Kat and let it out slowly. Kat loved it when Sarah would talk about all the places they needed to see. She felt Kat's head come to rest against her shoulder and smiled. It was intriguing. Being close to Kat could make Sarah's entire being erupt in nervous excitement one second and in the next Kat's presence could calm Sarah like nothing else in the world. Sarah closed her eyes. "Where do you want to go?" she asked Kat.

"Wherever you want to take me," Kat replied.

Sarah felt her lips curl into a smile. She imagined taking Kat everywhere. Sarah wanted to see the world. She craved adventure and there was no one she'd rather share any adventure with than Kat. "How about we go to London?"

"Do we get to ride on one of those buses?"

Sarah giggled. "That's what you want to see?"

"Well, yeah." Kat shifted and looked at Sarah. "They have two stories."

Sarah shook her head. Kat made her laugh. Of all the things Kat could find intriguing—castles, dungeons, sweeping estates, historic sites—the first thing that bounced into Kat's mind were double decker buses. A bus it would be. Sarah would ride a bus all day if that's what Kat wanted to do.

"Do you think we could ride the bus to a castle?"

Kat smiled. "Castles are good," she replied, nestling back against Sarah. "Are there princes at the castle?"

Sarah felt a strange tug at her heart. Of course, Kat would dream about finding her prince. Sarah closed her eyes again. Anything for Kat. "A handsome prince who slays dragons," she said.

Sarah swore she could feel Kat smile against her. She took a deep breath and started to spin her story, taking them both to another world, one that blended fantasy and reality, history and modern conveniences like buses.

"It's a long ride past green fields and small villages to reach the castle," Sarah began. "The bus bumped along the road—up and down—jostling them about as they watched the scenery pass by…"

Kat was content to let Sarah's voice carry her away. She never ceased to be amazed by Sarah's imagination. Sarah's room was full of books, most of them books Kat would never have thought to read without Sarah. Some nights when Kat slept over, Sarah would read to her. Kat delighted in Sarah's animated voices and the frequent explanations she needed to give about the story she was reading. Reading was a form of escape and adventure for Sarah. Kat understood that. It had left Sarah with a colorful imagination and a vocabulary far beyond her thirteen years. Kat wondered if Sarah might one day write one of the books she was so keen on reading. She hoped that if Sarah did, she would be able to lie right here and listen to Sarah read it. Her thoughts drifted to Sarah. I wonder what she'll do? Probably end up ruling a small country somewhere. Kat pictured Sarah wearing a colorful headdress sitting atop a makeshift throne surrounded by a tribe of men and women holding spears. She giggled.

"Are you listening?" Sarah stopped her tale momentarily.

"Mm-hm."

Sarah looked down at Kat's head on her shoulder and frowned. "You were dreaming, weren't you? You fell asleep again."

Kat sighed. She might have drifted off into another world. She decided not to give Sarah the pleasure of being right. "Well, if you'd hurry up and get to the part with the prince…"

Sarah huffed. "Right—the prince…"

July 10, 1996

Some families kept a swear jar, a place to deposit coins when your mouth ran away with your senses. Deborah often thought that the Masters should consider implementing a Kat jar. It seemed that one of her children was always in the window, eyeing the house just up the street. Hardly a day passed when Kat Summers did not appear on the doorstep looking for Sarah. The exception to that rule came each July when Kat left for a week to see her grandparents. Deborah dreaded that week almost as much as she knew her daughter did.

"Why don't you take a walk over?" Deborah suggested.

Sarah's shoulders slumped. "You know Kat's mom," she said. "She'll just say Kat is busy packing or something."

"You won't know unless you try."

"I called earlier, and she said Kat was busy."

"Well, that was earlier," Deborah offered.

Sarah turned to her mother, half hopeful and half forlorn.

Deborah smiled. "I have an idea." She beckoned Sarah to follow her to the kitchen.

"What kind of idea?" Sarah wondered.

"Well, I baked a couple of pies this morning. Why don't I wrap one up, and you can take it over to Mrs. Summers? Tell her I know how much Kat loves them, and I promised I would send one to her grandmother."

A mischievous sparkle took shape in Sarah's eyes. Her mother always seemed to know the right thing to do. They shared more than the same color eyes. Deborah Masters was interested in everything. At least, that's what Sarah thought. Her mother could be found baking pies in the morning, reading Tolstoy in the afternoon, and watching a horror film in the evening. Sarah thought that her mother could have been anything—an astronaut, a doctor, a movie star, maybe even the president. Her mom knew the secrets to the universe, Sarah was sure of it.

Deborah finished wrapping the apple pie she'd made that morning and handed it to Sarah. "Pie solves everything," she said with a wink.

Sarah nodded, a slight skip in her step returning.

Deborah giggled as Sarah practically leaped through the door and skipped down the street.

"Where's Sarah off too?"

"Where do you think?" Deborah asked her husband.

"Those two are inseparable. You know, they have a lot of success now with that?"

"What?"

"Separating conjoined twins," he joked.

Deborah's eyes stayed with her daughter. She sighed inwardly. Sarah was rounding the corner to sixteen. She suspected that her daughter's feelings for Kat differed from that of a twin for her sister.

"Stop worrying about her," Jack said.

"I wish I could."

Jack looked over his wife's shoulder as Kat appeared in the doorway up the street. He shook his head. "It's probably a phase," he commented.

Deborah reached for his hand and squeezed. *I'm not sure about that.*

———— ◆◆ ————

"I love your mom," Kat said.

"Me too."

"I don't know why my mom thinks it takes a whole day to pack."

Sarah shrugged.

Kat looped her arm around Sarah's. "Let's walk down by the lake."

"Our spot?"

"Our spot."

"I wish you weren't leaving," Sarah admitted.

"Me too."

"Really? I thought you loved going home to visit?"

"That's not home anymore," Kat said.

"But your family is there."

"I guess. It's boring there."

"Boring?"

"Yeah."

"It's boring here," Sarah commented.

"I don't think so."

"Oh, come on," Sarah said. "What is there to do here?"

"You just want to see the world," Kat replied.

"Don't you?"

"I don't know. I don't think it's boring here."

"Think of all the places we could go," Sarah said.

"Like?"

"I don't know. What about Greece or Rome?"

"You just hope you'll find one of those mythical creatures you're obsessed with," Kat poked.

"Who says I wouldn't?"

"You're crazy, you know that?"

"Maybe they aren't real. People thought they were once."

Kat giggled. Sarah possessed a vivid imagination. She entertained Kat for hours with the tales she created. Everything seemed to fascinate Sarah. Before Kat could finish a chapter in a book, Sarah had flown through it, and was onto another one.

"What's so funny?" Sarah asked as they approached their favorite, secret spot.

"I was just picturing you sitting at the top of a pyramid."

"The pyramids are in Egypt."

"I know."

"And, you cannot sit on top of them. That'd hurt."

Kat burst out laughing. How could life ever be boring with Sarah by her side? She didn't need to climb aboard a train, a boat, or a plane to visit exotic places. Sarah took her on an adventure every time they were together.

"You know what we should do when you get back?"

"What?" Kat asked.

"We should go explore that cave Neil found."

"A cave?"

"Sure."

"Aren't there bats in caves?"

Sarah shrugged. "Probably."

Kat shuddered and pulled Sarah down to sit next to her. "No thanks."

"Why not? Bats won't bite you."

"No way. You can go in. I'll hold a light or something."

Sarah laughed. "You'll go in."

"No way."

"Yeah, you will. I'll protect you."

"What if there are snakes?"

"Snakes don't live in caves."

"How do you know?"

"I know."

"What if there is a creepy man in there?" Kat asked.

"Neil's not old enough to be a man."

Kat poked Sarah.

"We could dispose of that creepy doll he still has in his closet in there."

"Sarah!"

"What? He's almost thirteen."

"It probably has sentimental value."

"Yeah, until it strikes."

Kat laughed. For three years, Sarah had maintained one goal—dispose of Neil's redheaded doll.

"You laugh now. Bats are harmless. Dolls…"

"Stop."

"One day, you'll see."

Kat laid her head in Sarah's lap. "Tell me a story."

Kat always wanted a story. "About what?"

"Anything?"

"The cave?"

"Anything but that."

Sarah snickered. "Why don't you tell me a story for a change?"

"I don't have any."

"Sure, you do. What do you daydream about?"

"Not bats and no cyclops either," Kat said.

"Okay, so no bats or creatures. Tell me."

"I don't know. Last night I had a dream about Prince William."

Figures. Another prince. "Oh, yeah? Was he slaying dragons?"

"No, but he did kiss me."

What could Sarah say to that? Of course, Kat kissed the prince. There was always a prince. There would always be a prince. Sarah swallowed the lump in her throat. "Tell me the story," she said.

Kat smiled and began to recount her journey to the castle.

Sarah closed her eyes and pretended that the prince was a princess. Why not? After all, it was only make-believe. She listened as Kat spun a story about a majestic palace, armor standing in the doorways, giant chandeliers dangling from vaulted ceilings, butlers and maids running about, and Kat wandering through it all, hand in hand with her prince…ss. She sighed with contentment.

Kat opened one eye. A peaceful expression swept over Sarah's face. *See? She does want to find a prince.* "And, then…."

———◆•◆———

One Month Later

"No way," Kat protested.

"Oh, come on! I'll go first."

"No way, Sarah."

Sarah put her hands on her hips. "Neil and his friends were in there while you were gone."

"Yeah? And, there are *bats*!"

"One or two."

"No."

Sarah huffed. "What if your prince got lost in that great big castle?"

"Very funny. And, castles don't have *bats*."

"How do you know? Castles are *old*. Now, come on! Where is your sense of adventure?"

Sense of adventure? Bats? Bats were not Kat's idea of adventure, more like horror. Sarah liked to push Kat's limits. "How do you know Neil really went in there?" Kat asked.

"He told me."

"He told you? Sarah…"

"What?"

Kat peered into the opening of the cave. Neil was a chicken-shit, at least, that's what Sarah called him on almost a daily basis. Neil crawling into a dark cave seemed unlikely. Neil telling his sister he'd conquered some quest she had yet to, however, made perfect sense. Kat shook her head. "I don't think it's a good idea."

"What's going to happen?" Sarah challenged her friend. "I told you, I'll protect you."

"Who's going to protect *you*?"

Sarah scoffed at the notion that she would ever need protection. No, not Sarah. Sarah was a conqueror. That's how she saw herself. Life was a mystery to be solved, a quest to be conquered, and a challenge to be mastered. Why was Kat so afraid of wandering into a stupid cave? Sarah scratched her brow, considering how to approach this current conundrum. Her mouth wrinkled in time with her forehead. She licked her lips and nodded her head. "Are you afraid of the dark?"

"I'm not afraid of the dark," Kat said.

"Most people are."

"Sarah, you don't know what's in there."

"Which is why I want to go in there."

"It could be dangerous."

"Lots of things are dangerous."

Kat groaned.

Sarah grabbed the flashlight she had brought and knelt down at the entrance to the cave.

"Sarah! Stop."

"You wait here."

Sarah disappeared into the darkness. Kat knelt down and peered inside. "Sarah!"

"It's deeper than I thought," Sarah called back.

"Come back here!"

"It's cool." Sarah shimmied through the narrow opening. She struggled to hold the flashlight and propel herself forward. Eager to find some hidden treasure, Sarah pressed on. The natural corridor widened slightly. She was sure she could see an opening ahead. Her pace quickened. She shifted when the gravelly path gave way to a large room, and flipped onto her back, shining her light in the air. "Bats!"

"What?" Kat yelled into the hole.

"I said, there are bats!"

"Sarah, get back here before you get hurt!"

"There's dozens of them!"

"Sarah!"

"I'm fine! You should see this, Kat! It's like something out of a horror movie!" Sarah called back. "I could totally throw Chucky in here."

"Please," Kat called again. "Sarah, please come back." There was no way that Neil and his friends crawled into the hole. Kat felt it in her bones. Neil would never go by himself. Sarah barely fit inside. Neil might have been a bit smaller, but… "Sarah!"

"I'll be there in a minute!"

How long was a minute? There was a minute, and then there was a Sarah Masters' minute— those could last for hours. Kat's pulse quickened as the seconds continued to tick. There were times when she'd like to throttle Sarah. A cave? Who did Sarah think she was—Gertrude Bell? Sarah had read a book about female explorers and adventurers. Afterward, she'd been determined to out-do every single one. She could help establish a new culture. Why not? After reading about Ms. Bell's exploits, Sarah had briefly maintained that she would become an archeologist. Although, Kat suspected that had more to do with watching *Indiana Jones* than reading about some woman who lived in Iraq. Whatever the reason, it was pure Sarah. The littlest things inspired Sarah to want to discover something new. It was the same reason she decided she was determined to master soccer. Pele. Her father had a strange obsession with Pele. Pele and Gertrude Bell. Why couldn't Sarah choose something else to intrigue her? Betty Crocker, perhaps?

Sarah wiggled to turn herself in the tunnel. Did it shrink somehow? Sarah huffed. "Damn."

"Sarah?"

"I'm coming back," Sarah shouted. "I hope," she whispered.

Minutes passed. Kat strained to see into the crevice Sarah had crawled through. It was futile. She took a deep breath. "Sarah?"

"I'm coming."

"You said that. *When* are you coming? Are you stuck?"

Sarah muttered a few curses. The last thing she intended was to tell Kat that she *was* stuck. A few more unmentionable words. Kat hated it when Sarah swore.

"Sarah!" Kat called urgently.

"Fuck!"

I knew it! Kat laid down on her belly and started forward.

The sound of rustling dirt and rocks startled Sarah. "Kat? Is that you?"

"Just stay where you are!" Kat yelled.

"Like I have a choice," Sarah mumbled. "Go back, Kat!" Kat would likely kill her if they survived this escapade. "I mean it!" Sarah called out.

"If we survive, I'm going to kill her." Kat wiggled forward. "Can you shine the flashlight?"

Sarah flipped on the light and pointed it ahead. Kat came into focus.

"What happened?" Kat asked.

"I think my foot is caught on something."

"Behind you?"

Sarah looked at Kat as though she were insane. "My feet *are* behind me."

Kat glared.

"Sorry."

"Can you shake it loose?" Kat asked.

Sarah shook her head.

A deep sigh preceded Kat's next idea. The passageway was wider where Sarah was. "Can you turn on your side?"

"I think so."

"Good."

"Kat, you can't. What if we get stuck together?"

"Then I guess we'll die in this stupid cave." Kat shifted next to Sarah and inched forward. "If a bat flies at me, I swear…"

Sarah couldn't help but giggle. Kat may have been furious, but she still made Sarah laugh. A cool head always prevailed when Kat was around. Where Sarah tended to rush head-first into things, Kat took the time to measure the pros and cons of a situation. "I should listen to her more."

"What was that?" Kat asked.

"Nothing."

Kat managed to grip Sarah's leg. She felt around in the darkness, praying that nothing slithered over her hand, or worse, her head. She dug her hand into the rocks around Sarah's foot. "See if you can pull it out," she told Sarah.

Sarah moved her foot a few inches. "Not yet."

"Shit," Kat grumbled.

"Did you just swear?"

"Shut up."

Sarah laughed.

"Keep laughing while we die in here with a hoard of bats!"

Sarah laughed harder.

"Sarah!"

"Sorry."

"Help me."

Sarah's heart skipped. "Help you?"

"Help me help you, you fool!"

"Oh…"

"Keep moving your foot."

Sarah did as she was told. She could faintly make out Kat's string of, "I'm going to kill her. Shit. Shit. If I die in here. I'm going to kill her. Shit."

Sarah finally pulled her foot free.

"Ouch!"

"Shit! Kat, are you okay."

Kat huffed. A foot to the face was almost as bad as a bat in the hair—almost. She jostled herself into a better position and pulled herself backward to face Sarah again. "You are so dead."

"Saved me just to kill me, huh?"

Kat rolled her eyes. "Let's go, Indiana."

"Who?"

"Just follow me out of this hole."

Sarah was a few seconds behind Kat. She was stunned when Kat threw herself into Sarah's arms the moment she emerged. "I thought you wanted to kill me."

"Don't ever do that again."

"What?"

"Try something that stupid." Kat began to cry.

"Kat, why are you crying? I'm fine."

"Shut up," Kat said. She held onto Sarah tightly.

"Kat…"

Kat pulled back and smacked Sarah in the arm. "You could have been killed!"

"Oh, come on. It was just a…" Sarah began to protest. Kat's glare stopped her. She nodded. "I'm sorry."

"You're not Indiana Jones."

"I could be…"

Kat held up a finger.

"Okay, okay. I get it. Thanks, by the way."

"For what?" Kat was still shaken. She wasn't sure what she felt more—relief or anger.

"Saving my ass."

"You are so lucky no bat shit on me."

Sarah's laughter lifted them both.

"It's not funny," Kat tried helplessly to stop laughing.

"I'm sorry, I've never heard you swear so much."

"I've never been that scared," Kat said.

Sarah sobered. "I'm sorry. I should've listened to you."

"What did you just say?"

"Oh, okay! You were right."

Kat gloated. She might as well enjoy the moment. In another day, Sarah would have some new scheme cooked up to get them both into trouble.

"You don't have to look so happy," Sarah said.

Kat took Sarah's hand. "Let's go home."

"It was pretty cool."

Kat shook her head.

"Well, it was!"

"I give up."

Chapter Three: Inseparable
April 24, 1997

"You're going to rule the world," Kat laughed.

"I don't want to rule the world," Sarah replied with a smile.

Kat turned on her side so that she could look at Sarah. Sarah was gazing up at the sky. Kat studied the whimsical expression on her best friend's face. Sarah was always thinking, always dreaming of faraway places, imagining journeys and adventures that Kat could scarcely comprehend. Sarah was fearless. Kat envied that.

"Yes, you do," Kat disagreed.

Sarah turned her head slightly and looked in Kat's eyes. "No," she said. "I just don't ever want to say I didn't try. I don't mean to rule the world," she explained. "You know what my dad says?"

"What?"

"The only regrets you'll have are not trying. If you want something, no one can make that happen but you. The only way you fail is if you fail to try," Sarah said.

Kat smiled at her best friend. "Well, that might be true, you've never failed at anything."

Sarah turned her attention back to the stars. "Maybe. I haven't tried everything yet to know if he's right."

"Why Harvard?" Kat asked.

"Because it's the best and no one thinks I can or will. And, if I can, I think I should."

Kat laughed. "You will."

"What about you?" Sarah asked.

"What about me?" Kat returned the question.

"Oh, come on, Kat. What do you want after we leave here?"

"Who says that I want to leave here?"

"Well, okay, but you must have things that you dream about—I mean other than going to the prom with Derek Brooks."

Kat snickered. "It's a start," she replied.

"Yeah, but a start to what?" Sarah teased.

"Listen, you could go with Derek yourself if you wanted to," Kat said.

Sarah wrinkled her nose. "No, thanks. I'd rather go with Neil," she joked.

"Weird," Kat commented.

"Why? Do you want to go with Neil?" Sarah asked.

"Why? Do you want to go with Derek?"

Sarah sighed. "I don't really want to go with anyone."

Kat's forehead crinkled in confusion. "What do you mean? You don't want to go to the prom at all?" she asked. Sarah made no reply. "Sarah?"

"Not really—no."

"Hey, if you really want to go with Derek, I'm sure I can find someone else to take me," Kat offered. "He'd probably rather take you anyway."

"I doubt that," Sarah said. "And, anyway I don't really want to go with anyone."

"Why not?"

"I don't know," Sarah replied.

"Yeah, you do. Why not?"

Sarah huffed. "It's like the last big thing in high school," she said.

"Exactly!" Kat answered. "You're like Miss School Everything."

"Miss School Everything?"

"Well, you are," Kat said. Sarah glanced at Kat and rolled her eyes. "Most Likely to Succeed, Ms. Soccer Captain, Ms. Debate Team… Come on, you can't make me go alone," Kat begged.

"Um, I must've missed something. How is you going with Mr. Perfection going alone?"

"Mr. Perfection?"

"Yeah—Derek," Sarah replied.

Kat flinched at the animosity in Sarah's voice. Sarah had never mentioned disliking Derek Brooks. Lately, anytime the football player walked by them or whenever Kat mentioned his name, Sarah's mood seemed to shift dramatically. Derek had fawned over Sarah since the eighth grade. Then again, most of the boys tended to follow Sarah around with puppy dog eyes. Sarah was beautiful, intelligent, outgoing, and she was aloof. Sarah's standoffish attitude seemed to make her even more intriguing to their male classmates. Kat understood that. Sarah was the most interesting person Kat had ever known. She doubted that she would ever meet anyone that could make her laugh, force her to think, or for that matter, challenge her patience more than Sarah Masters. You only got one best friend in life as far as Kat was concerned. Kat's was Sarah, and she had no intention of letting any boy come between them—ever.

"You don't like Derek much," Kat guessed. Sarah kept her eyes skyward. "I don't want to go without you," Kat said.

Sarah sighed and closed her eyes. Disappointment colored Kat's voice. Sarah could tell Kat was close to tears. She couldn't help how she felt. Sarah had no desire to go to the prom. She was not inclined go anyplace where she might be subjected to watching Kat dance with someone else, Kat being held by some boy, or God forbid, Kat being kissed in her presence. She'd endured that a handful of times over the years. It had always left her stomach churning and her chest aching. If Kat wanted to go, Kat should go. Why did Sarah need to be there too?

"Sarah?"

Kat's voice was meek and insecure. Sarah hated herself for being the cause of that. She pulled Kat over and felt Kat's head come to rest on her shoulder.

"You should go with Derek," Sarah said.

"What about you?"

Sarah could feel the flips beginning in her gut at the mere thought of enduring a night of Kat's arms wrapped around Derek Brook's neck. "Why is it so important to you that I am at the prom?" Sarah asked.

"What do you mean?" Kat shot up. "You're my best friend. I can't go to our senior prom without you there! It's not right. We're supposed to be together for all the big stuff."

Big Stuff—sometimes Sarah had to admit that she and Kat had drastically different ideas about what equated to *big stuff*. Derek Brooks would have been lucky to rate a pebble's weight on any importance scale in Sarah's world. Then again, proms wouldn't have fared much better than Derek. What did top the significance scales in Sarah's life was everything that meant anything to Kat. And, for reasons that Sarah found un-fathomable, Derek Brooks and a high school senior prom seemed to fall into that category for her best friend. She painted on her best smile for Kat's benefit, and pulled Kat back down onto the blanket.

"If it means that much to you, I'll get a date," Sarah promised. She felt a small sense of satisfaction in Kat's audible sigh of relief.

"I don't want you to go if you don't want to," Kat said sadly. "I just don't want to go without you there," she said.

Sarah heard Kat sniffle and pulled her closer. "It's only a dance, Kat. Why are you so upset?"

"It's not only a dance," Kat said. "It won't be long after that and you'll be gone."

"I won't be gone forever," Sarah said. "I'll be back at Thanksgiving. And, anyway, you'll be busy with classes too, and if you get your way probably with Derek," Sarah offered as lightly as she could manage. If she had the courage to be honest, Sarah would have told Kat right then that she loved her. Sarah hated the idea of being apart. The longest she'd gone without seeing Kat in the last six years was one week each summer when Kat visited her grandparents. Sarah dreaded that week every year.

"Derek isn't you," Kat mumbled.

Sarah closed her eyes. *And, I can never be Derek.*

⸻

Kat scanned the room for any sight of Sarah. A sea of tuxedos and bad prom dresses obstructed her view. Where did Sarah disappear to? She felt Derek pull her closer, and she stiffened.

"Stop worrying about Sarah," he told her. "She's not your date."

Not my date? That was obvious. Sarah seemed to grow more distant from Kat as prom night had approached. She'd wrangled a date and picked out a dress. She'd smiled for pictures in front of Kat's house, flashing pearly white teeth at the camera. They'd laughed over dinner, and Sarah had even joined Kat and their dates on the dance floor for a few songs. As soon as the music had shifted to a slower beat, Sarah had performed her vanishing act.

Derek held Kat to him, breathing in her ear heavily.

Kat felt ill. She liked Derek. He was handsome, popular, and funny. It seemed clear that his intentions for their evening differed from hers. She struggled to pull away in his grasp. "Derek," she said firmly. "I need to find Sarah." He gripped her tighter.

Sarah emerged from the bathroom and searched out Kat. Even at a distance, Sarah could see the evidence of Kat's discomfort. Derek's hands gripped Kat's arms. As Sarah, approached, she noted a hint of fear in Kat's eyes.

"What's going on?" she asked when she reached the pair.

"Where's your date?" Derek snapped.

Sarah held his gaze. "Last I knew, he was dancing with Jodie Pritchard."

"Don't you think you should go get him?" Derek asked.

"No." Sarah looked at Kat. She reached over and took hold of Kat's arm. "I need your help with something."

Derek glared. "Now? What do you need her help with?"

Sarah grinned maniacally. Several replies lingered on the tip of her tongue. The feel of Kat's arm looping around hers stopped her inclination to prolong any banter with Derek. She's never cared for him. By Sarah's account, he was cocky, abrasive, and entitled, all qualities Sarah found obnoxious. She guided Kat a step away and flashed Derek a smile. "It's girl stuff," she told him. "You should know *all* about that."

Derek bristled.

Sarah offered him a wink over her shoulder as she led Kat away.

"Can we leave?" Kat asked.

"Leave? Kat, you've been obsessing over this prom for months."

"Can we? Please?"

"Where do you want to go?" Sarah asked.

"Our place," Kat replied.

Sarah nodded. *Our place it is.*

"I am so not dressed for this," Sarah grumbled.

"You look beautiful," Kat said.

Sarah's pulse began to race. If only Kat meant that the way Sarah wished. She spread the blanket from the trunk of her car on the ground. "Did Derek slip something into your soda?"

"Why do you always do that?"

"What do I do?"

Kat shook her head.

Sarah collapsed beside her on the blanket. "What did I do?"

"You do look beautiful," Kat said. "Everyone's head turned the minute we walked into that hall."

Sarah's eyes swept over Kat. The moonlight glistened on the blue of Kat's dress, and it seemed to reflect in the gentle brown of Kat's irises. Beautiful? Kat was always telling Sarah how "beautiful" she was. It confused Sarah. No one in the world could ever hold a candle to Kat. Sarah was reluctant to tell Kat what she saw when she looked at Kat—what she felt. She smiled. "It's not me they were looking at."

"Yeah right."

"It wasn't," Sarah said. "It was you."

Kat's eyes grew teary.

"Hey," Sarah cooed. "What's with the tears?"

"You were right."

"I was right? What was I right about?"

"Derek is a jerk, and it was only a dance."

"Oh, Kat. No, I wasn't. Well, maybe I was right about Derek, but it was a lot more than some dance to you."

Kat sniffled. "We should have just come here."

"Well, we're here now." Sarah leaned back against the tree and pulled Kat into her arms. "I'm sorry, Kat. I know you wanted tonight to be special."

"It is," Kat said.

"I know this isn't the same."

"You made it special," Kat said. "You always make it special," she muttered.

Sarah kissed the top of Kat's head. "I just want you to be happy."

"Don't let me date any more jerks."

Sarah chuckled in spite of the knot in her stomach. The fact was, she was likely to deem anyone Kat dated a jerk. Kat could fall in love with a real-life Prince Charming, and Sarah would still place him squarely in the "jerk" category. It was selfish. Sarah knew that. No one would ever be good enough for Kat in her eyes. She would never be good enough for Kat, but if Kat ever thought to give her the chance, Sarah would move heaven and earth to make Kat happy. *Pipe dreams and fairytales.* Sarah sighed.

"Sarah?"

"Yeah?"

"What are you thinking?"

Feeling Kat against her, Sarah was tempted to tell her best friend exactly what she was thinking. She wished she could be Kat's Prince Charming. For a moment, she would indulge in the fantasy. Here, underneath a warm star-lit sky, Sarah would pretend that Kat was hers. She closed her eyes. "I hope your fairytale comes true, Kat."

"Promise me something?"

"Anything."

"Promise me that this will always be *our* place."

Sarah pulled Kat closer. "I promise."

"I love you, Sarah."

Sarah pushed back her tears. "I love you too, Kat."

<hr/>

Two Months Later

Why did the room feel so small? Sarah was sprawled across her bed, looking at the ceiling. It felt close, as if it were pressing in on her. Is this what they meant when they said the sky was falling? Was the sky falling? Were the walls closing in? She tried to take a deep breath. In two days, Sarah would be off to college. It wasn't an ocean away, and yet Sarah had a nagging sensation that it was too far—much too far. Who was she kidding? A mile away from Kat seemed like a continental divide. She closed her eyes. "I shouldn't go." A knock on the door forced a sigh from her lips. "Come in."

"What are you doing? Napping?"

Sarah pried one eye open.

"I thought you were packing?" Kat scanned the mess in Sarah's room. A pile of clothes was heaped on her desk chair. A large suitcase sat open on the floor. Two boxes remained completely empty. Nothing from Sarah's desk had been packed. The posters and pictures that Sarah had purchased for her dorm room sat in the corner in a pile. "Sarah?"

"I'm not going."

"To college?"

"Yeah."

"Don't be silly. Of course, you're going."

Sarah shook her head.

"Hey." Kat took a seat on the bed next to Sarah. "It's not that far."

"It's far enough."

"Sarah…"

"I should've stayed here."

"No," Kat disagreed. "You want to go to law school, Sarah. You've always wanted to see the world."

"Yeah, with you."

Kat grinned. "Well, we're not dead *yet*."

"It doesn't feel right."

"You can come home on the weekends. I can visit."

But will you? Sarah closed her eyes again.

Kat flopped down beside her. "Move over."

"I thought you came to help me pack."

"You thought I came to do your packing."

Sarah sniggered.

"No way, Masters. If you're napping, so am I."

"Did you go out with Jared last night?" Sarah asked.

"Yeah."

"And?"

"And, what?"

"You know…"

"He's Jared."

"You like him," Sarah observed.

"I don't *not* like him."

"You like him."

"Hey, I'll bet you'll have a boyfriend within a week when you get to school."

I doubt that. "Mmm."

"What? Too busy for a relationship?"

"Relationship? No thanks."

Kat giggled. "You're waiting for Pele or something."

"Pele? Pele is older than my dad."

"Well, you're waiting for *someone*," Kat observed.

"Waiting is pointless," Sarah said. She opened her eyes and heaved herself off the bed. "If you want something, you have to go after it."

"Or him?"

Sarah shrugged and grabbed a pile of clothes. She threw them haphazardly into her suitcase. "See? It's not going to pack itself."

"I don't think it's the same thing."

Sarah shrugged and continued her task. "So, you're going?"

"Kinda have to."

"Yeah, that scholarship and all."

"Mm-hm."

"Just don't take over the whole campus."

"Why not?"

Kat laughed. "Or take it over."

Sarah smiled.

"I'll miss you," Kat whispered.

"Well, just think, it'll give you a little more time with Jared."

"Not the same."

Sarah nodded.

"Neil said that Don asked you out," Kat said.

"Don's a dick."

"Sarah!"

"What? He is. No thank you."

"He's super smart—like you."

"He's super creepy like Chucky."

Kat laughed. Don Matson was a sophomore at The University of Connecticut where Sarah was headed. He'd been hovering anywhere Sarah was all summer. Boys did that. Sarah ignored it. She didn't ignore them, but she paid little mind to their overtures. Protests aside, Kat was certain that Sarah was waiting for someone. She could only imagine what constituted Prince Charming in Sarah's mind. "Indiana Jones," she muttered with a chuckle.

"What are you talking about?" Sarah asked.

"Oh, nothing. I was wondering if you might change your major to archaeology when you get there, is all."

"Ha-ha. That was a long time ago."

"Funny, feels like yesterday."

Sarah rolled her eyes. Kat had never let her live down getting stuck in the cave. Sarah also understood that Kat's obsession with that day stemmed from her fear. Sarah had felt the shaking in Kat's body the entire walk home that day. She'd hated herself for being its cause.

"Some people might think being a lawyer is the same thing."

Kat was puzzled.

"Digging up dirt."

"Sounds more like a journalist," Kat offered.

"Both jobs people hold in high esteem," Sarah replied with a note of sarcasm.

"You'll probably do both and then become an archeologist."

"You never know," Sarah said.

"Nothing would surprise me. I envy you."

"Why?"

"You're fearless," Kat said.

Sarah smiled. *Not really, Kat—not really.* "There are a lot of things scarier than crawling into a cave."

Kat nodded. "Like Chucky?"

Sarah shivered. "One day, I will burn that box."

Kat threw a T-shirt at Sarah. "Get packing."

November 28th

"I thought you were going to the library?"

Sarah closed the door to her dorm room. "I did."

Eliza lifted a suspicious brow at her roommate.

"I did."

"You made it across campus and back in fifteen minutes?"

Sarah flopped down onto her bed. She was caught. She had no intention of admitting she'd been caught. How did Eliza even know that she had been headed to the library?

Eliza Martin had become her closest friend—aside from Kat, of course. She counted herself lucky in the dorm-mate category. Eliza was quirky, smart, and possessed a wicked sense of humor. She loved adventure. Eliza wasn't only eager to explore the world, she intended to change it. Sarah admired that. The first few weeks away from home had challenged Sarah more than she'd expected. She missed her family. She missed the familiarity of home. Most of all, she missed Kat. Eliza had eased Sarah's anxiety. She made Sarah laugh. She coerced Sarah into investigating every nook and cranny of the campus. Sarah loved her new friend. Eliza seemed to understand her in ways that no one else ever had. Lately, Eliza challenged Sarah's ability to think straight. The thought made Sarah snicker. *Accurate.*

Sarah had never given a second glance to anyone except Kat. She'd endured countless sleepless nights, wishing that she could tell her best friend what she felt. *Impossible.* She'd listened to Kat's musing about boys since the sixth grade. She'd watched Kat kiss boyfriends and hold hands in the hallway at school. Each time, she swallowed the lump in her throat, pressed down the ache in her heart, and painted on a smile. Her brief visit home for Thanksgiving had tested Sarah's resolve to continue loving Kat at a distance. Kat's relationship with Jared seemed to have blossomed in a couple of months. Sarah had barely seen Kat alone that weekend.

Jared had become the fixture in Kat's life that Sarah had once been. In two months, everything had changed. It drove reality home for Sarah. Kat had someone in her life. Sarah was alone—still.

Lying in her childhood bedroom, brewing over reality, combing through memories, and feeling sorry for herself had led Sarah someplace unexpected. Without any debate, she had rolled over, lifted the phone and called Eliza.

"Sarah?"

Eliza's voice pulled Sarah from her thoughts. "How did you know I was going to the library?" Sarah wondered.

"I know things," Eliza teased.

"Oh, so now you're psychic?"

"Maybe I am."

"Changing your major?" Sarah returned.

Eliza moved from her bed to Sarah's. "Tell me what's wrong."

"Nothing is wrong."

"Right."

"I…"

Eliza smiled at her friend. "What are you so afraid to tell me?"

Let me count the things. Sarah had yet to tell anyone about her sexuality. The last thing she wanted was to alienate the one person who was keeping her sane. Sane? That was laughable. After their Thanksgiving Day phone call, Sarah found herself imagining kissing Eliza. Kissing Eliza? What was wrong with her? She'd chastised herself repeatedly. *Stop falling for your friends.* Oh, God, was she falling for Eliza? No. She loved Kat. She did love Kat. Sarah was tired of being alone, of kissing scruffy boys. She either felt nothing or slightly nauseous every time she tried. The only sparks that had been ignited in Sarah told her to flee, and to flee fast. Why should she have to be alone? Telling someone about her feelings terrified Sarah. And, fear was not an emotion that Sarah cared for. After all, she was a conqueror.

"Sarah, please tell me what's wrong."

"Why do you think anything is wrong? It's too cold to walk all the way across campus."

Eliza held Sarah's gaze. Sarah was never deterred by cold weather.

"It is," Sarah argued.

"You don't have to tell me. I know something is bothering you. You've been weird ever since Thanksgiving."

"You always think I'm weird," Sarah joked.

"Weirder than usual."

Sarah sighed.

"You've kept your distance from me all week."

Sarah startled.

"Why?" Eliza wanted to know the answer.

"I haven't…"

"You have."

Most nights, Sarah ended up lying on Eliza's bed talking. That, or Eliza ended up on hers. More nights than Eliza could count, they fell asleep in the middle of a conversation. Suddenly, Sarah was determined to stay on her side of the small room.

"Did I do something?" Eliza asked, unable to keep the hurt out of her voice.

"What?"

"Did I do something?"

Sarah nearly choked on the emotion that bubbled in her veins. Yes, Eliza had done something. She'd made Sarah miss her. She'd somehow managed to conjure desire in Sarah.

Only one person had ever done that. Only one person, unless you counted Jennifer Aniston or Lucy Lawless, and Sarah was reasonably sure neither of those people *did* count. Fear flashed in her eyes. She lived with Eliza. How could she possibly tell her the truth?

"Please tell me," Eliza begged. Tears welled in her eyes.

"Nothing," Sarah promised. "It's not you, it's me."

"It *is* me. I can feel it. You've barely looked at me this week. You only came back here because you expected me to be out."

True. Caught. "It's just something I have to figure out," Sarah offered. The sensation of a warm hand on her knee made her stomach flip and her eyes close.

"Please," Eliza said again. "I don't want to lose you."

Sarah's eyes flew open.

"Is it me?" Eliza asked again.

Before another thought could form in Sarah's head, her lips pressed to Eliza's. Warmth flooded her veins. Eliza's arms pulled her close as she deepened their kiss. Was the room spinning? Was she breathing? Sarah's tongue brushed against Eliza's. She forced herself to pull away and sighed. "I'm sorry."

"Are you?" Eliza asked. "Because I'm not."

The thought that a team of horses had taken up residence in her chest briefly crossed Sarah's mind.

"Are you? Sorry?" Eliza asked again.

"No."

Eliza pulled Sarah close. "I don't want you to be sorry."

"Liza, this is a bad idea."

"Why?"

"Because I don't want this to ruin…"

"Ruin what?"

"I'm not curious."

"Really?" Eliza flirted.

Nervousness laced Sarah's laughter. "Okay, maybe I *am*, but that's not what I mean."

"Are you gay?"

"Are you?"

"I don't know," Eliza admitted. "I don't. I know I want to be close to *you*. You're not the first girl I've kissed. So…"

Sarah was stunned.

Eliza giggled. "Sarah, was that the first time you kissed another girl?"

Sarah didn't answer.

"It's okay," Eliza said.

"Liza, I don't want to screw up…"

"If you say our friendship, I will have to punch you."

Sarah laughed.

"I like you." Eliza shook her head. "No, I don't just like you. I mean…"

"I think I get it," Sarah replied. "Yes."

"Yes?"

"Yes, I'm gay," Sarah said. A million pounds of weight seemed to instantly lift from Sarah's shoulders, even as her tears began to flow.

Eliza laid back on Sarah's bed and pulled Sarah into her arms. "It's okay," she promised. "I'm glad you are."

"Why?"

"Because I'd really like to kiss you some more."

"You're not freaked out?"

"Did you hear anything I just said?"

"Yeah. I heard you say you're not sure if you're gay."

"Do I need to be sure?"

"No, but I…"

Eliza rolled over and looked at Sarah. "Can it be enough that I want to be with you?"

"I don't know. Do you?"

"I don't want to be with anyone else," Eliza said.

"I missed you last weekend. I was so glad when you called. I didn't think you would."

"Why not?"

"Because you were going to be with Kat."

Sarah sighed deeply.

"See what I mean?" Eliza said. "You're in love with her."

There was no point in denying the obvious. Sarah didn't think that her feelings for Kat were of any consequence. It was a dead-end. She knew that. Deep down, she'd always known it. She never let herself think about anyone else. That would be a betrayal of Kat. Kat was likely cuddled up with Jared, kissing him, planning her future with him. Why shouldn't Sarah be able to cuddle with someone she cared about?

"I missed you too." Sarah sought to change the subject. "I thought about you a lot."

"Really?" Eliza's voice lightened.

"Yeah."

"In what way?"

Sarah cleared her throat.

Eliza giggled. "Want the good news?"

"Please?"

"I thought about you too." Eliza felt Sarah tremble against her. "Sarah, I'm not going to tell anyone, if that's what you're scared of."

"I didn't even think about that."

"What are you thinking about?"

"Would you care? If people knew about me?"

"No."

"What about if they knew about *us*?"

Eliza smiled. "Not really—no."

"Really?"

"Why should I? Hell, my aunt is a lesbian. My parents won't care who I bring home. And, they love you. You look surprised."

"I am."

"Why?" Eliza wondered.

"You're not even sure if you're…"

"Gay? No, but I'm not straight."

Sarah seemed to be confused.

Eliza laughed. "You are too much, Sarah." She leaned in and captured Sarah's lips. "Do you mind if I do that again?"

Sarah shook her head.

"Good."

The next hour passed in a blissful blur of arousal, emotion, and gentle discovery. Kisses—all they shared were kisses. Sarah's body was on fire. Her pulse raced. Amid new sensations, her mind had suddenly gone quiet; thought and reason gave over to acceptance. Eliza accepted her. Eliza cared for her. Eliza was attracted to her. Maybe one day Eliza could even love her. Maybe she could love Eliza. For now, it was enough; no, it was more than enough to be seen. Someone finally saw who Sarah was, and she didn't run away. It was liberating. She sighed with contentment when Eliza's arms surrounded her.

"We should get some sleep," Eliza said.

"Will you…"

"I'm not getting out of this bed unless you kick me out."

"I would never kick you out of bed."

Eliza roared with laughter.

"That's not what I meant."

"I know. It was still funny."

"Liza?"

"Yeah?"

"Nothing."

"I'll still be here tomorrow, Sarah. I promise."

Sarah closed her eyes and let Eliza hold her. *I hope so.*

Christmas Eve

Soft white light illuminated the room. Sarah had always loved Christmas. Of course, she suspected that was because Kat was mildly obsessed with the holiday. For the last six years, Sarah had enjoyed a Christmas Eve tradition. After family dinners had ended, Kat would wander across the street to Sarah's house. They would exchange presents, watch old Christmas movies by the light of the Christmas Tree, and sip hot chocolate. For the first few years, the festivities had been short-lived. Sarah's mother or father would walk Kat home by nine-thirty. Now, Kat would wander home when she was too sleepy to watch another movie. Sarah was pleasantly surprised that Kat wanted to continue the tradition. She'd expected that Kat would spend Christmas Eve with Jared.

"I'm glad you wanted to come over," Sarah said.

"Why wouldn't I?"

"I don't know. I guess I figured you'd want to be with Jared."

"I saw him earlier."

Of course, you did.

"I would never change our tradition."

Sarah nodded.

"Unless you wanted to?" Kat wondered what was going through Sarah's mind. "Is everything okay with you?"

Sarah took a deep breath and held it. "There's something I need to tell you."

"Okay."

"I met someone."

Kat held Sarah's gaze steadily. "You mean, you have a boyfriend?"

"No."

"Okay?"

"I have a girlfriend."

Kat stared at Sarah dumbly.

"Okay, not the reaction I expected."

"You have a *girl*friend?"

Sarah nodded.

"Who?"

Sarah felt sick. Why was this so hard? "Liza."

"Liza? As in your roommate, Eliza?"

Sarah nodded again.

"Like a *girlfriend?*" Kat tried to make sense of Sarah's revelation.

Sarah had come out to her parents on one of their weekend visits, going as far as to explain that she was involved with her roommate. She wasn't sure what she expected their reaction to be. Deborah and Jack Masters embraced their daughter and suggested they take Sarah and Eliza out to dinner. That was it—no fanfare, no questions, no tears.

"Liza is a sweetheart," Deborah offered.
"Why don't you call her and see if she'd like to join us for dinner?" Jack suggested.

Sarah had broken her news to Neil that morning. His reaction made her laugh.

"You just figured out that you're gay?"

Now, it was time to tell Kat. Kat's response threw Sarah for a loop. She'd prepared for anger. She'd considered tears. She'd entertained the possibility that Kat would hug her and say that she knew all along. Kat seemed to have difficulty processing what Sarah said at all. "Yes," Sarah said. "Liza is my girlfriend. I'm sorry I didn't tell you sooner. Not just about Liza, that I'm a lesbian."

Kat's eyes stayed with Sarah's. "How long have you and Liza…"

"A month."

It was Kat's turn to nod. "Do you love her?"

What? The question caught Sarah off guard. Did she love Liza? She felt something for Liza. Looking at Kat, the answer to that question seemed clear. Sarah loved Kat. She also missed Liza, more than she was willing to admit. Eliza was due to visit for New Year's. Sarah wasn't sure how Kat would handle that. Kat had never seen Sarah with anyone, romantically speaking, that was. Sarah would never be comfortable watching Kat with someone else. She had been forced to press down the pain she felt, wear a smile, and offer her support. What was shining in Kat's eyes?

"I like her," Sarah finally replied. "A lot."

Another nod.

"Are you mad?"

"Huh?"

"Are you mad that I didn't tell you?"

Kat smiled. "No." *I'm not sure what my problem is. What is your problem, Katelyn? You've been bugging her for years to find someone.*

"Is it because I told you that I'm gay? Are you freaked out?" Sarah grew fearful.

"What? No," Kat promised. "Sarah, no."

Sarah began to cry. It wasn't the admission she longed to make. Telling Kat about her sexuality made Sarah feel more vulnerable than she ever had in her life. It reminded her a bit of the panic that momentarily swept over her in that cave years ago. True to form, Kat rescued her again.

Kat scooted across the sofa and wrapped Sarah in her embrace. "No," she promised. "Why didn't you tell me?"

I couldn't. Now I have to.

"I'm sorry," Kat apologized. "I'm not freaked out. A little surprised, maybe. Only because you've always had boyfriends."

Sarah feared her tears were endless. If only she could tell Kat the truth. Half-truths felt empty. At least, she wouldn't have to hide who she was anymore.

"Sarah. Please don't cry. Liza's great," Kat said. Eliza was great. Kat had met Sarah's roommate a handful of times on visits. Eliza always engaged Kat in conversation when Kat called Sarah. It wasn't difficult to understand someone being attracted to Eliza Martin. She was tall, blonde, athletic, and outgoing. If Sarah was a lesbian, it made sense that she would choose someone like her roommate.

Slowly, Sarah's tears abated. "I'm sorry, Kat."

"For telling me the truth?"

"No, for not telling you sooner. I didn't want to tell you over the phone. It happened so fast, you know? I didn't expect to feel this way. And…"

Kat pushed Sarah away a few inches, wiped away Sarah's tears, and smiled. "You can tell me anything. That's what best friends are for."

"Are we? Are we still best friends?"

The insecurity in Sarah's voice stopped Kat's heart for a second. Seldom did Sarah falter. "We'll *always* be best friends." She kissed Sarah's forehead and giggled.

"What?"

"I was just thinking that this explains a few things."

"Like what?"

"Like your *Friends* posters, and that weird fascination you have with *Xena*. I always thought that was about the mythology." Kat laughed. "Turns out it was about leather."

Sarah smacked Kat lightly. "It's not the leather, Kat. It's what's *inside* the leather."

Kat laughed. "You're nuts. Are we going to watch a movie, or what?"

Sarah felt a lump form in her throat. *Or what?* "Movie it is."

Chapter Four: Making Plans
December 23, 1999

*F*ew things compared to waking beside Liza. Softness pressed against softness, a hint of Liza's perfume mingling with Sarah's on the pillow made the thought of fully waking painful. Sarah wrapped her arm around Liza's hip. Her lips leisurely cascading kisses down the back of Liza's neck. She heard Liza mumble. Or was that a moan? Sarah grinned and nipped lightly at Liza's shoulder. Two years had flown by—two years waking beside the woman in her arms. There was a definite advantage to being a lesbian in college. There was if you were fortunate enough to room with your girlfriend.

"Just what are you doing?"

Sarah's hand wandered up Eliza's hip. "Want me to stop?" Sarah asked.

"Why are you awake?"

"Why are you talking?"

Eliza turned over and looked at Sarah.

"Good morning," Sarah said.

"It is now."

"Might get better," Sarah offered.

"Oh?"

Sarah's fingertips lifted to Eliza's breast and faintly caressed her nipple.

"It might," Eliza agreed. She caressed Sarah's cheek and brought their lips together. "I love you."

Sarah's heart flipped. They'd exchanged many endearments in two years. "I love you," had passed between them only a handful of times. She kissed Eliza in reply.

"Do you?" Eliza asked. "Love me?"

"I love you," Sarah said.

"Are you just saying that to get me into your bed?"

"Unless I'm missing something, you *are* in my bed."

"Mm. I guess I am."

Sarah's eyes sparkled. What was love? Perhaps it was possible to be in love with more than one person. Her hand fell softly down Eliza's side, skimming the curve of Eliza's breast and then her hip. No matter how many times her fingertips made this journey, Sarah's heart skipped and her skin tingled. She delighted in the wispy sighs that passed through Eliza's lips, floating between them, lingering in exchanged breath and pleading glances. What was love? Was it defined by yearning or was it found in a moment—a shared connection? Sarah let her lips fall against Eliza's. Her heart thundered in her chest. Her hand tracked inward, finding the warm softness of Eliza's excitement. "I do love you."

"Sarah…" Eliza kissed Sarah softly. Her hands drifted up and down Sarah's back, urging her to continue. Sarah was gentle. She'd always been gentle. It astounded Eliza. From their first kiss, she understood that Sarah would be tender and loving when they touched. That had never changed. Sure, Sarah had pushed her against the door of their room a few times, kissed her passionately, undressed her, and descended her body as if Eliza were her prey. Desperation never equated to demanding. Insistent? Yes. Persistent? Definitely. Forceful? Perhaps. Sarah's touch remained tender.

"God… Sarah…"

Sarah's kiss fell from Eliza's lips down her throat to the swell of her breasts. She glanced up, eager to watch desire burn in her lover's eyes.

Warmth covered Eliza's nipple and spread through her veins to the place where Sarah's fingers continued to explore. She thought it was strange how her insides could flush with heat while her skin erupted in goosebumps. She watched as Sarah's tongue flicked over one of her nipples. Sarah knew exactly how to touch her, where to linger, and when to continue. They'd spent many hours discovering each other. She closed her eyes and reveled in Sarah's attention.

Did anyone ever tire of this? Sarah loved touching Eliza. She sometimes found herself wondering how anyone could not love women. She did. She counted herself lucky. Eliza was the first person Sarah had ever touched, had ever allowed to touch her. Eliza was patient. Sarah had fumbled the first few times they'd made love. Eliza had gently guided her hand where she needed it, and she encouraged Sarah to give voice to what she needed, how she wanted Eliza to touch her. They'd giggled through mishaps and minor embarrassments. Eliza was more than her girlfriend. She wasn't only a roommate. She'd become Sarah's best friend away from home. It occurred to Sarah as her kiss meandered over Eliza's stomach that she trusted the woman beneath her more than anyone in her life, maybe even more than she'd ever trusted Kat. It took her breath away. She'd never had the courage to tell Kat the truth. Then again, she'd left a few things out with Eliza too. She shook away the thought and fell into Eliza, tasting the length of her in a languid stroke.

Eliza picked up her head to watch Sarah making love to her. "Perfect," she mumbled.

Sarah hummed against Eliza's center. It did feel perfect; Eliza's hips rotating against her, the haunting sound of deep moans and short gasps that preceded a thundering release that begged to be unleashed. She slipped two fingers inside Eliza.

"Sarah!"

Sarah pumped deeper, over and over until Eliza's body shook. *Perfect.*

"Jesus," Eliza muttered. "You are fucking amazing."

Sarah crawled up Eliza's body, gliding against her sensually. "You think so?"

"Think? Who could *think* when you're doing that?"

Sarah chuckled.

"Do I get to return the favor?"

"Liza…"

"What?"

"It's never a favor," Sarah said seriously.

Eliza recognized the storm brewing in Sarah's eyes. She'd witnessed it many times. It hurt. There would always be a barrier between them. A smile tainted with sadness graced her lips. Sarah loved her. Eliza didn't doubt that. She felt it pass between them many times. Sarah would never banish the ghost that hovered in the space between them. Eliza knew that too. That ghost promised their end. It wouldn't be long, and they would part ways as lovers. Eliza sensed the impending doom. She might love Sarah. She wanted more than Sarah could give her. She wanted to see the world. She wanted a family. She wanted someone who wanted the same things. Sarah might daydream about taking her kids to soccer practice. If she did, she'd never shared that with Eliza. And, if Sarah thought about those things, Eliza was sure someone else painted those dreams. "I love you," she said.

"I love you too."

"I know," Eliza replied. What else could she say? Would they last until graduation? Would they try to make something work at a distance? Would Sarah wake up one morning and realize that Eliza was her future, and Kat was her past? She let her head rest on Sarah's chest and listened to the even rhythm of Sarah's heart. What was love?

"You okay?"

"Perfect," Eliza lied.

"It's not working," Jared said.

"And, you thought that telling me this two days before Christmas was a good idea?" Kat asked.

"We don't want the same things."

"The same things?" Kat questioned her boyfriend.

"You're thinking about proposals and wedding dresses. I'm thinking about…"

"This is because we haven't slept together."

"It's been two years, Kat."

Kat's pulse quickened. She'd been dating Jared for just over two years. She'd allowed him to touch her. She'd touched him. She'd felt his arousal grow, and she had released it for him. That was as far as Kat was willing to go. His frustration had been building for months. Kat felt it. Something told her that Jared would not be the person to propose. He didn't look forward to a future with Kat. He looked forward to a time when she would let him have her as his lover.

"And, if I said yes?"

"You won't," he replied.

"So, this *is* about *fucking*."

Jared swallowed hard. Kat never swore. An occasional, "oh shit," or "damnit," might fly from Kat's lips. He was positive he'd never heard her say the word *fuck*.

"That's what I thought," Kat said.

"Two years, Kat. I'm twenty-two."

"I see."

"Do you?"

"I think so," Kat sighed. "I'm sorry you feel this way."

"How am I supposed to feel?"

"I've no idea," Kat confessed.

"I'm not trying to hurt you."

Kat nodded. "I need to go."

"I'll take you home."

"I'll walk."

"Kat, it's freezing out there. Let me take you home."

"I'll be fine," she told him. Kat grabbed her coat and opened the front door.

"Kat, please. It's a fifteen-minute walk. Let me…"

"I could use the air."

"I know you don't want to be in the car with me. I get it. It'll take five minutes to drive you."

Five minutes was five minutes too long. "I've been able to find my way home since I was twelve." Kat opened the door and walked through.

Jared felt sick. He should follow Kat. She was in no mood to be followed. He made his way to the phone and called the one person he was sure Kat would talk to.

Sarah heard the phone and rolled over. She was entirely too comfortable pressed against Eliza to worry about a late-night caller. A rap on her bedroom door prompted her to open one eye. The door creaked open an inch and Deborah peered into the room. "It's for you," she said.

Sarah tried to shake herself awake. Who on earth would be calling this late?

"It's Jared," Deborah said.

A jolt of fear ripped through Sarah. She nodded and reached over to the bedside table to lift the receiver. "Jared?"

"I'm sorry, Sarah."

"What's wrong?"

"Kat took off."

"What are you talking about?"

"I sort of broke it off, and she left."

"You broke up with Kat?"

"Yeah, and she walked out. I…"

"You didn't stop her?"

"She…"

"Are you telling me she's walking home at this hour by herself?"

"I offered…"

Sarah was already out of bed. "I'll get her." She hung up the receiver.

Eliza kept her eyes closed. "Is Kat okay?"

"I don't know," Sarah said. She leaned in and kissed Eliza on the head. "I need to…"

"Yeah."

"I'll be back in a few minutes."

Eliza nodded in the dark. Kat could call any time of the day or night and Sarah would answer. Sarah would drop *everything* if Kat needed her. She opened her eyes, reached up and stroked Sarah's cheek. "Go."

Sarah placed her lips against Eliza's. "Go back to sleep."

Eliza closed her eyes. She doubted that sleep would claim her until Sarah returned, and something told her that would take longer than a few minutes. She listened as Sarah finished dressing and the door opened and closed again. Kat was single again. Eliza wondered how that might change all their lives.

———⬧•⬧———

Sarah drove the route she was sure Kat would take home—no Kat. There was only one place Kat might head. It was barely thirty degrees outside. "Kat," Sarah mumbled. She turned the car onto the old dirt road that led to their special place and flicked on the car's high beams. "Kat," she muttered again. She sped up slightly and pulled the car over, placed it in park, leaving the engine running and the lights on. "Kat!" Sarah jogged a few paces up the road. "What are you doing?"

Kat stopped without turning.

Sarah moved in front of her best friend.

Kat. "Come on," Sarah said. "Let me take you home."

Kat shook her head.

"Kat, please. Let's get in the car. It's cold out here."

"I don't want to go home."

"Where do you want to go?"

Kat looked at Sarah helplessly.

Sarah needed no further explanation or information. "Okay, but we'll take the car. Please?"

"You don't need to be out here with me," Kat said.

"Yes, I do." Sarah took hold of Kat's arm and led her to the car. Once they were both safely inside, Sarah started the car forward.

"There's something wrong with me," Kat said absently.

"There's nothing wrong with you," Sarah disagreed. She pulled the car into a grassy spot near the tree she and Kat called theirs. "What are you talking about?"

"There is. The worst part is that I don't blame him."

"Jared?"

Kat nodded.

"What happened?"

"It's not what happened. It's what *hasn't* happened."

Sarah was confused.

"Maybe I should have."

"Kat, what are you talking about?"

"You have, haven't you?"

"Have? I don't…"

"You've slept with Liza," Kat guessed.

Gut punch. Sarah tried to breathe. The one topic she avoided exploring with Kat was sex. If she opened the door to that conversation, she would inevitably be confronted with information she preferred to ignore. Kat told her everything. She told Kat everything—everything except what they did sexually. A few references and plenty of inferences had been made over the years; neither shared details. Sarah assumed that Kat and Jared were lovers. Two years was a long time. Of course, Sarah had sex with her girlfriend. "Kat, are you telling me that you and Jared haven't had sex?"

"I know. I'm a freak."

"No. I just assumed—I mean, last time you visited, it sounded like you two…"

"We've touched each other," Kat said. She threw her head back against the seat and sighed. "It didn't feel right."

"Kat…"

"I am, I'm a freak."

"You're not a freak."

"I'm probably the only virgin either of us know."

Sarah smiled. She reached across the seat and pulled Kat to her. "I doubt that. And, Kat? If he's not willing to wait until you're ready, that's his loss." She meant it. As she said the words, a sense of guilt nagged at Sarah. Kat was worth waiting for. Those were empty words. Sarah had given up waiting too. She told herself that was different. Maybe it was different. It didn't matter. "Anyone would be a fool not to wait for you," she told Kat.

Kat cried in Sarah's arms.

"It's okay. It's okay, Kit Kat."

"What if it never feels right?"

"It will," Sarah promised.

"I'm sorry," Kat said.

"Why?"

"Liza probably hates me right about now."

"No one hates you." The notion that anyone could *hate* Kat Summers was laughable.

Kat held onto Sarah. "We should go."

"We're not going anywhere until you tell me you're ready."

Kat sniggered through her tears. "You might be waiting a long time."

Sarah closed her eyes. Kat's words lodged in her chest. Part of her would always be waiting for Kat. She'd tried to deny that for years. What was the point? It was true. If Sarah had the slightest inclination that Kat might one day—any day—return her affection, Sarah would wait forever. It would take longer than that for Kat to see the truth in Sarah's eyes. She stroked Kat's hair, and breathed her in. This was Sarah's destiny. She wasn't certain if loving Kat was a gift or some punishment for a past-life deed. Loving Kat was the single most wonderful and painful thing in Sarah's life. She had no choice. "I told you," Sarah said. "You *are* worth waiting for."

May 5, 2000

Neil paced nervously outside Kat's door. He offered her a slight wave when she opened it.

"Neil?"

"Yeah. I… Umm…"

"What's up?" Kat asked casually.

"Well, umm… I'm driving down to see Sarah tomorrow. I thought maybe you'd like to go. You know, Mom asked me to bring her some boxes and stuff."

"Sure."

"Oh… Okay… Great. So, I'll pick you up around eight. Is that cool?"

"Sounds good."

"Kat?"

"Yeah?"

"Have you talked to her?" Neil asked.

"Yesterday."

"Was she…"

How was Sarah? Kat couldn't say for certain. Sarah never liked to appear vulnerable. Ending a three-year relationship had to be painful. Kat suspected that Sarah was hurting more than she would ever admit. From what Sarah had said, she remained friendly with Eliza, but felt that they both required some distance. Sarah had accepted an internship for a State Senator in Connecticut. She would be transferring campuses and working part-time. Sarah's parents had rented her a small apartment for her last year at the University of Connecticut. Eliza would be keeping the off-campus apartment she and Sarah had shared for the last year.

"I think she's okay," Kat said. "Hurt. You know Sarah, she'll never admit it."

Neil nodded. "So, you don't mind hanging out with me on the way there?"

"Not at all." Kat flashed him a smile. Neil could be adorable, in an entirely different way than he had been when she'd first met him. "I'll see you at eight."

"Okay. Hey, Kat?"

"Yeah?"

"I'm glad you're coming."

"Me too," Kat replied.

"I should go," Eliza said.

"Why?"

"Neil with be here with Kat anytime now."

"And?"

"Sarah."

"Liza, Neil and Kat both love you."

"I doubt that."

"Why? Because we're not together anymore?"

"That's a good place to start."

Sarah felt sick. She reached over and pulled Eliza into her arms.

"What are you doing?" Eliza asked.

"No one hates you."

Tears gathered in Eliza's eyes. "Why is this so hard?"

"Three years is a long time," Sarah offered.

"I'm going to miss you, you know?"

"You'll see me."

"You know what I mean."

"I do. I think Jamie might ease that," Sarah said.

Eliza tensed.

"Jamie's terrific," Sarah said. She meant it. Recently, Eliza had been spending a lot of time with their friend Jamie Flannagan. Jamie was a year older and working on her Master's Degree in Psychology.

"We're not…" Eliza began to protest the idea that she and Jamie were involved.

"Mm. Not yet. I think we both know you're headed that way."

"I didn't plan on…"

"I know that," Sarah said. "It's okay."

"What about you?"

"Me?"

"Is there anyone on your radar?" Eliza asked.

Sarah laughed. "No."

"Oh, come on."

"Nope. I think I'll enjoy my last year of college as a single woman. That's an experience I've never really had." She winked at Eliza.

"Do you regret it?"

"Us? No way."

"Neither do I. I still love you," Eliza said.

Sarah looked at her ex-girlfriend lovingly. Eliza had opened her up to all kinds of things. She allowed Sarah to accept the truth about her sexuality, and even her feelings for Kat. Their parting had been inevitable. They'd outgrown each other. Sarah kissed Eliza's forehead tenderly. "I love you too."

"But you're in love with someone else."

A wan smile took shape on Sarah's face. "Like I said, I'm looking forward to the single life."

"Maybe you should tell her," Eliza said.

"I don't think that's a good idea," Sarah said.

"You know, she might surprise you."

"Oh, I'm sure there would be some *surprise*. I'm okay."

"I'm going to go." Eliza pulled away.

"Liza?"

"Yeah?"

"I love you too."

"I know."

———•◦•———

"You suck at packing," Kat observed.

"I do not."

Kat looked around the small apartment. "Second thoughts?"

"About what?" Sarah asked.

"Leaving Liza."

"No."

"Really?"

"Really."

Neil busied himself putting together some boxes, listening to his sister and Kat's conversation with interest.

"Seriously?" Kat questioned.

"I'm looking forward to being single."

"Hoping to conquer the capitol?" Kat teased.

"Ha-ha."

"Just asking."

"You never know," Sarah quipped. "I might."

Kat laughed. "I've no doubt."

"What about you?" Sarah asked.

"Conquering capitols has never been a goal of mine."

"Very funny."

Kat folded a few of Sarah's T-shirts. "There's no one at the moment," she said.

Sarah nodded.

Neil tossed a couple of boxes toward his sister. "Are you gonna feed us?"

"Feed you?" Sarah laughed. "You're the one with the job. We're the starving students."

"You don't have any food here?" Neil asked.

"Well, Liza's decided to try being vegan, so unless you want sprouts and beans—no."

"Pizza?" he suggested.

"Sure. You're paying," Sarah said.

"That's messed up," he fired back. "Aren't you the one who wants to be a lawyer?"

"And?" Sarah challenged him.

"What about labor law?"

Sarah shrugged. "You offered to help."

"No, Mom offered me to help."

"And, probably sent you with money," Sarah guessed. "Besides, like I said, you're the one with the job."

"I thought that's why you were moving," he replied. "For a *job*."

"I don't get paid," Sarah explained.

"That's *fucked* up," he commented.

Kat giggled.

"Nice mouth," Sarah said. "Do you kiss our mother with that mouth?"

"Not our mother." He wiggled his eyebrows.

Kat laughed.

Sarah threw a box back at her brother. "I pity the poor girl."

Neil grinned. "Girls, as in *plural*."

Sarah rolled her eyes. "Well, there's no accounting for taste. Have you told them about your buddy?"

"Screw you, Sarah," he shot back.

"You still have him, don't you?"

"I'm going for pizza," he said.

"I knew it!" Sarah gloated.

"Are you coming or not?" Neil asked.

"Depends? Do we need a booster seat for your friend?" Sarah teased him. "Is he in one of these boxes?" Sarah peered inside a box.

Kat shook her head and grabbed Neil's hand. "Let's go, Sarah," she said.

"Oh, I see how it is. I go away for a few years and you get Kat to protect you."

"You're the one afraid of a doll," he said.

"Ha! I'm not afraid of anything." Sarah followed her brother and best friend out the door. *Well, maybe there is one thing.*

July 3, 2000

Kat loved the Fourth of July. It had long been her favorite holiday. She'd spent it with Sarah every year for the last seven years. It seemed strange without Sarah. Kat had planned to walk out to the tree by the lake and watch the fireworks alone. Sarah had been invited to spend the holiday in Washington DC for the week by one of her fellow interns whose father was a congressman. She would be watching the fireworks over the Potomac with powerful lawyers and lawmakers. Kat's pride in Sarah's accomplishments and her happiness for Sarah didn't eliminate the disappointment she felt. Things changed. Things always changed. For some reason, Kat had always thought that their Fourth of July tradition would remain static.

Kat needed a distraction. A hot, sunny July day seemed like the perfect excuse to wash her car. She threw the sponge in her hand into a large bucket and grabbed hold of the hose.

"Hey!"

Startled, Kat lost control of the hose in her hand. Neil's scream sent her into a fit of laughter. He stood at the end of the driveway, sopping wet. She bit her lip in the hopes of containing her amusement.

Neil looked down at himself and back at Kat. "You think this is funny?"

Kat shrugged.

"Uh-huh." He started toward her.

"Neil," she warned him.

He continued his steady pace forward.

"I'm warning you!" Kat pointed the hose at him. "I'm armed."

Neil sprinted toward her, accepting another spray of cold water. He wrestled the hose from her hand.

"Don't you dare!" Kat warned him again.

"What was that?" Neil asked. "I think I have some water in my ear." He opened fire on her.

"Neil!" Kat ran through the front yard.

Neil's aim followed Kat's every step, drenching her from head to toe. He released his grasp on the trigger. "Give up, yet?" he called out.

"No!"

"Okay." He opened fire again.

"Neil!"

Neil laughed and dropped the hose. "You're wet," he observed.

"You're an asshole."

"Kat, did you just swear?"

Kat glared at him.

"Hey, you started it," he reminded her.

"Uh-huh. What are you doing here?"

"Well, I came over to see if maybe you wanted to go to the fireworks with me tomorrow. Doug is going to take the boat out to watch them."

Kat made no reply.

"If you don't want to…"

"Neil?"

"Yeah?"

"Are you asking me out?"

"Huh? No. I mean, yes? I don't know. I mean, I know you usually hang out with Sarah for the fireworks. I thought maybe you…" he stopped and tipped his head. "Do you? Want me to? Ask you out?"

Kat grinned. "Can I trust you to keep me dry on this excursion? Or are you planning on throwing me overboard?"

Neil shrugged. "I'd bring a towel—just in case."

Kat laughed. "What time?"

"Huh?"

"What time tomorrow?"

"Oh! Six? We were going to cook out at Doug's before we take the boat out."

"Okay."

"Seriously?"

"Did you hope I would say no?"

Neil shrugged. "No."

"Then I'll see you at six."

———◆———

Kat picked up the phone, instinctively knowing who the caller was. "How's DC?"

"Hot. How's Webster?"

"Boring."

"Miss me?"

"I'm still mad at you," Kat replied lightly. "I can't believe you're at some swank party and I'm stuck here at the lake by myself."

"You know, I'd rather be with you."

"Sure, you would." Kat laughed. She heard Sarah sigh. "I know. It's a terrific opportunity for you," she said.

"What are you doing tonight?" Sarah asked.

"Actually, Neil invited me to hang out with his friends." She rushed to complete her next thought. "I think he feels sorry for me."

"*I* feel sorry for *you*. Did you say yes?"

"Yeah. It's Doug and his girlfriend, and a couple of the guys from the garage." Kat waited for a reply. "Sarah?"

"Sorry. Well, that sounds fun."

"It would be more fun if you were here."

"Well, I'll be home Saturday for a whole week. You'll be sick of me."

"Not likely."

"Have fun tonight."

"Sarah?"

"Yeah?"

"You too."

———

"How many people are here?" Sarah asked.

Elaine laughed. "Who knows? My father probably doesn't even know."

"Thanks for inviting me."

"To tell you the truth, I was surprised you accepted."

"Why?"

"It hasn't been that long since you and Liza broke up."

Sarah's eyes twinkled with recognition. She wondered if Elaine might have a secondary agenda to her invitation. "It's been longer than most people realize."

"Still, I…"

Sarah smiled and leaned into her friend's ear. "I'm glad you invited me."

Elaine's breath hitched. She'd been eyeing Sarah Masters for a year, wondering if she might ever have the chance to get closer to Sarah.

"What do you say we find someplace to watch the show?" Sarah suggested.

"I know just the place."

"Lead on."

———————•• •••———————

Sometimes, Kat thought she had a memory problem. It had been a hot, humid day. Now, with the sun down, out on the water, Kat shivered. Why hadn't she brought a sweat-shirt?

"Cold?" Neil asked.

"I'm okay."

The first cracking sound of the evening erupted, followed by a bright burst of light.

"Here," Neil said. He leaned against the side of the boat and pulled Kat to sit between his legs. "Better?"

Kat felt the heat from Neil's body pressed against her back. He *was* warm, so why did she shiver again?

Neil wrapped his arms around Kat and pulled her closer. "Is this okay?"

Was it okay? What had she expected to happen? *Oh, God.* Neil's arms were around her. *Oh, God.* She wanted his arms around her. Kat closed her eyes and nodded.

"Tell me if it's not," he said.

"It is." Kat heard the booms in the distance, she saw the lights in the sky, but none of it seemed to register. The strength of Neil's arms, the warmth of his chest, the tickle of his breath against her neck made Kat dizzy. *It's Neil. Stop this, Kat. It's Neil.*

Kat suspected that Neil had developed a slight crush on her. This did not feel *slight*. He was a far cry from the little boy she and Sarah teased endlessly. She let herself fall against him.

"I'm glad you said yes," he whispered.

Kat closed her eyes. "Me too."

———— ••• ————

Sarah imagined the fireworks show was spectacular. The sensation of Elaine's hands roaming over her thigh made it difficult for her to concentrate on anything. She'd hesitated to accept her friend's invitation to spend a few days in the nation's capital. Something told her to bite the bullet and agree. Now, she knew what that something had been. She'd met Elaine Brody during her sophomore year. Elaine lived on the floor above Sarah and Eliza. Sarah often joked that the fates had smiled on her—two lesbians in a two-floor radius. What were the chances? Elaine had gently corrected her, explaining that technically, there were three lesbians in a two-floor radius, and the chances were excellent that number would rise. As usual, Elaine's assessment proved correct. Sarah giggled at the memory.

"Did I tickle you?" Elaine asked.

The answer to that question was a resounding, no. "Mm, no. I was thinking about when we met."

"You barely noticed me."

"Not true."

It was Elaine's turn to giggle. "You were completely wrapped up in Liza."

"Maybe. I noticed you."

"What *exactly* were you thinking about?" Elaine wondered.

"I was thinking that you were right."

"About what?"

"About the number of lesbians that could be crammed into a two-floor radius."

"I'm not sure they're all lesbians."

"Well, they certainly are curious."

"Curiosity killed more than one cat," Elaine offered.

Sarah leaned over and let her lips hover a breath from Elaine's.

"Yes?" Elaine asked.

Sarah kissed her in reply.

"Thank God," Elaine whispered.

"What are you thanking God for?"

"I thought you were going to make me do that."

Sarah laughed. "That would have been a travesty."

"I'm a wallflower."

"Right. A wallflower who invites a woman away for four days to stay in a hotel suite complete with a jacuzzi tub and a king-size bed."

Elaine shrugged. "I didn't choose it."

"Is that so?"

"Mm-hm."

"Does that mean you don't want to *share* them?"

Elaine's breath caught again. "Stop talking, Sarah." She claimed Sarah's mouth with hers.

"Don't you want to watch the fireworks?" Sarah whispered against Elaine's lips.

"No."

Sarah grinned. *I am so glad I accepted this invitation.*

December 19, 2000

Neil snuck a kiss from Kat. "You know, she's going to find out that we've been dating."

"I know."

"I get it."

"Neil, Sarah is my best friend. I don't know how she'll feel about this."

"Okay."

"Okay?"

"We won't tell her anything now."

"Thank you."

Neil nodded. "But Kat, if we're going to keep seeing each other, she's going to find out."

"I know." Kat did know. "We're not seeing each other exclusively."

"No."

"So, let's just…"

"I get it."

"Neil, I just—I don't want stress during the holiday, okay? Last year Jared broke up with me, and then Sarah started having problems with Liza after New Year's. It's not like we're walking down the aisle. It's a few dates."

He nodded again. "You're right. Can I kiss you one more time before I leave?"

Kat smiled and pressed her lips to Neil's. "Better?"

"I'll see you," he said.

"You will."

"Kat?"

"Yes?"

"We're still on for New Year's?"

"It's a date."

Neil kissed Kat's cheek. "I'll see you later."

Kat let out a long sigh. She liked Neil. She was attracted to Neil. She'd been careful to keep things casual. They'd shared a few kisses. She would like to claim that they were chaste. Neil's kiss did not conjure images of life in a convent, not unless she was visiting to beg forgiveness for her carnal thoughts. She chuckled. *Only me.* Casual was best. Neil had been out with a few other girls since their Fourth of July date. Kat had agreed to dinner and several excursions with collegemates. Only Neil had passed the test to make it to a second date, and a third, and a fourth. She sighed again. *Bad idea, Kat. It's a bad idea.*

———⦁◆⦁———

Scrooged. Again. "Why do you love this movie so much?" Kat asked.

"What's not to love?" Sarah replied in kind.

"I don't know. I'm not a Bill Murray fan, I guess."

"I love Bill Murray."

"Yeah, I know."

"He's sexy-ugly."

"What?" Kat laughed.

"What? He is."

"Gross."

"Oh? What do you find sexy?"

"Not Bill Murray."

"Ha-ha."

Kat raised an eyebrow. "So, would you sleep with Bill Murray?"

Sarah considered the question and shrugged. "Maybe."

"*You* would turn to the dark side of heterosexuality for Bill Murray?"

"Stranger things have happened."

Kat laughed. "I doubt that."

"Why? Come on, Kit Kat, there has to be someone you would turn to the dark side for."

"Maybe."

"Who?" Sarah asked, genuinely curious to hear the answer.

"Sandra Bullock."

"Doesn't count."

"Why not?"

"Everyone I know would sleep with Sandra Bullock."

"Yes, but almost everyone you know sleeps with women."

"Still doesn't count. Pick someone else," Sarah said.

"You won't believe me. And, you'll make fun of me."

"No, I won't."

"You shouldn't. You picked Bill Murray."

"Stop stalling," Sarah said.

"Candice Bergen."

Sarah stared at Kat.

"You asked."

"She could be your mom."

"Bill Murray?"

Sarah snickered.

"Have you ever?" Kat asked softly.

"Have I ever what?" Sarah asked.

"You know… Fooled around with a guy."

"In high school."

"Yeah, I know that. But that was just heavy petting." Sarah guffawed.

"Stop laughing at me."

Sarah couldn't have stopped laughing if she wanted to. Heavy petting? Who had Kat been hanging out with while Sarah was away? Mrs. Stearns? Mrs. Stearns lived two houses down from Kat's parents. She was a retired school teacher who Sarah guessed had to be at least two hundred.

"Sarah, stop."

Sarah looked at Kat and caught her breath. In an instant, she fell into another fit of laughter.

"You're a jerk."

Sarah tried unsuccessfully to regain her composure.

"A jerk who wants to sleep with old men," Kat added.

Sarah tossed a pillow at Kat. "At least I don't call out for Murphy Brown in bed."

Kat tossed the pillow back. "Jerk."

"Ohhh… Murphy… I mean, Candice, I mean… Oh, Murphy!"

Kat pounced on Sarah. She imitated Sarah's voice. "I've always wanted to sleep with a ghostbuster. Scrooge me…"

"Scrooge me?" Sarah wrestled Kat and pinned her. "What does that even mean?"

"Oh, right. It's the *meat*balls." Kat grinned.

Sarah glared then grinned evilly. She dropped a hand to Kat's side and started tickling her.

"Sarah, stop! Please!" Kat laughed. "I'm going to pee! Stop!"

"Maybe Candice can loan you some Depends."

"Stop," Kat begged.

Sarah finally complied. Kat's head fell into her lap.

"Would you really sleep with Bill Murray?" Kat asked.

"Hard to say," Sarah replied. "And, the answer to your other question is no."

"What question?"

"No, I haven't fooled around with any guys since high school."

"Have you ever wondered about it?"

"Not really."

"Really?"

Sarah sighed. Why was it so hard for people to understand that she was attracted to women? "Do you think about touching women?" Sarah asked pointedly.

"No."

Gut punch number two million. "So, why can't you understand that I don't think about guys?"

Kat looked up at Sarah. Hurt flickered in Sarah's eyes. "I do understand."

"Do you?"

Kat took Sarah's hand and held it. "Yeah, I do."

"I feel like that disappoints you somehow," Sarah said. "That I'm not attracted to men."

"Oh, Sarah, no." Kat squeezed Sarah's hand. "You're the one person who I don't think could ever disappoint me." *Me, on the other hand, might disappoint you one day.* Kat closed her eyes. "Are you and Elaine seeing each other?"

"Do you mean are we in a relationship?"

"I guess."

"No. I told you I'm happy being single."

"Until Ms. Right finds you," Kat said.

Sarah ignored Kat's comment. "What about you? What about that guy you went out with? What's his name? Bentley?"

Kat laughed. "You mean, Royce."

"Because that's better."

"Beats Bill Murray."

"Very funny. Are you still seeing him?" Sarah wondered.

"Seeing, yes. Dating, no."

"So, we're both single for once."

"Looks that way," Kat said. "Something tells me that your single life is more interesting than mine."

"I doubt it."

I don't.

"Do you want to watch something else?"

"You mean besides your boy crush?"

"You're not going to let that go, are you?"

"Not likely," Kat admitted.

"How about I see if there's an old Murphy Brown tape downstairs?"

"Shut up."

"No, huh? How about…"

"How about we just stay here and watch the tree."

"Why? Is it going somewhere?"

Kat gripped Sarah's hand a little tighter. She missed Sarah when Sarah was away. Kat sometimes thought she led two distinct lives—the one when Sarah was home, and the one when Sarah went away. "Can we?"

Sarah slid down next to Kat. "Check. Tree watching it is." Sarah sensed that Kat's eyes had fallen shut. She placed a faint kiss on Kat's head. *I love you, Kit Kat.*

Chapter Five: That Old Dirt Road
March 22, 2001

Sarah watched the taxi pull away and flung her bag over her shoulder. She was relieved to be home. And, she was anxious to see Kat. She'd devised the perfect plan. She would stop at the corner store for some ice, head down the old dirt road to their secret spot by the lake and lay out a celebration picnic. Sarah couldn't wait to see the expression on Kat's face when she announced that she'd been accepted to Harvard Law School. She imagined Kat would jump up in excitement. But then, she also imagined that when Kat reached out to her, just maybe she would have the courage to finally tell Kat the truth. Maybe this was the right time. Everything in Sarah's life was going as she had planned. She'd only be a couple of hours away from home for the next two years. She could visit every weekend if she wanted. Maybe, just maybe it was time. *Maybe*.

"What are you doing here?" Kat asked.

Neil shrugged and grinned. "Thought you might want to take a ride out by the lake."

"Is that so?"

Neil nodded. "I even have food."

"Well, you know me," Kat replied. "I can never resist food."

"Is that the ticket to your heart?"

Kat stepped up to Neil and wrapped her hands around his neck. "One of them."

Neil fought to swallow. He'd been planning this afternoon for weeks. "So?"

"Now?"

"Do you have someplace else to be?" he asked.

Kat shook her head. "What do I need to bring?"

"Nothing."

"Really?"

"I told you, I have everything we need."

Kat smiled. *I'll bet you do.*

⁎⁎⁎

Sarah laid out the blanket on the ground and placed the champagne she purchased into a bucket. She dumped a bag of ice in and smiled at the scene. "She's going to freak," she chuckled.

Now, it was time to execute the second part of her plan. She'd make the trek to Kat's door. Kat would be excited. Sarah was confident of that. Kat was always thrilled when Sarah came home unexpectedly. The picnic by the lake and Sarah's news would be the icing on the cake. She took a deep breath and started forward, smiling ear to ear.

"I can't wait to see her."

⁎⁎⁎

Neil pulled the truck into a secluded spot near the end of the dirt road. He hopped out and opened Kat's door. He hoped that she would be receptive to his attempt at romance. They had casually dated for more than a year. Recently, he had felt things shift between them. Kat was graduating college in a month. She'd already lined up a teaching job. People in town had become acquainted with Neil's talent for fixing and restoring automobiles. That had resulted in a healthy influx of business at Gerry's garage where Neil worked as a mechanic. So much work in fact, that Gerry had suggested Neil become a partner in the business. The overture surprised Neil. He was only twenty. The thought of owning a business made him feel old. How much responsibility would that require? Then there was Kat.

Kat made Neil think about the future. He found himself considering Gerry's offer more and more. There were things that Kat wanted. Neil knew that. For years, he'd heard her talk to Sarah about her dreams for the future. Now, she had begun to share those with him. Neil wondered what role he might be able to play in fulfilling those dreams. He often found the friendship between his sister and Kat interesting. Sarah dreamed big. Kat was inclined toward simple things—family, home, a place to land. When he stopped to think about it, they seemed unlikely friends. Kat's aspirations seemed to align far more with his than with his sister's.

"Hey," Kat called to Neil. "You okay?"

Neil smiled and nodded. He took Kat's hand and led her to the back of the truck. He lowered the gate, jumped into the back and offered Kat a hand up.

Kat watched as Neil laid out a couple of blankets and pillows and placed a cooler in the middle of them.

"It's nothing fancy," he said as he opened the cooler.

Kat looked at him lovingly. She felt sure she knew where the afternoon was headed. Her heart fluttered. She reached out and brought his lips to hers. "It's perfect," she whispered.

———◆·◆———

Sarah hummed while she walked down the grass path that led to the dirt road into town. She looked up at the sky which seemed to be threatening to spill over. *Oh, well. If it rains we'll just go to Plan B. Not that I have any idea what Plan B is.* Sarah laughed. She'd planned the afternoon carefully. In fact, she had been planning this visit for years. The only wrench in her plan was Neil. *Neil.* What to do about Neil? Sarah sighed. It didn't take a brain surgeon to see that Neil had a massive crush on Kat. Sarah had noticed that when they were still in school. She knew that Kat had gone out with Neil a few times. But Kat always downplayed their "dates." Sarah had come to believe that Kat simply didn't have the heart to burst Neil's bubble. After all, they'd all grown up together. She sighed again. *He'll get over it.* She forced herself to banish thoughts of Neil from her mind as she continued toward the road. She glanced back overhead. *Now, don't let me down.* Sarah chuckled. *I'm taking to the sky. You've lost it, Sarah—completely. Now, what about a Plan B...*

———◆·◆———

Kat looked at Neil with anticipation. When, she wondered, had she fallen in love with Neil Masters? It seemed crazy. Little Neil—little Neil wasn't so little anymore. Long gone was a young boy's attachment to a Buddy doll. Neil had traded that fascination for cars in about the sixth grade. In fact, Kat had come to believe that Neil had only held on to that stupid doll for so many years to torture Sarah. That thought brought a smile to her lips. God, how Sarah hated that doll. There were traces of that innocent boy still evident in Neil. It amazed Kat that after all the years they had known each other, Neil could still grow timid and shy in her presence. He was different from his sister; at least, he was with Kat. He'd grown into a handsome, compassionate man; a man who made Kat laugh and who made her tremble with his kiss. Those eyes–it was his eyes that lured her. As they looked into hers now, Kat fell into them. They twinkled with hope, excitement, and just a twinge of insecurity. Kat was certain that her eyes reflected the same feelings. She'd already made her decision before Neil had shown up unexpectedly that afternoon. She'd been reluctant to move toward a relationship with Neil. He was her best friend's little brother. Somehow, that seemed wrong to Kat. She'd avoided the inevitable long enough. She loved him. Kat felt confident that he loved her. The only question in her mind was if he wanted the same things that she did.

"What are you thinking?" Neil wondered.

"I guess I'm wondering where you hope this will lead—other than the obvious."

Neil nodded. "You mean do I want more than to kiss you in the back of my truck?"

"I do."

Neil leaned in and kissed Kat tenderly. He heard her sigh and pulled away to look at her. "I want you," he answered. "And, not just in the back of a pick-up," he chuckled. "I kind of hoped you might want to try this."

"*This?*"

Neil shook his head. *Smooth, Masters—real smooth.* "I'm saying this all wrong."

Kat understood Neil's sentiment, even if it had gotten lost in his words. She cupped his cheek. "No, you aren't," she replied. She kissed him gently, inviting him to search and explore. Her fingers threaded together behind his neck as their kiss deepened. She forced herself to pull back, feeling breathless and exhilarated. "What is *this* that you want to try?" she asked.

"Us," he said.

"Us?"

"Together. Kat," Neil took a deep breath, "I do want this. I mean that I want to be with you... I... Not just like this... I love you," he said the words.

Kat smiled. "I love you too."

Neil was stunned. "You do?"

Kat chuckled. "I wouldn't be here like *this* if I didn't."

Neil leaned in and captured Kat's lips again. Their kiss deepened quickly, nervous anticipation driving them both. His hands dropped to Kat's waist, winding their way up her sides. He hesitated.

Kat took hold of the bottom of her shirt and lifted it over her head. She almost laughed at the expression on Neil's face. They had been talking about "this." She wondered now what he had thought "this" meant.

"Kat, we don't have to... You don't have to..."

Kat took Neil's hand and placed it over her breast. Her hand went to his chest and she smiled at the feel of his racing heart. "If you're not ready," she said.

Neil licked his lips. "I've only ever done this with one person," he confessed.

"Well, that's once more than me," Kat tried to reassure him. She felt his hand gently begin to knead her breast and she closed her eyes. "Neil," she sighed.

Neil lowered Kat beneath him. He smiled when she met his gaze. Kat's hands ran over his shoulders to his back. His fingertips reached around her back and unhooked her bra. They tracked inward, enjoying the feel of Kat's skin, exploring her softness. His palm grazed over Kat's nipple and he heard her gasp. *Oh, God. Please let me get through this.*

Kat sensed Neil's nervousness. She felt the evidence of his arousal against her leg, and she reached down to unzip his jeans. "It's all right," she assured him.

Neil leaned in and kissed her passionately. *Slow down, Neil. Slow down.* He kept repeating the mantra in his head. *It's Kat. It's Kat.* "I love you," he whispered.

"I know."

———— ·•·•· ————

Sarah reached the road and glanced up at the sky again. *Just great.* She shook her head ruefully. *So, what's your brilliant plan, Masters?* She chuckled remembering some of the stories she used to tell Kat. Kat always gravitated to the simple things. That's why Sarah had made this plan. It was simple. It was "them." She groaned. *Simple, Masters. Think. Think.*

Sarah was always thinking, always planning. Dreaming had always seemed pointless without planning to Sarah. A person could spend her whole life dreaming and never get to realize one of her dreams. Planning was required. She firmly believed that any dream could come true with careful planning. There were times, however, when all of Sarah's planning eclipsed Sarah's ability to enjoy the dreams she realized.

Planning didn't only serve to achieve goals; planning was also an escape. If Sarah kept her mind busy with preparations and directions, then she had less time to revel in her emotions. And, appearing emotional was not something Sarah Masters enjoyed. Emotions made a person vulnerable. Emotions, like dreams without plans led to disappointment. *Plan B.* Sarah began to mull over possible alternatives to a picnic by the lake. She pictured Kat and smiled. *Kat.* She missed Kat. They spoke frequently, but the phone had always been a pathetic substitute for Kat's company. Sarah sighed. Maybe Plan B didn't matter. No matter where they went, no matter how Sarah delivered her news, she would be with Kat. That's all that had ever mattered to either of them. Sarah let out a contented sigh. It wouldn't be long until she saw Kat. *It doesn't matter where just so long as she's there.* Her ears tuned to a sound in the distance. "What the...."

"Neil?" Sarah muttered. She was almost positive that the truck she saw in the distance was her brother's. "Now, what are you doing out here?"

Sarah meandered closer. Maybe Neil had come out to drink some beers with his friends. That wouldn't surprise her. Maybe she would join them for a few minutes. She could use a dose of liquid courage.

"Neil..."

Sarah's ears perked at the sound of Neil's name. "Kat?" Sarah slowed her pace. She stopped a few feet from the truck and leaned against a tree. "Kat?" she whispered in disbelief.

Neil was positive he heard something. He kept his head next to Kat's, listening to her soft pleas and desperate sighs. He tried to concentrate on his rhythm. Kat was holding onto him tightly, and he was determined to be gentle with her. He heard another rustle and lifted his head to look out into the woods. *Sarah? Shit.*

Sarah's heart plummeted rapidly. She wanted to run, but it seemed she had become rooted in the ground. Her eyes briefly met Neil's. She shook her head, certain he had seen her. She watched as he lowered his head and claimed Kat's lips. She closed her eyes and nodded. *Looks like it's Plan B, Masters.* Sarah swallowed hard and turned back in the direction she had come from. She heard Kat's voice call out Neil's name in the distance just as the skies opened. She walked numbly down the road until she reached the grass path, not caring about the rain that gathered in droplets on her skin. Planning, thinking, dreaming—maybe sometimes there just was no happy ending. She reached the blanket now soaked from the raging storm. Sarah collapsed against a tree. The storm would pass. It would pass. Just like everything in life, the storm would pass.

———◆•◆———

Kat loved watching a storm. She was content to sit on the front porch with Neil and watch the rain fall. Rain seemed magical to her. The entire day had felt magical. She had known that she and Neil were headed for something more than a few casual dates for some time. She wasn't sure when she had fallen in love with him. She'd resisted the urge to be close to him for more than a year. Neil was Sarah's little brother. Other than Kat, Neil was the person closest to Sarah. That was something the two shared that had made their bond grow quickly. They both admired Sarah, they both reveled in her attention, and they both missed her sorely.

Kat strained to make out a figure in the distance as it approached. "Sarah?"

Neil tensed.

Kat stood up slowly. It *was* Sarah. Kat made her way to the edge of the front porch. "Sarah?" she called out.

Sarah took a deep breath and tried to swallow her sadness. *Kat.* Normally, the sight that greeted her would have immediately sent her into a sprint. Now, Sarah's pace slowed to a crawl. She hesitated for a second before continuing forward.

Kat spun on her heels. She ran in the house and grabbed a blanket from the couch. She burst back through the screen door and down the steps to greet her best friend. "Sarah?" Kat wrapped the blanket around a shivering Sarah. "What are you doing home?"

Sarah did her best to smile. It was hopeless. She was drenched to the bone, freezing, and she didn't even care. The only thing that Sarah could feel was heartbreak.

Kat wrapped her arms around Sarah and pulled her close. "Why didn't you call?"

Sarah offered little more than a shrug in reply. She feared that any attempt to speak might result in a complete breakdown. She'd spent hours sitting alone in the special spot she had shared with Kat. She'd cried for so many hours, she thought perhaps all her tears had gone dry. Seeing Kat with her head on Neil's shoulder, feeling Kat's arms around her, Sarah now feared her tears might be endless.

"Neil, tell your mom that Sarah's home."

Neil nodded and made his way into the house.

"You're shivering. Why didn't you call?" Kat asked again.

"I wanted to surprise you." *Well, at least that was honest.*

Deborah stepped out onto the porch just as Kat helped Sarah up the stairs. Immediately, she realized that something was wrong. "Sarah? Why didn't you call?"

"Why does everyone keep asking that? I know the way home," Sarah replied.

Kat flinched. Sarah rarely sounded angry. *Something is wrong.*

Deborah's brow furrowed in concern. She had the ability to read her daughter. She could wager one guess what might be driving Sarah's sullen yet irritable disposition. She would have to comb a million memories to find the few times Sarah had ever snapped at Kat. She let her eyes drift to her son. Neil's gaze had fallen on his feet. *Oh, no.* Deborah pulled Sarah closer to her.

"Let's get you into a hot shower," she suggested. "Kat, can you go find something dry for Sarah in her old room?"

Kat nodded. She looked at Sarah. "I'm glad you're home."

Sarah refused to meet her gaze.

Kat's heart lurched in her chest. "I'll find something," she said.

Deborah led Sarah to the bathroom and shut the door. "Want to tell me what's going on?"

"I got caught in the rain."

"I can see that. Your wet condition explains your disposition?" Deborah asked.

Sarah shrugged. She peeled the wet clothes from her body.

Deborah took them and put them in the sink. "Sarah?"

"I don't want to talk about it—not right now."

Deborah nodded. "Okay. I'll have Kat bring you something."

Sarah grabbed her mother's arm. "Can you bring it in here?"

The fearful look in Sarah's eyes nearly stopped Deborah's heart. She wanted to gently pry some more. Instead, she offered Sarah an understanding smile. "Sure."

"Thanks."

Deborah grabbed Sarah's clothing from the sink and stepped through the door. She let out a heavy sigh.

"I found some sweats." Kat began to make her way toward the bathroom door.

"Here." Deborah moved to hand Kat the clothing in her hand. "If you could have Neil throw those into the washing machine, I'll get these to Sarah."

Kat nodded sadly and made the exchange. "Is she…"

"She's tired," Deborah tried to offer Kat some reassurance.

"Is she mad at me or something?"

Kat's despondent tone cut through Deborah like a knife. *Oh, Kat.* "No, sweetheart," Deborah said.

"Something's wrong," Kat observed.

Deborah's lips curled into the hint of a smile. "I know," she said. "I think we just have to wait for Sarah to tell us what that might be."

Kat nodded again before wandering off to find Neil.

Deborah sucked in a long breath and released it slowly. *If she'll tell any of us what that is.*

"Are you okay?" Kat asked.

Sarah met Kat's eyes for the first time since arriving home. Nothing had changed, and everything had changed. Kat's gaze melted her heart. She wanted to be angry—to lash out at Kat and Neil. What was the point? Maybe it was better to face reality now. Sarah couldn't deny that she had always expected one day Kat would fall in love with someone. She'd tried not to imagine Kat's glee over Derek Brook's proposal for years. Then Derek had become Jared. She'd never entertained the notion that the person who would steal Kat away would be Neil. That made it worse. How would she ever avoid them? She'd tried to deny and distance herself from the inevitability for years. Sarah allowed herself the delusion that maybe one day Kat could love her the same way. She'd permitted herself daydreams and love poetry. She'd fallen asleep more nights than she could count imagining Kat. She'd awakened each morning, wishing the pillow in her grasp, the occasional coed, even that Eliza was Kat. All along, somewhere in the deep recesses of her mind, Sarah knew it would never come to pass. She had no one to blame but herself for the heartache she felt. *Idiot.*

"Sarah?"

"I wanted to come home and tell you all about law school," Sarah said.

"You got accepted!"

"To a few," Sarah replied evenly.

Neil stepped into the room. "Hey," he greeted the pair.

Sarah offered her brother a strained smile.

"So?" Kat asked.

Sarah sighed. She was certain that her news would surprise everyone. She'd contemplated what to do for hours before making her way home. She needed distance—distance from her delusions. "UCLA," she said.

Kat's jaw dropped. "California? You're going to California?"

Sarah nodded. "I've got a full ride there." That was true, and it was about the only thing that let Sarah justify the choice.

"Congratulations," Neil said. "Los Angeles, huh? Lots of hot blondes there," he offered.

Sarah stared at him blankly. He moved to put his arm around Kat.

"I thought you were going to say Harvard," Kat said.

"Things change," Sarah replied.

Kat looked up and held Sarah's gaze. *What aren't you telling me?*

Neil looked down.

Sarah sipped her tea and allowed silence to fill the room. What was there to say? Kat had made a choice. She'd chosen Neil. That was obvious. Sarah made a choice too. *Life goes on—whatever that means.*

Two Days Later

"I can't believe you're leaving already," Kat said.

Sarah shrugged and shoved a few things into her backpack. "Might as well go home."

"You are home."

Sarah ignored Kat's comment. "So, you and Neil, huh?"

"Sarah, I wanted to tell you that things had changed."

Sarah nodded.

"You knew we'd gone out a few times."

Sarah held back her desire to scream.

"I didn't mean to hide anything," Kat promised.

"It's okay. He could've told me."

"Are you mad?"

Mad? Was Sarah mad? She'd combed through her thoughts and feelings for the last forty-eight hours. Anger? She'd felt it. Heartbreak? That had come in spades. Mostly, Sarah felt like a fool. Kat had mentioned going out with Neil. Sarah hadn't given it much thought. They'd all been friends for years. As far as Sarah knew, Kat had been dating casually. That belief was partly responsible for Sarah's determination to remain single. Sure, she'd slept with Elaine on and off. She'd enjoyed the company of a few women. Single suited her. Eliza had moved on from their relationship. Apparently, so had Kat. But then, there was nothing for Kat to move on from, was there? Other than a peculiar crush on Candice Bergen, and an admission that she wouldn't kick Sandra Bullock out of bed, Kat had never given Sarah any reason to believe they could ever be more than friends. All the reasons, the hundreds of moments that Sarah had managed to create into possibilities amounted to nothing more than fantasy. She had no right to be mad. She didn't even have a reason to be hurt. That didn't change that fact that she was. Distance was the only remedy Sarah could think of. She needed space, and she needed it now.

"No," Sarah said. She wiped a tear from Kat's cheek. "I'm not mad. I want you to be happy."

"I can't believe you're going to California," Kat said.

"It's just another place." *Isn't that the truth?*

"It's so far."

"You can come visit." *You and Neil.*

"Do you really have to leave now?" Kat asked. "I thought we could go to our place and talk for a while."

The last place that Sarah wanted to travel was to *their* place. "I wish I could," she lied.

"We haven't been out there since last summer," Kat said.

"It's not going anywhere."

No, but you are. Kat had a sinking feeling. Sarah's eyes refused to give away what she was thinking. One thing was obvious, Sarah wasn't in the mood to talk. "I can drive you," Kat offered.

"Thanks. Mom's going to take me. I think she wants to take me shopping before I get on the train. Something about law students and holey jeans."

Kat nodded.

Sarah's hurt lurched in her chest. She would never be able to stand seeing Kat hurt—never. "I'll talk to you," she promised. She hugged Kat and felt Kat hang on. "Hey," Sarah softened her voice. "I'll be back."

Kat nodded and wiped away a few tears.

"Are you ready?" Deborah asked from outside the room. She offered Kat a sympathetic grin.

"Yeah, I'll be right there," Sarah promised. "Guess that's my cue."

"Sarah?"

"Yeah?"

"Nothing."

"We'll talk," Sarah said.

Kat nodded dumbly. *But what will we talk about?*

Sarah winked and threw her backpack over her shoulder. "You should take Neil out there."

Kat's brow wrinkled in confusion. "Where?"

"To the tree," Sarah said. She forced herself to smile, waved, and left the room.

Kat stood in place. "It's *our* place," she muttered.

Chapter Six: Distant Shores
October 5, 2004

*C**ute*. Beth Greer looked across the Law Library at a feisty woman who appeared to be reading one of the pages the riot act. She'd noticed the woman on campus a few times. She'd even attempted to approach her once. She chuckled as the young man behind the counter grew flustered. His face had deepened to a shade that looked faintly purple. Beth pushed out her chair and strolled across the room.

"What don't you understand?" Sarah asked the man behind the counter.

"I'm sorry. I can't access it on the computer," the young man explained.

"What *can* you access on that thing? I called twenty minutes ago to have that held. I was assured it would be here."

Beth stepped up to the counter. "Sorry," she apologized for the intrusion. "I called earlier..."

The young man flushed again.

Beth looked at his nametag. "Bad day, Brian?"

"System issues," he explained.

"Ah. So, what are the chances you'll be able to help me right now?"

He shook his head.

Beth heard the woman beside her grumble. She offered a smile. "Guess we're both shit out of luck. How about a coffee?"

"Excuse me?"

"How about I buy you a coffee," Beth repeated.

"Why?"

"Well, I can't get what I need here, and based on what I overheard, you're not having much luck either. So, how about a coffee? Unless you'd prefer a beer." Beth watched as the stranger beside her considered the offer, measuring her silently. *Can't tell she's a law student.* "Beth," Beth extended her hand. "Beth Greer—in case, you know, you wanted it on record."

"Sarah. Masters—in case you wanted a witness." She gestured to Brian.

"I guess that would be you, Brian," Beth said. "So, Sarah Masters, coffee or beer?"

"Martini."

Beth raised an amused brow.

"Dirty," Sarah said.

Beth grinned and gestured to the front door. "Martini it is," she said. *The dirtier the better.*

———◆·◆———

"Where are you taking me?" Kat asked.

"I thought you loved an adventure?"

"You're worse than your sister sometimes."

"I wouldn't go that far."

"What are you up to?"

"I'm not up to anything," Neil said.

Kat looked across the front seat skeptically. She'd willingly followed Sarah into insane schemes thousands of times. The twinkle in Neil's eyes was unmistakable. He was plotting something. He shifted in the driver's seat and gripped the steering wheel tightly exactly the way Sarah would when she had concocted one of her "Masters" plans—that's what Kat called them. She looked back out her window and tried not to laugh. Keeping secrets was never an easy task for the Masters' siblings. "I can only imagine," she mumbled.

"How's the martini?" Beth asked.

"Dirty."

"Subtle isn't your forte, is it?"

Sarah shrugged. "What made you decide to save me?"

"I didn't."

Sarah chuckled.

"I saved Brian."

"I don't usually lose my temper like that," Sarah said.

"Bad day?"

"I've been trying to get my hands on that journal for the last four days."

"Frustrating," Beth offered.

"A little. So? I'll assume you're a student."

"What gave that away?" Beth asked.

"Other than the obvious?" Sarah countered.

Beth smiled. Sarah Masters was going to be a tough nut to crack.

"Where are you from?" Sarah asked.

"Here."

"Los Angeles?"

"Orange County—and don't judge me."

Sarah winked. "No judgment."

"You?"

"Massachusetts."

"Long way from home," Beth observed.

"I guess that all depends on your definition of home."

"Oohhh. Lawyer speak already."

Sarah shrugged.

Oh, I will figure you out yet, Sarah. Just you wait.

———◆•◆———

"What on earth?" Kat mused.

"What do you think?" Neil said.

"I don't know. What am I thinking about?"

"The house," Neil said.

"I've always loved this house," Kat said.

Neil beamed. "Yeah, I remember."

"It's a shame no one has ever fixed it up."

"What if someone did?"

"Huh?"

"What if someone fixed it up?" Neil asked.

"I'll bet it'd be amazing."

"Amazing enough to live in?"

Kat's gaze narrowed in questioning.

"I sort of bought it."

Kat leaned forward slightly. "What?"

"Well, I've been saving for a few years. It was cheap. I can do most of it myself—with some help. I kind of hoped you might like to live in it—with me, I mean."

Kat shook her head.

"I mean, it won't be for another year or so. It'll take time to…"

Kat leaned in and kissed Neil soundly.

"Is that a yes?"

"That depends."

"What does it depend on?"

"You *sort of* bought it?" Kat teased.

Neil blushed. "I…."

"I love you, Neil."

"I love you too," he said. "Maybe it seems crazy. I mean, I haven't even proposed yet."

Kat raised her brow.

"I will," he said without thinking.

"Thanks for the heads up."

"I suck at this," he admitted.

"What's that?"

"Romance."

"I don't think so," Kat disagreed. She kissed him again.

"Do you want to go inside?"

"Can we?"

"Yep."

"Neil?"

"Yeah?"

"I hope you do someday."

"What?"

"Propose."

He smiled. "Let's go take a look."

One Year Later
December 21, 2005

"You're not nervous, are you?" Sarah asked.

Beth blushed.

Sarah closed the distance between them. "My family is going to love you."

"What about Kat?"

What about Kat? Kat would love Beth too, and if Sarah's divination skills were on point, Kat was destined to become more than an honorary member of the Masters' family. She wasn't sure when that would come to pass. She spoke with Kat every Wednesday. It had taken time for Sarah to grow comfortable with their weekly phone calls. This would be her fourth visit home since finding Neil and Kat in the back of Neil's truck. Living on the opposite coast, intense studies, and a part-time job gave Sarah the perfect excuse to limit her travel. Last Christmas had tested Sarah's patience and her emotions. Even their Christmas Eve tradition had fallen flat. Until recently, Sarah had seriously considered making an excuse and staying in Los Angeles for the holidays. She had every reason not to make the trip. She'd just started at a large law firm in downtown Los Angeles. To her surprise, she'd been thrown directly into the fire. Her caseload was enormous, and her stress level through the proverbial roof.

"Kat will love you."

Beth nodded doubtfully. Sarah's affection for Kat Summers was undeniable. Sarah lit up like a Christmas tree when she told tales about their childhood exploits. And, she often grew solemn when the topic of Kat's romance with her younger brother arose. Love took many forms. Beth understood that. She'd pursued Sarah unfailingly for nearly a year. She'd fallen in love with Sarah over their first shared martini. No matter how many protests Sarah waged about getting involved, Beth refused to give up. She would be forever thankful to a dead car battery. Driving past the law library late one night, she stumbled across Sarah standing in front of her car with the hood up. It was Beth's second rescue attempt. The first ended with a martini. The second ended in Sarah's arms. Sarah made Beth laugh. She challenged Beth to consider new ways of thinking, and she encouraged Beth to stretch. Sarah was Beth's future. At least, she hoped so. One thing was evident, any future with Sarah meant Kat Summers would figure prominently. She prayed that winning over Sarah's best friend would be easier than convincing Sarah they should have a second date had been.

"I hope so," Beth said.

"I know so."

"Still baking?" Kat asked Deborah.

"It's what I do."

"Six pies? Mom, even Neil can't eat that much."

Deborah laughed.

"Are you worried about meeting Sarah's new girlfriend?" Kat asked.

"Worried? No. I suppose it will be a bit strange seeing her with someone."

"Why? She was with Liza for three years."

"I'm not sure that was quite the same," Deborah said.

"Probably not," Kat agreed. "She seems sweet."

"Beth?"

"Yeah."

"I don't think Sarah would get involved with anyone who wasn't," Deborah said.

"Sweet?" Kat tried to clarify.

Deborah nodded. It amazed her that Kat still failed to see what drove everything Sarah did. Whether Sarah traveled home or chose to fly far away, Kat was always the reason. Deborah prayed that one day, someone would come into Sarah's life and change that reality. The closest she'd seen was Eliza. Sarah's college romance had opened her to the possibility of sharing her time, and parts of herself with someone other than Kat. Deborah wasn't convinced that anyone had stolen Sarah's heart, not from Kat. Kat possessed lingering innocence and gentleness that drew people to her naturally. Her personality had always balanced Sarah's—complemented Sarah's. Any woman who managed to get close to Sarah would need to possess several qualities: intelligence, honesty, and gentleness.

"She seems happy," Kat said. "Happier than I've heard her in a long time."

Happier than the day she came home to tell us about law school. Deborah agreed. She hoped that Sarah had finally found someone new to put at the center of her life. "I hope so," she told Kat. *I hope so.*

———————•◆•———————

Christmas Eve

"Relax," Sarah said.

"I feel like I'm intruding on your tradition."

"Impossible."

"Sarah, you and Kat have…"

"We've shared our tradition with other people plenty of times."

"You haven't had any time at all to spend with her."

Sarah grinned.

"What?"

"Not many women would be worried about that."

"She's your best friend."

"And, you're my girlfriend," Sarah said. "Besides, I would never subject you to my mom alone on the first visit home."

"Why not? Your mom is terrific."

"Did you see all those pies?"

"Yeah?"

"That's all the evidence you need."

"Of what?"

"The coming Inquisition," Sarah said.

Beth laughed. "You're insane."

"Probably." Sarah offered her hand. "Come on, let's go watch *Scrooged*."

"*Scrooged*?"

"Yep."

"Why?"

"I like to torture Kat."

Beth laughed.

"So, you two watch *Scrooged* every year?" Beth asked.

"Only because I can't find a *Murphy Brown* Christmas special," Sarah said. A pillow hit her in the face. "Hey!"

"Watch it," Kat warned. "I'll tell Beth your dirty little secret."

"Yeah? I'll tell Neil yours."

"He already knows."

"You told my brother you want to sleep with old women?" Another pillow strike.

Beth laughed. "Is this normal?" She looked at Neil to answer.

"Pretty much."

"And, it has nothing to do with age. It might be a blonde thing," Kat said.

Sarah coughed. "What? Sandra Bullock isn't blonde."

"Sandra Bullock?" Neil asked.

"Don't ask," Kat advised. "She's the reason we arrived at Candice Bergen."

"You can't choose Sandra Bullock. You know the rules."

"Am I the only one who's lost?" Beth asked.

"Nope," Neil said. "I learned in the fourth grade to pretend I understand."

Kat grinned. "Do you know why Sarah wants to watch *Scrooged* every year?"

"Because it's funny?" Neil guessed.

"No," Kat drew out the word.

Sarah shot her best friend a warning glare.

"Why?" Beth asked innocently.

"Do you want to tell her?" Kat asked Sarah. "Or shall I?"

"You've gotten mean. When did you get mean?" Sarah asked.

"You deal with twenty-five second graders all day long," Kat said.

Sarah huffed.

"Why?" Beth asked again.

"Sarah has a boy crush," Kat offered.

"Everyone has a boy crush," Beth said.

"Thank you," Sarah said.

"I don't," Neil chimed.

"Right." Sarah rolled her eyes.

"I don't!"

"Rusty Wallace?" Sarah said. "Your bedroom was plastered with his picture."

"Because he's cool!"

"Oh, Rusty! Rev it up," Sarah teased.

Beth and Kat both giggled.

"It's okay, honey," Kat told Neil. "Apparently, the one man who could turn Sarah straight for a few hours is Bill Murray."

"Eww!" Neil commented.

"He's funny!" Sarah defended herself.

"What was it? Sexy-ugly. That's what you said," Kat offered. Bam! Another pillow strike.

"Can't take the heat?" Kat threw the pillow back.

"Oh, I can take the heat, Miss Geriatric lover," Sarah replied. She tossed the pillow back.

Neil beckoned to Beth. "It's gonna get ugly," he said.

Beth followed Neil to the kitchen. "Are they always like that?"

"Not always," he said. He grabbed a pie and unwrapped it. "They just better hope they don't break any of mom's decorations."

Beth smiled.

"So, how did you meet Sarah? Not her version," he clarified.

"Well, the first time we *met*, she was dressing down one of the student workers in the law library."

Neil seemed puzzled.

"She was scolding him—to put it mildly. I saved him from certain death."

Neil chuckled. "I thought she said something about a dead car?"

"That came later. Almost a year later," Beth explained. "If I'd known killing her car battery was the way to get a date, I'd have found a way to accomplish that months earlier."

"Sarah mentioned that you two are moving in together."

"When my lease is up next month."

"That's great," Neil said. He handed Beth a plate with a piece of pie.

Beth detected a hint of worry emanating from Sarah's brother. "Neil? Is something wrong?"

Neil shook his head. He'd planned to propose to Kat on Christmas morning. Sarah seemed more relaxed at home than he had seen her in years. He guessed that the woman standing in the kitchen was the reason. Kat's laughter filtered to his ears. She was happy too, happy to have Sarah home. He couldn't spoil the holiday for any of them. He'd wait until Sarah and Beth made their move. "Nope," he answered with a smile. "Just doing a little planning in my head."

"I hope it doesn't involve a pie fight."

Neil laughed. "She told you about that, huh?"

"She did."

"Mom was so pissed."

"Did they really throw pies at each other?"

"Yep. Sarah started it, though," he said. "That was the year Kat moved in. After that, they stuck with pillows."

Beth smiled. "There's nothing quite like a best friend."

Neil's heart dropped. Sarah was his, and he was about to break her heart. "No, there isn't."

February 14, 2006

Kat wasn't sure what to make of Neil's behavior. He'd paced around the kitchen that morning nervously. She'd come home from school late in the afternoon to find him doing the same thing. Now, he was drumming his fingers on the arm of the couch. "Is the move that bad?" Kat asked.

"Huh?"

"You." Kat covered Neil's hand with hers. "What's with you today?"

"Nothing."

"You can't lie to save your life."

"I'm not lying."

"Uh-huh."

"I should've taken you out to dinner."

"Why?"

"It's Valentine's Day," he reminded her.

"Yes, I know. I loved the flowers, and the candy, and the dinner your mother sent over." She giggled.

He groaned.

"Neil?"

Neil scratched his brow, another nervous habit he'd possessed since childhood.

"Did something happen at work?" Kat asked.

Neil dropped to his knee.

Kat held her breath when he took her hand.

"I looked up different ways to do this. None of them made sense to me. I'm not good with poetry and stuff. I fix cars."

Kat smiled.

"I know we've talked about having a family and all that. I think… No, I want to have that with you. I guess, most people buy the ring before the house. We've never been most people." He took a deep breath and pulled a ring from his pocket. "I was hoping that maybe you might marry me."

Kat caressed Neil's cheek. "Of course, I'll marry you."

"Really?"

Kat laughed. "My mother will be thrilled that I won't be living in sin anymore." She kissed him.

"I love you," he said as he slipped the ring on Kat's finger.

"I love you too."

Beth walked into the apartment and lost her breath. Sarah was a hopeless romantic at heart. She counted four vases filled with roses. Candles adorned the coffee table, end tables, and mantle above the fireplace. Three weeks, that's how long they'd been living together. While it was true that they'd spent few nights apart over the last couple of years, sharing the same space as partners had already changed their relationship. Few things surprised Beth. Sarah was one of the exceptions.

"Long day?" Sarah emerged from the bedroom.

"I thought you were working late?"

"I lied."

"Is that so?"

"Practicing my attorney gig," Sarah joked. She walked over to Beth and kissed her. "I knew today was going to be rough for you."

Beth's head fell onto Sarah's shoulder. She was part of a team representing two young boys who'd been molested by their uncle and grandfather. "It sucked."

"I'm sorry," Sarah said. She kissed Beth's head and held her close. "How did it go?"

"Another continuance. How much longer do these kids have to be put through this?"

Sarah stroked Beth's back. "You're amazing."

"I don't feel amazing."

"I know you don't. You are." Sarah pulled away. "Are you hungry or would a strong martini be in order?"

Beth smiled lovingly. "I love you, Sarah."

"Where did that come from?"

"I do."

Sarah smiled. "I love you too."

"What if I told you that all I want right now is you?"

"Is that right?"

"Mm."

"And, how would you like me?"

"Preferably naked, without any arguments," Beth said.

"Oh, counselor, do I even get a chance for rebuttal?"

"I'm hoping my summation will be enough."

Sarah laughed. "I can't wait to hear it."

———◆·◆———

February 15, 2006

Sarah answered the phone without any thought. "Stuck at work again?"

"No."

"Kat?"

"That would be me."

"Sorry. I thought you were Beth."

"I figured. Are you busy?"

"Not really, why?"

"I was hoping we could talk."

"Uh-oh. That doesn't sound good."

"No, it is. Well, I think it is."

"Okay?"

Kat took a deep breath. She'd wanted to call Sarah as soon as Neil slipped the ring onto her finger. The longer she waited, the more she seemed to dread placing the call. It was ridiculous when she thought about it. She'd been living with Neil for over a year. The logical next step was marriage. She'd always imagined that she and Sarah would be each other's maid of honor. She pictured Sarah as the godmother to her children. Sarah was the first person Kat called with every important piece of news—her first kiss, her first job, her college acceptance letter, and the house Neil had purchased. There were two exceptions: the first time she'd made love and her engagement. She swallowed hard. "Neil proposed last night," she said in one breath.

Sarah heard the words. She seemed unable to process them.

"Sarah? Are you there?"

"Yeah. Yeah, I'm here. That's great, Kat," Sarah replied. Gut punch.

"Who knows? Maybe you'll be next."

True to form, Sarah reached for her humor. "I think I prefer living in sin," she said.

"You never know," Kat said.

"So? When do you think this momentous occasion might be?"

"I don't know," Kat said. "Next year sometime, I think."

"Well, I will be sure to mark my calendar."

"Sarah?"

"Yeah?"

"Are you all right?"

"Sure. I'm happy for you, Kat. Really, I am. It's been a tough week here." She needed a go-to, something—anything to change the subject. And, it had to be true. Kat would see through her in an instant if she lied.

"Why? What's wrong?"

"Beth's working on a tough case—emotionally speaking," Sarah explained. It was the perfect reason to justify the stress Sarah was sure Kat heard in her voice.

"Is she okay?"

"I think so," Sarah said. "It's taking its toll, though. She hasn't slept in days."

"You're worried about her."

"I am."

"She'll be okay, Sarah. She has you."

"I'm not sure I'm the solution."

"Maybe you're the support."

Sarah sighed. She was close to tears. Hearing Kat's news hadn't surprised her. It stung. It still stung. Why did it have to hurt? What was wrong with her? Hadn't she dealt with this for years? What difference did it make? Kat lived with Neil. Kat slept with Neil. God knows, Sarah knew that. Why was the idea of Kat marrying Neil so unnerving? *Permanence*. That was the answer: permanence. Sarah was terrific at offering support. Maybe she should've been a bra. Asking for support? That was not something Sarah enjoyed. And, who would she go to? Beth? That was laughable. "Honey, I'm sorry, I can't help it. I love you, but I've always been in love with Kat. Now, she's gone. Worse, she's marrying my brother." No, that wouldn't be a great plan. Maybe she could talk to her brother. Oh, right, he was in love with the same woman. Another bad idea. Perhaps, Sarah should do what most people did when their heart broke. She should call her best friend. Wrong answer—again. On top of all of it, she was genuinely concerned about Beth. She'd pour her heartache into that.

"Maybe," Sarah said. "I hate seeing her so torn up."

"You love her."

I do love her, but she'll never be you. "Yeah, I do."

"Just keep telling her that."

"That's your solution?" Sarah chuckled.

"You might be surprised how much it helps."

No. Sarah wouldn't be surprised at all. "I'll try that."

"If you need to talk…" Kat offered.

"I know. Listen, don't let me rain on your parade."

"You're not," Kat said. "I love you, Sarah. I don't want you to keep things from me. You never have before."

Oh, Kat, if only that were the truth. "Thanks," Sarah said. "I love you too, Kat." *God, help me, I do.*

<hr/>

A Week Later

Sarah tried to concentrate. Coffee. Maybe she should make some coffee. No. Bad idea.

"Hey." Beth walked into the kitchen. "You're still up?"

"Yeah. I need to be prepared for tomorrow."

Frustration poured off Sarah in visible waves like heat off the summer pavement. Beth reached over and closed the folder Sarah was studying.

"What are you doing?" Sarah asked.

"You can't drown yourself in work."

"I'm not."

Beth refused to release Sarah's gaze. Sarah had been avoiding life for the last week. More to the point, Sarah searched for constant distraction. First, Sarah poured herself into supporting Beth. When that didn't accomplish banishing her emotions, Sarah immersed herself in work. Sarah had taken on at least three new cases in the last week. "You're not going to find the answer in there." Beth pointed to the folder.

"I certainly hope I do or I'll lose this case."

"That's not what I mean." Beth took a seat at the kitchen table. "Talk to me."

"About the case?"

"No, Sarah. Tell me what's bothering you that you are so determined to avoid."

"Avoid?" Sarah pointed to the folders and papers spread across the kitchen table. "Does *this* look like avoidance to you? Because it looks like *immersion* to me."

Beth held Sarah's gaze firmly.

"What?" Sarah snapped.

"You've been restless ever since Kat told you about her engagement."

Gut punch. Sarah felt sick. What should she say?

"Talk to me."

"What is there to say?" Sarah asked. "My brother is marrying my best friend. We all saw that coming."

"That might be true. That doesn't mean it sits well with you."

"Why wouldn't it? Neil and Kat have been together a long time, Beth."

"Restating the obvious is not your best argument," Beth said.

"What do you want me to say?"

"How about what you *feel?*"

Like that ever mattered. "How I *feel?* Gee, I don't know. Let me think about that."

"Sarah, I wish you would trust me enough to talk to me."

Shit. "I do trust you." Sarah mentally smacked herself. She did trust Beth. She loved Beth. Kat and Neil? Sarah had convinced herself she'd accepted the inevitable long ago. Now, the inevitable was staring her in the face like one of the mythical giants she'd been fascinated by in her youth. A giant that had been stalking her and suddenly was ready to strike. She rubbed her face. Talk to Beth? What was she supposed to say? *I love you, but the truth is that I've wanted to be with Kat since I was twelve. I never thought she'd marry my brother.* No. That was not the best answer to give. Beth deserved more than Sarah's denials. Sarah settled on part of the issue that continued to plague her thoughts. "What if it doesn't work?" Sarah asked.

"You mean, what if something happens that comes between Neil and Kat?"

Sarah nodded.

"Babe, that could happen now."

"True. They're not married now, Beth. Call me crazy, I think that ups the stakes a bit. What happens if it falls apart?"

Beth smiled. "I don't think you will ever lose Kat."

"How can you be so sure?"

"Because she loves you, Sarah."

Sarah groaned. "I don't know."

"You don't know that Kat loves you?"

"No, I know that."

"So, does Neil."

Sarah shook her head. Neil loved her. Neil also seemed to enjoy hurting her, just a little bit. Sarah still couldn't understand why her younger brother was determined to stick it to her. She knew that he had gone out with Kat a few times. That hadn't bothered her. Sarah had expected it to pass the moment Kat met someone new. The day she saw them together in the back of Neil's truck changed everything in Sarah's world. Kat's news sent Sarah careening off the memory ledge—the memory of that rainy afternoon. The look in Neil's eyes when they met with hers in the distance continued to haunt Sarah. For a brief second, she noted regret, perhaps even apology. In less than an instant, Neil's eyes sparkled with an odd sense of accomplishment, as if he had defeated Sarah in one of their childhood games. It made Sarah sick. More than the sound of Kat's voice speaking her brother's name, it had been the joy she saw in Neil's eyes that day that twisted the knife over and over in Sarah's heart, or was it her back?

"Neil might love me," she agreed. "He has a funny way of showing it sometimes. I never thought anything could come between us—any of us."

"Has it?" Beth asked.

That depends on who you ask. "No," Sarah lied. "Not really."

"Why do you think Neil and Kat getting married will?"

"I don't. I think it *could*."

Beth nodded. "Not everything falls apart."

Sarah smiled. Beth was forever an optimist. It was one of the qualities Sarah admired most in her girlfriend. Beth saw the best in people, much like Kat did. Beth saw possibility in situations where most people would see only grief and despair. "Forever the optimist," Sarah commented affectionately.

"I'm not sure I'd say that. Bad things happen," Beth admitted. "Things can fall apart. Sometimes, the worst things that can happen lead to the most wonderful places."

"Like I said…" Sarah began. She leaned over and kissed Beth's lips. "Forever the optimist."

"You can talk to me about anything," Beth said. "Remember that."

"I will."

"I hope so."

Chapter Seven: Hello and Goodbye
December 24, 2008

One year. That's how long Sarah had been Kat's sister-in-law. She'd accepted the role she played in Kat's life as best she could. They spoke often. Oddly, more than they had in many years. Beth's presence and the physical distance between them had helped to ease Sarah's pain. Kat was usually full of stories when Beth and Sarah visited for the holidays. Kat had been markedly quiet all morning. That led Beth to suggest that Sarah and Kat rekindle their annual tradition—alone. To Sarah's surprise, Neil agreed. He took Beth out to the garage to see a couple of the cars he was working on, and she promised him a beer afterward. Twenty minutes into *Scrooged*, and Sarah could no longer bear the silence.

"Kat? Want to talk about it?" Sarah's heart stopped instantly when Kat looked at her. Tears streamed down Kat's cheeks. Twenty minutes, twenty years, twenty decades would never change the way Sarah loved Kat. She reached out and pulled Kat into her arms. "It can't be that bad." A million possibilities flooded Sarah's mind in an instant. Neil was cheating on Kat. *No way.* Neil was sick. *No, Mom would have told me that.* Kat was sick. *Oh, God.* "Kat, talk to me."

"I don't know if we're going to have children."

"What?" Sarah tried to make out Kat's words through her tears.

"I don't know, Sarah. I didn't get the best news."

"Tell me. It can't be that bad."

Kat caught her breath. "I don't know if I can get pregnant."

"Okay?"

"If I do, we'll… Well, we'll need help. And, that's expensive, Sarah. It's…"

"Shhh. Kat, please don't cry."

"I can't help it. What if he decides that…"

"Stop," Sarah said. "Neil loves you."

"Yes, but…"

"No way. Now, tell me what happened."

Sarah sat for the next hour and listened to Kat explain the results of her fertility tests. She heard all of Kat's fears and worries. At the top of the list was how they might afford fertility treatments. It could take years to be successful. It could take years and they might never be successful. Perhaps, they could adopt. The same concerns arose. Adoption was expensive and a long process.

"It'll happen," Sarah said.

"How can you be so sure?"

"Because if anyone is supposed to be a mom, it's you. It'll happen."

"I'm glad you're so confident."

"I am."

Kat giggled through a few remaining tears. "I'm scared, Sarah."

Sarah held Kat. More times than Sarah cared to count, Kat had rescued her. Now, Sarah thought it was her turn. "I promise, Kat. I promise you, you will be a mom."

"How can you promise that?"

"Because there isn't anything you want more, and there isn't anything I won't do for you to have that."

Kat closed her eyes. "Found a magic wand?"

"Maybe," Sarah replied. *Or my wallet.* "Whatever it takes, Kat. Whatever it takes."

———◆•◆———

"Can I talk to you for a minute?" Sarah requested.

Neil nodded. "She told you. I know she did. She told me."

"Take a walk with me?"

He nodded again and grabbed his coat. "I don't know what to do. Her insurance is great. It doesn't cover everything." Neil shook his head.

"I'll pay for it."

"What?"

"I said, I'll pay for whatever you need."

"No," Neil replied. "I'm not a charity case."

"I don't think that. I think you're my brother."

"I can't accept that, Sarah. She'll kill me."

"No, she won't."

"Sarah, it's my responsibility…"

"Look, I'm not here to look after Mom and Dad."

"Mom and Dad don't need help."

"Not yet. They will."

"That's your way of telling me that you're never coming home," he guessed.

Sarah looked ahead. "My life is in California."

"With Beth."

Sarah made no reply. "Yours is here. I always figured that whatever I saved would end up going to your kids anyway."

"Why? Maybe you and Beth…"

"I don't think so," Sarah said.

"You never know."

Sarah smiled. She knew. "So, instead of saving for their future, I'll invest in their beginning."

"I can't ask you…"

"You didn't. I offered. If it makes you feel better, you can pay me back. I'll just put it away for their college."

Neil chuckled. "Sarah…"

"Just accept the offer, Neil."

He nodded. "I still think you and Beth…"

"Don't think," Sarah advised. "It gets us both into trouble."

March 13, 2010

Kat toyed with her bottom lip and pressed her ear to the phone receiver. "Are you sure?" She listened. "Positive? Thank you." She placed the receiver in its cradle and let out a long breath. Neil was away at a NASCAR race in Florida. She'd never manage to get him in the phone mid-afternoon. She picked the phone back up and called the one person she was sure would answer.

"Yes, Claudia?"

"Kat's on line two."

"Kat?"

"Yep."

"Okay, thanks. Do me a favor? Hold my calls?"

"Already done," Sarah's assistant replied.

"Kat?"

"Hi. Sorry to bother you in the middle of the day."

"You're not bothering me. What's up?"

"Sarah?"

"What's wrong?"

"Nothing." Kat took a deep breath. "I'm pregnant."

"Seriously?"

"Seriously."

"Is Neil opening champagne?"

"He doesn't know yet."

"What?"

"He's in Daytona working on a crew. I couldn't wait to tell you."

"I'm excited for you, both of you."

"I still can't believe it's real," Kat confessed.

"I can."

"Yeah, well, you've always believed in magic."

"I wish I was there to celebrate with you. You should go over to Mom's and make her cook for you."

"I might. I think I want to tell Neil first."

"Yeah, well, don't tell him I know. I'll play dumb. I'm good at that." *I am really good at that.*

"Sarah?"

"Yeah?"

"Thank you for everything."

"*I* didn't do *anything*," Sarah joked.

Kat laughed. Leave it to Sarah to find a joke in an emotional conversation. "Yes, you did. We wouldn't have gotten here without you. I owe you."

"No, you don't. That's what best friends are for."

Kat doubted most best friends went to the lengths Sarah did to offer support. Sarah had loaned Kat and Neil the money to pursue in vitro treatments. Beth had a friend that specialized in fertility medicine. He had made the recommendation for a doctor in Massachusetts and promised to answer any questions if Kat and Neil needed someone to talk to. Sarah had taken late night calls and listened to Kat's fears for hours on end. Best friend seemed a pathetically inadequate description for Sarah. "I hope you know I would do anything for you too," Kat offered.

"I know that. I'm glad that I could help. Besides, Neil hates poop. He's always hated poop. He gags at the sight of it." Sarah chuckled. "Diapers? Oh, make sure you take *lots* of video for me."

"You really are evil sometimes."

"I'm happy for you, Kat."

"I know you are. I'm going to try to call him. I doubt I'll get him, but…"

"Congratulations," Sarah said again.

"I love you, you know?"

"I love you too, but I'm not changing diapers."

Kat laughed.

"I will, however, videotape Neil."

"I believe it. I'll call you later."

Sarah hung up the call and closed her eyes. She was genuinely happy for Kat, and for Neil. Kat's dreams were all coming true. Someone should be able to keep her belief in happy endings. If anyone deserved the fairytale ending, it was Kat. "I love you too, Kat."

December 22, 2010

"Shh," Kat hushed the baby in her arms. "Now, what's all this about?" She cradled her infant daughter and rocked back and forth until the baby quieted. "Oh, Brie," she cooed. "You know, you are going to have some special visitors for your first Christmas."

"How are my girls?"

Kat smiled at Neil. "We're both a little tired, I think."

"Why don't you go take a rest?" Neil suggested. "I'll take care of Brie for a bit."

"I thought you were headed to Mom's?"

"You know her," Neil said. "She insists she doesn't need my help with anything and there is no way she is going to let you jump in."

Kat sighed. "Feeding this family, all the festivities— it's a lot of work for Mom, Neil."

Neil shrugged. "She's excited. It's her first Christmas being Nana. Let her do it."

"She's hoping that Sarah will have an announcement, you know?"

Neil nodded. He was sure that Kat was right. Sarah and Beth had been together for five years. They seemed to be a solid couple. It was easy to see that Beth adored his sister, and Neil had noted the affectionate gazes Sarah cast in Beth's direction. Still, he doubted that Sarah would be giving his parents any Christmas present in the form of engagement announcements or ceremony invitations. If Sarah had any intention of that, Neil was positive Kat would have been the first to know.

"Well, I hope she's prepared for some disappointment," he said.

"Why? You don't think they're headed that way?"

"You'd know better than me."

"Not really," Kat disagreed. "Sarah's pretty tight-lipped when it comes to her relationship with Beth. Actually, she's always been quiet about her relationships."

Kat's revelation didn't surprise Neil. He remained confident that if Sarah decided to make a formal commitment to anyone, she would be inclined to tell Kat before anyone else. One thing Neil did know, Kat had always been and would always be first in his sister's heart.

"You know, Sarah," Neil began. "She's always got something big on the horizon."

"Yeah. I just wonder when that something might be a *someone*."

Neil reached over and took hold of the baby. "Go on," he instructed Kat. "Go get some rest. We both know once Sarah gets home it will be a whirlwind."

⸻

Sarah looked on as Kat cradled her niece. Brianna. Sarah shouldn't have been surprised by the name. Kat's favorite book to read her class was about a princess named Brianna who became a dragon slayer. Sometimes, Sarah thought that Kat should've become a writer instead of a teacher. Being with children suited Kat. No wonder motherhood looked good on her. If anyone had been destined to become a mom, it was Kat. Sarah's heart simultaneously sank and soared. For as long as Sarah could remember, Kat talked about being a mom. Kat dreamed about minivans and basketball hoops in the drive-way. She felt Beth's hand slip into hers.

"She's beautiful, Kat," Beth said.

"She looks like Neil," Kat said. "And Sarah."

Sarah shook her head. "She looks like a baby."

Kat's eyes met Sarah's playfully. "She whines like you too."

"I have never whined, Kat."

"Oh, I can think of a few occasions when you gave Brie a run for her money."

"Never happened."

"How about when you got stuck…"

"Do not say in the cave."

Kat smirked.

"What cave?" Beth asked.

"You never told her that story?" Kat asked Sarah.

"Didn't come up," Sarah replied.

"She suffers from selective storytelling syndrome," Kat explained. "Always has."

"Thank you for your diagnosis, Dr. Masters," Sarah teased.

"You do," Kat continued.

"What cave?" Beth inquired.

"When we were about fourteen, Sarah got it into her head that she should go spelunking."

"Hey! Neil did it," Sarah argued.

"No, I didn't."

"What?" Sarah looked at her brother to explain.

"Told you," Kat said.

"You said you went in that cave with your friends." Sarah pointed a finger at her brother. "You even told me about the bats!"

"Yeah, I lied."

Beth laughed. She continued to be amused by Sarah, Kat, and Neil. The connection all three shared was palpable. She never grew tired of hearing tales about her partner. She listened as Kat and Sarah bantered about what had happened in the cave. Neil occasionally rolled his eyes. Sarah groaned, and Kat smirked triumphantly. Sarah had been a precocious kid. It made Beth wonder what Sarah's children might be like. She held onto Sarah's hand, her thoughts spiraling to a future Christmas, one that might find her rocking the baby she and Sarah shared.

A Week Later

"So?"

Sarah looked up from the book in her lap at Beth. "So?" she returned the vague question. "Oh no, what's ticking in your brain?" Sarah inquired.

"There's nothing that says that couldn't be us," Beth replied. Sarah's brow wrinkled in confusion and Beth sighed. "Brie," she said. "I saw the look in your eyes when you held her," Beth explained.

"What look was that?"

"Do you want that?" Beth asked.

"Want what?" Sarah wondered.

"A family," Beth answered.

Sarah's heart dropped so rapidly in her chest she thought she might lose consciousness.

"Sarah?" Beth called with concern.

"You mean kids?" Sarah tried to clarify.

"Do you?"

"Do you?" Sarah returned the question in kind. Beth's face tightened measurably, and Sarah sighed. "Is that what you want, Beth?" Sarah asked gently.

Beth hesitated to answer. She wasn't certain what she saw brewing in Sarah's eyes—a storm of some kind. It left a pit in her stomach. "I love kids."

"I love kids too," Sarah replied.

"But?"

"Beth, I never thought about having children. I mean, we've never talked about that."

"Maybe we should."

Sarah nodded. "I think the fact that you want to talk about it tells me everything I need to know."

"And, that response tells me we are not on the same page at all."

Sarah wasn't sure what to say. *Kids?* There were days when Sarah was positive she resembled a petulant twelve-year-old. "You would want to do that with me?" Sarah questioned.

"Why wouldn't I want to have children with you?" Beth asked. "I think we could offer a child a great deal, don't you?"

"You mean stability and opportunity," Sarah surmised.

"Actually, I meant love."

Sarah scratched her brow. "Seeing Brie gave you the bug."

"The bug?"

"The baby bug," Sarah said.

"You think that I am raising this just because Kat and Neil had a baby?" Beth bit.

"I didn't say that."

"What are you saying, Sarah?"

"I'm just wondering where this is coming from."

"We've been together for five years. I'm not sure why it would surprise you that I want to discuss our future."

"And, you would like our future to include a family."

Beth nodded. "I would, but it's hardly my decision."

Sarah found herself at a loss. She had never considered having children. She and Beth had created what Sarah had thought was a comfortable and meaningful life together. She knew that Beth loved children. Until now, they had both been focused on building their careers.

"I know you love kids," Sarah commented.

"So, do you."

"I do, but I never thought I'd have any."

"Why not?"

Sarah shrugged. *Why haven't I?*

Beth sat down beside Sarah and took her hand. "Sarah? Talk to me."

"I'm not sure what to say."

"How about telling me how you feel."

"You mean about having children?" Sarah took a deep breath. "I'm not sure that's what I want."

"What do you want?"

That's an excellent question. "I like our life the way it is."

"You *like* our life?"

"Don't you?"

Beth held Sarah's hands in hers. "Yes, I like our life. I love you, Sarah. There isn't anything I wouldn't give you or want to do with you. I thought you knew that."

Sarah squeezed Beth's hands. "I love you too." *I do love you, Beth.*

"There is a but coming."

"I don't think that being a parent is what I want," Sarah said honestly.

Beth nodded. "And, that's all there is to it, I take it."

"What do you want me to say? If I tell you that I need to think about it, that would just be leading you to have false hope. How would that be fair?"

"I suppose it wouldn't be."

"We have a great life. Why do you want to change that?"

Beth's eyes grew sad. "In my experience, life changes whether we want it to or not."

"That might be true, but this is something we would have to choose."

"It is."

Sarah closed her eyes. Part of her was screaming to give Beth what she wanted. After all, what Beth had said was true. They had a great deal to offer a child. Sarah did like her life with Beth. She'd never considered that it would end. She also had never put much faith in the idea of forever. Beth was right. Life changed whether you wanted it to or not. Sarah was certain hers was about to take an unexpected turn.

"I want to give you what you want," Sarah said.

"But you can't."

"Not this," Sarah replied.

Beth nodded and made her way to her feet.

"Where does that leave us?" Sarah asked.

Beth shook her head. "I honestly don't know."

Sarah sat on the bed watching Beth pack. "Beth…"

"Please, don't make this harder than it is."

"I don't understand why this is happening."

"Sarah, please."

"I love you."

"I love you. That's not the issue."

"Why is there an issue? We've been together for how long? You never mentioned wanting kids."

Beth shook her head. "Things change, Sarah."

"Yeah, I guess so."

"That's not fair."

"What's not fair?" Sarah asked.

Beth closed her suitcase, shook her head again and walked out of the room. She was tired of discussing why she felt the need to leave and exhausted by their arguments.

Sarah followed. "Beth, please."

"Sarah, you might want to ask yourself why you always hold back."

"What are you talking about?"

Beth tried to explain to Sarah how she felt and what she needed. Sarah seemed unable to fathom Beth's perspective, or maybe Sarah was unwilling to understand. For years, something kept Sarah at a slight distance. Sarah loved her. Beth believed that. Sarah cared about the life they'd built. Beth didn't doubt that either. There would be no point in denying that Beth wanted Sarah. More than anything, Beth wished that Sarah would walk across the room, pull her close, and tell her that they would make things work. Sarah wouldn't.

"I love you more than anything in this world," Beth said. "I fell in love with you the moment I saw you, Sarah."

"I love you too."

"But not enough," Beth replied. "Not enough to look down the line and see me at its end. I need that. I want that. I want someone who sees me when she closes her eyes. I want a woman who looks at me and dreams about the future—everything a future can hold. I thought one day, if I could be patient, I would be that person for you. God knows, I want to be."

"Beth…"

Beth put her hand on the door knob and turned. "Something holds you back." She smiled at Sarah. "If you love her, Sarah—if you love Kat that much, you owe it to yourself to let her know. You owe it to her." She smiled. "I'll see you."

Sarah sat dumbfounded. Her chest tightened, her gut twisted, and her eyes burned. How could she let Beth walk out the door? Her face fell into her hands. Beth knew. How did Beth know that Sarah loved Kat? Had Beth always known? "What am I doing?" Sarah fell onto the couch and sobbed. "What have I done?"

Kat rolled over and grabbed the phone. "Hello?" The only sound she could hear was a faint whimpering. She sat straight up in bed. "Sarah?" No reply. "Honey, what's wrong?"

"She left."

"Who left?" Kat couldn't make out Sarah's words. "Sarah, are you telling me that Beth left?"

"Yes."

A forceful jolt traveled through Kat's heart. If ever she'd seen someone in love, it was Beth Greer. Beth's eyes rarely left Sarah when they were together. It made no sense. "What happened?"

"I guess she wants different things."

"Oh, Sarah. I'm sorry. What can I do?"

Nothing. Why had she called Kat? Did she think hearing Kat's voice would ease her pain? It did. It always did. Kat's voice had always possessed the power to calm Sarah. She cradled a pillow on the couch. "I'm sorry. I didn't mean to wake you."

"You can call me anytime. You know that."

"I miss you," Sarah mumbled.

Emptiness echoed in Sarah's voice. It cut through Kat like tiny glass shards piercing her heart. She pictured Sarah's face. A memory of Sarah soaking wet from the rain as she walked toward the Masters' front porch played like a movie in her thoughts. "I wish I could be there."

Sarah struggled to breathe. Fresh tears surfaced. Would they ever cease? Would Sarah ever feel whole? No. She was broken, too damaged to ever be put back together again. Humpty Dumpty—that's who Sarah had become.

"Sarah." Kat's eyes grew moist. "It'll be okay. Come home."

Home? Sarah looked around the condominium. There were so many pieces of Beth left— pictures of trips they'd taken, holidays they had shared. Sarah noted Beth's reading glasses lying a few feet away on the end table. She reached out for them and choked on the sob that followed. Wasn't love supposed to bring happiness? Sarah wanted to laugh. Here she was wishing that she could crawl into Kat's embrace. What was she mourning? Was it Beth's departure or was it the reason for her exit? Sarah gathered her emotions and set them aside. A deep breath. A long, audible exhale. "I wish I could."

"Why can't you?" Kat asked.

How long did Kat want to continue this conversation? Sarah's list of reasons was endless. She could give Kat all the expected answers. *I have to work. I have my condo. I have my friends. I have my life here.* All of it would be accurate; none of it spoke the truth. "I can't," Sarah replied. "I just can't."

"I wish I could be there," Kat said honestly. Had it not been for Brie, Kat would've boarded the next plane to Los Angeles. There was Brie to think about.

"I'll be okay."

Sure, you will.

"I'm always okay," Sarah said. "I'm sorry I woke you."

"Don't you dare apologize. I'll call you later and check on you."

"You don't have to."

"Don't be stupid."

Sarah chuckled despite the pain she felt. "Stupid?"

"If you think I'm not going to worry about you, you *are* stupid."

"I'll be all right, Kit Kat."

"You haven't called me that in a long time."

Sarah resisted the temptation to reply, *Because you aren't my Kit Kat anymore.*

"Call me if you need to talk," Kat said.

"I will, but I won't."

"I mean it."

"I know."

"I love you, Sarah."

Sarah gripped the pillow in her arms tighter. "I know you do, Kit Kat."

Kat swallowed the lump in her throat. "I do. Get some rest."

"You too." Sarah tossed the phone aside. She closed her eyes and squeezed the pillow in her arms. Sleep. She needed sleep. At least, she could disappear into her dreams for a few hours. Who needed reality? Who needed *home*? "Sleep."

———— ••• ————

Three Years Later
December 24, 2013

"Sarwah!"

"Who?"

Brie giggled.

"Are you looking for someone?" Sarah teased her niece.

"You!"

"Me?"

"You!"

Kat sniggered from her seat on the sofa. "I think she might have finally met her match."

"Who? Sarah or Brie?" Deborah asked.

Kat shrugged. "They're so much alike."

"Sarah and Brie?"

"Yeah."

Deborah looked back at her daughter and her granddaughter. There was no sense in denying Kat's observation.

Brie resembled Sarah in numerous ways. She was lanky, and she sported curly blonde hair. It would be easy to look at a childhood photo of Sarah and mistake her for Brie. That was until you looked in Brie's eyes. Brie's eyes were just like her mother's, a soft, golden-brown that reflected intellect, sweetness, and just a hint of mischief. Years of living, loving, and mothering had taught Deborah valuable lessons about people. Most people didn't see with their eyes, not when it came to the people they loved. Most people saw with their heart. Kat saw Sarah in Brie because she loved Sarah and missed her desperately. Sarah remained the person that Kat trusted and admired most. Kat's expression as she watched Sarah and Brie was a roadmap to her heart.

"She misses you too," Deborah offered.

A weak smile did little to conceal Kat's doubt.

"She does," Deborah promised.

Does she? Little by little, the late-night conversations and confessions that Kat had enjoyed for nearly twenty years with Sarah had dwindled. Sarah's life existed in what equated to a foreign land for Kat. Kat lived life three hours ahead in time from Sarah. That was the excuse they both used. When Kat was coming home from work, Sarah was in the middle of her day. When Sarah was winding down from dinner, Kat was putting Brie to bed. Endless lame excuses crept into the time Kat once shared with Sarah. She waited all year for Sarah's holiday visit, for Sarah to pop home at Brie's birthday. It had been years since Kat and Sarah had enjoyed their Christmas Eve tradition together. Kat sighed.

"Why don't you and Sarah rekindle that tradition of yours?" Deborah suggested.

"I'm not sure she's up for that."

Deborah patted Kat's knee. "Only one way to find out."

Kat's gaze fell on Sarah. "I guess so."

———— •—•———

"I'll get the movie," Sarah said.

Kat grabbed her hand. "I was hoping maybe we could just talk."

Sarah flopped onto the sofa with a thud. "Talk, huh? What's up, Kit Kat?"

"I miss you."

"I miss you too."

"No, I really miss you, Sarah. I feel like we don't talk anymore."

Sarah nodded. "We talk."

"Not like we used to. I don't have any idea what's going on with you."

"There's not much to tell," Sarah said. "Work, work, and more work."

"No girlfriend?"

"I have lots of girl *friends*."

"Very funny."

"No one worth mentioning," Sarah said.

"How's Beth?"

Sarah sighed. Kat's line of questioning was one of the reasons Sarah sought distance from her entire family. Not everyone needed to get married and have babies to be happy. She didn't. Why couldn't everyone accept that? "Beth is good," Sarah said.

"Do you like her partner?"

"Soon to be wife, and, yes, I do. Donna's great."

Kat nodded. "You know, Mom still hopes…"

"Mom loves romance novels," Sarah said. "Beth is my friend. I'm happy for her." *I'm happy for everyone.*

"What about you?"

"Me?"

"Are you happy?" Kat asked.

"Depends on how you define happy, I guess." It was the most honest answer Sarah had in her arsenal of excuses and justifications. She wasn't *unhappy*. That was enough for Sarah.

"That's lame, Sarah."

Sarah chuckled. "Why is it lame? It's the truth. I love my job. I have friends—even Beth and Donna. I don't have anything to complain about, Kat."

"And, that makes you happy?"

"I see people every day with a reason to be unhappy," Sarah offered. "I see families torn apart, and kids who are afraid to be in the same room with their parents. There's a lot of shit in this world, Kat. It reminds me that happiness is never permanent."

"That's depressing."

"Why? Because it's true. You can be happy for a few minutes, maybe even a few weeks. No one is happy all the time," Sarah observed. "Maybe the reason so many people are miserable is that they have some crazy idea they're supposed to be happy twenty-four hours a day. I don't think happiness is an attainable goal."

Kat's heart clenched. Sarah's observations held more than a nugget of truth, but the reason behind the philosophy tore at Kat. Loneliness danced in Sarah's eyes. Sarah might be able to hide that from most people, not from Kat. "I don't know," Kat said. "I don't think you can be happy forever, but I think you can be fulfilled. Maybe that's what happiness really is."

"Maybe," Sarah said.

"Do you still love your job? Honestly?"

"Yeah, I do." *Now, that is one-hundred-percent true.* "I do. If I can help, I have to try."

"See? You do still believe in fairytales."

Sarah smiled. "For some people, I do."

"For some people?"

"Yeah. Maybe there are some of us who are meant to invent them so other people can live them," Sarah said. "Speaking of fairytales…" Sarah hopped up from her seat. "How about we watch *Scrooged?*"

In that instant, a piece of Kat broke. *Oh, Sarah.*

Chapter Eight: Falling Apart
May 14, 2016

"Brie!" Kat called up the stairs.

"Coming, Mom!"

Kat shook her head and turned to make her way to the front door. Unexpectedly, she collided with Neil. "You're off early today," she observed.

"I have a meeting," he commented absently.

Kat smiled. "You all right?" she asked.

"Yeah, sure," he replied. He leaned in and placed a chaste kiss on her cheek.

Kat looked at him curiously. She wasn't certain what she saw in his eyes. Neil had been unusually reserved in their conversations of late. Kat chalked up his quiet demeanor to stress at work. He had started traveling more over the last year. He'd been working on and off with a NASCAR team. It was his lifelong dream. While Kat was certain that Neil loved what he was doing, she wondered if the distance was beginning to cause a rift between them. She sighed and took hold of his hand. "Are you sure you are okay?" she asked him again. Neil's weak smile tugged at Kat's heart.

"Just tired," he told her.

"Are you taking me, Daddy?" Brie asked excitedly.

"No, honey. I'm taking you to school," Kat replied as she let go of Neil's hand.

Neil looked at Brie and smiled sadly. "I can take her. It will give you a little extra time this morning," he offered.

Kat tipped her head and narrowed her gaze. "Are you sure? I know you have a lot to do."

"Sure, I'm sure," he put her argument to rest. "Get your backpack," he told his daughter.

"You don't have to take her," Kat said.

Neil kept his focus on Brie as she scurried into the living room to retrieve her backpack. "No, it's okay. It's on my way."

Kat sighed inwardly. "Neil?"

"Yeah?" He finally looked at her.

Kat's face scrunched in concern. "Are you sure?"

He nodded.

"Ready!" Brie announced as she bounced back into the room. "Bye, Mom!" She waved to Kat.

Kat chuckled. At six, a ride to school from Daddy was an adventure—any deviation from the normal daily routine heralded an adventure for Brie. "I'll see you at Nana's later," Kat said.

"'Kay!" Brie called back, already halfway to her father's truck.

"I'll see you tonight," Kat told Neil.

Neil nodded. He leaned in and kissed Kat's cheek. "I'll see you," he whispered.

Kat stepped out on the front porch and waved goodbye. She was grateful for a short reprieve. Neil's simple gesture would add an extra half an hour to her morning. That meant that Kat could sit and enjoy a full cup of coffee on the porch before she had to leave for school. It was a luxury that she was rarely afforded. She closed the front door and headed off to pour herself a second cup of coffee.

———— ·•· ————

"I'm glad you called," Sarah said.

"You just wanted a free breakfast," Beth teased.

"That's a bonus." Sarah was about to continue when the waitress approached their table.

"Ready to order?"

Sarah nodded. "Since she's paying I'll have an extra-large Bloody Mary, banana pancakes, and coffee. Larger than the Bloody Mary if possible."

Beth laughed. "Hungry?"

Sarah grinned.

The waitress turned to Beth. "And, you?"

"Just some fruit and a cup of decaf."

With a nod, the waitress left.

"Decaf?" Sarah puzzled over the order. "Miss Caffeine Addict is ordering decaf? What gives?"

Beth smiled. "That's why I wanted to see you."

"To tell me you quit your one vice?"

"No," Beth chuckled. "Donna and I are expecting."

Sarah's gaze narrowed. "Expecting what?"

"Sarah, I'm…."

Sarah guffawed. "I'm not *that* dense." She reached across the table and took Beth's hand. "Congratulations."

"Thanks."

"But nine months with no caffeine? God, poor Donna."

It was Beth's turn to laugh. She'd met Donna Brasefield a year after her split from Sarah. They'd started as friends, slowly winding their way to marriage. "I know. I'd better hope she doesn't lock me up somewhere."

Sarah's gaze softened. After their break-up, Sarah had remained single. The longest she'd managed to stay involved with one person was six months. It suited her. Two failed relationships had taught her an important lesson. Sarah did hold back. Some part of her felt that moving forward would betray her love for Kat. It was ridiculous. Kat and Neil were happily married. Kat had the job she'd always wanted, the family she dreamed of, and the life she desired. Sarah had distanced herself from Kat too. Year by year, she found more excuses to avoid visiting home. She poured herself into work, taking on pro bono clients, and building her firm. She missed Beth more than she had expected to. She missed Kat. Sarah was tired of missing people, even if it was her doing that caused her pain. In time, she and Beth had built a new dynamic. They were friends—best friends, in fact. She did love Beth Greer. Just like Kat, Beth deserved everything the world could offer—everything Sarah was incapable of giving her.

"I'm happy for you."

"I know you are. What about you?"

"Me?" Sarah winked. "The only thing I am expecting is to end up paying this tab."

Beth's expression communicated concern and understanding. "Sarah."

"Oh, come on, this date isn't about me. Let's keep talking about you."

Beth sighed, but obeyed Sarah's wishes. Someday, she hoped Sarah might give herself a break, give herself a chance, and stop feeling responsible for everyone's happiness or misery. "You win," she said.

"What do I win? The tab?"

"You can have that too," Beth promised.

Sarah smiled. For an instant, she wondered what it might have been like to have Beth tell her this news as a partner. The moment passed quickly. It left a mark. Funny, how that worked. She was relieved when the waitress set her drink on the table. "Ah, it's Bloody Mary, the girl I love!"

Oh, Sarah.

Kat's hand trembled. The note fell from her grasp, floating like a leaf on the wind to the floor. Her head was spinning yet everything seemed to be moving slowly. She collapsed into a kitchen chair and stared blankly ahead. "This can't be happening."

Sarah looked at the number on her cell phone. "Hey, Mom."

"Sarah…"

"Mom? What is it?"

"It's Kat, honey."

Sarah's heart stopped for a split second.

"Sarah, Neil left her." No answer. "Sarah?"

"What do you mean he left her?"

"I wish I knew."

"I don't understand."

"He left her a note this morning," Deborah said. "I don't know what he's thinking. I do know that Kat is a wreck."

"I'll get the first flight I can."

Deborah nodded.

"Mom?"

"Are you sure that's what you want to do?"

"I'll let you know as soon as I have it arranged," Sarah promised. "Is she…"

"She's confused. She's hurt."

"I'll be there as soon as I can."

Deborah stared at the phone in her hand. Sarah would quit everything, put anything on hold if Kat needed her. She shook her head. She had spent years watching Sarah struggle with unrequited love. For most of that time, she believed that in time, Sarah's heart would be captured by someone new. Eliza had given her hope. When Beth appeared in Sarah's life, Deborah was convinced that Sarah was ready to let go of Kat. Sarah had let Kat go. She'd never let go of Kat. There was a difference between those two things. Sarah accepted Kat's decisions. She supported her best friend with as much manufactured enthusiasm as she could muster. But Sarah never released Kat from her heart. Running home now to pick up the pieces of Kat's broken heart could lead many places. Deborah prayed it did not lead to more fragments in her children's lives.

"Mommy?" Brie tugged on Kat's shirt.

"Yes, love?"

"Where's Daddy?"

"Daddy went on a trip for work," Kat explained.

Brie frowned. "When's he back?"

"I'm not sure," Kat admitted. She saw Brie's frown deepen. "But you know what?"

Brie shook her head.

Kat smiled. "Someone is coming to visit you tomorrow."

"Who?"

"You don't know who?" Kat teased.

"Auntie Sarah!"

"That's right."

Brie brightened. She didn't see her aunt often. She did talk to her every week, most times when she was at her nana's house. Sarah made her laugh, and Sarah encouraged her to tell stories. She looked forward to Sarah's calls, and to calling Sarah. Most of all, she loved to hear her mother tell stories about her aunt. Her mother always smiled when she talked about Auntie Sarah. "Can she stay here?"

Kat sighed lightly. "If she wants to. She might want to stay with Nana."

"We can ask her."

"Yes, we can ask her," Kat agreed. "Now, let's get you pajamas. Tomorrow will be a busy day."

"'Cause Auntie Sarah is coming?"

"Right."

"Mommy?"

"Yes?"

"Will you tell me a story?"

"I can read you a story before bed."

Brie shook her head again. "About Auntie Sarah," she said.

Kat smiled genuinely. "Sure."

"Want to talk about it?"

Deborah looked up from the book in her lap at her husband.

"Who are you more worried about?"

"Honestly, I'm not sure. I don't know if Sarah running home is the best idea."

"You knew she would."

"I did."

"Why did you call her?" Jack asked.

Deborah tossed her book aside haplessly. "Kat needs her."

He nodded. "Probably so."

"I don't know how they're all going to get through this, Jack—not this."

"I wouldn't underestimate any of them."

"I'm not."

"But?"

"Sarah is in love with Kat."

"We all know that," Jack said.

"All of us?" She raised her brow.

"You don't think Kat knows?"

"I'm not sure what I think," Deborah confessed. "I know that sooner or later the truth always surfaces—no matter how deep you bury it."

"They'll be okay, Deb."

"I'm glad you're confident."

"They love each other—all of them. They always have."

"I know. That's what worries me."

Jack pulled his wife over and wrapped an arm around her. "They'll find their way, whatever it is supposed to be."

"How can you be so sure?"

"Because we all do eventually. We have to."

———••—••———

"How come Auntie Sarah called you Kit Kat? Like you're a candy bar!" Brie giggled with delight.

Kat laughed. "Who told you that?"

"Daddy."

Kat's heart lurched violently. "Daddy told you that Sarah calls me Kit Kat?"

"Yep. He says it's 'cause she thought you were sweet."

Kat pushed back her tears. She never asked Sarah why Sarah chose that nickname. She always assumed it was because it went together. One day, Sarah started calling her Kit Kat, and it stuck.

"What do you call Auntie?"

"Other than crazy?" Kat winked. "I never called her anything but Sarah," she said.

"How come?"

"I don't know. I guess that was special enough. Your Auntie Sarah is one-of-a-kind. She's the silliest and the smartest person I know. Except for you." Kat tickled Brie's belly.

"Yeah, 'cause I look like her too."

"Yes, you do."

"Daddy says that too."

Daddy says a lot of things. "Does he?"

"Yeah. He said Auntie Sarah made you crawl into a cave."

168

"Oh, did he? Well, she did."

Brie's eyes grew wide.

"Because she got stuck in the cave."

Brie laughed. "She got stuck!"

"Yep."

"Was it dark?" Brie grew serious.

"It was very dark."

"You didn't get lost?"

"No. It wasn't big, just dark. And, Sarah never let me get lost," Kat said. "She's a good navigator."

"What's a nabigrator?"

"Navigator," Kat corrected her daughter. "It's someone who knows how to find their way."

"Even in the dark?"

"Especially in the dark," Kat offered.

"But you can't see in the dark."

"Well, a good navigator uses the stars like a compass."

"Like Grandpa's compass?"

"A bit," Kat said. Neil and Sarah's parents took their children camping frequently when they were kids. Jack and Neil planned to start the tradition with Brie over summer vacation. Another swift plummet of her heart made Kat's stomach roil. She forced herself to smile.

Brie sensed her mother's sadness and wrapped her arms around Kat's neck. "Don't worry, Mommy."

Kat closed her eyes.

"Auntie Sarah will help Daddy get home."

"You know, Brie, she just might," Kat agreed.

Neil picked up his phone, looked at it, and placed it in his pocket. He wanted to call home. He wanted to know how Kat was. He wanted to talk to Brie. Why had he left that stupid note? It was a cop-out. Sarah has teased him for years that he was a "chicken." Maybe she was right. A note to tell your wife you were walking away was cowardly at best. He couldn't face her. He couldn't look into Kat's eyes and tell her. That would lead to questions. Neil didn't have any answers, not the answers Kat deserved. He needed a break to sort through the questions. The only thing he remained clear about was the end of his marriage to Kat. It wasn't a marriage. It was an existence, and it was slowly killing them both. For the first time, he understood how Sarah felt over the years. Existing might have seemed preferable to some people. After all, love had the ability to cause pain. He didn't care about flowery rhetoric and love poems. Neil heard many people say that if it hurt, it couldn't be love. Total bullshit, that's what he thought about that sentiment. Love could hurt like hell. Existing was just existing. It wasn't loving. It was safe. Or was it safe? Neil had come to believe that nothing was more painful than living an existence, playing a role, pretending to feel.

Love? Neil loved Kat. Some part of him wondered when he'd fallen out of love with her. When had she fallen out of love with him? He gripped the steering wheel in his truck. Who had she fallen in love with? Neil wondered about that too. Who had he become mesmerized by? He always wanted to be like Sarah. He wanted to impress his sister. Everything Sarah did, everything Sarah had, Neil strived to master it. He'd always felt inadequate in those pursuits, save one—Kat. "Shit," he groaned. Now, he'd hurt the three people he loved most, his wife, his daughter, and his sister. Kat and Sarah had been his best friends for a lifetime. Marry your best friend;

isn't that what he's heard people advise a million times? "Just make sure it's the right one," he mused.

———— • • ————

Kat sat in the dark sipping a glass of wine. Her fingers fumbled through the pages of an old photo album. She laughed at a picture of Sarah outside what was now her house. For years, Kat had ogled the Victorian house of Maiden Lane. It had been abandoned for years. Sarah had concocted some insane story about the ghost of a pirate that would appear in the upstairs windows. Kat had to remind her repeatedly that pirates did not traverse lakes in Massachusetts. Sarah scoffed at the argument. She would prove it.

Sarah was thirteen in the picture that Kat's thumb caressed. It was taken the day that Sarah decided to investigate the old house. Thankfully, she didn't fall through loose floor boards or have any ceiling tiles bury her alive, which were all possibilities Kat had considered. No, Sarah had survived the excursion. She came out covered in a few cobwebs, sporting a handful of Polaroid photos she had snapped. Kat flipped the page in the album. "Ghosts and pirates," she chuckled. Sarah had a vivid imagination. Kat looked at one of the pictures Sarah had taken inside the house. She glanced up at the ceiling. Neil had found tiles that closely matched the originals. Kat had half-hoped Neil would find some ghostly evidence during the renovations. The only ghosts that lingered here now were Neil's and Sarah's. Kat sipped her wine.

The perfect house, a childhood dream come true. No, a childhood wish that Neil had granted. Kat loved this house. She loved it because it reminded her of the tales Sarah told, and the adventures that Sarah led them all on. She traced another picture of the three of them. Love was endless. Kat understood that. Once you loved, you could never forget that love. It clung to you, even when you tried to shake it free. There were two people that Kat loved beyond measure—Sarah and Neil. Without them she would not be sitting in this house. Without their love and their generosity, the little girl who held her heart like no other would not be tucked in upstairs. Every important moment in Kat's life had Neil and Sarah at its center—every, single one. She let her finger circle the faces in the photo. Love might linger, time had a way of moving on. Kat closed the album, set down her wine, and sprawled out on the sofa. Where had it all gone wrong? First, Sarah left. Now, Neil was gone. She reached for the afghan behind her and wrapped herself in it like it was a protective cocoon. Her eyes closed. *Why does everyone leave?*

May 16, 2016

"Kat?"

Kat looked up from the front porch swing. Sarah stood at the foot of the steps staring up at her with apologetic eyes. Kat closed her eyes hoping to force her tears into submission.

"Kat," Sarah stepped up onto the porch and wrapped her sister-in-law in a warm embrace.

Kat didn't speak. She collapsed into Sarah and fell apart in the safety of Sarah's arms. Somehow, she knew Sarah was the one person who would understand her pain.

Sarah closed her eyes and held on as if her life depended on it. There were no words that she could offer to quell Kat's pain. No one understood the pain of loving someone who simply couldn't love you the same way better than Sarah Masters—no one. She led Kat to the swing, careful to keep Kat close.

"What am I going to do?" Kat finally asked. "What am I supposed to tell Brie?"

Sarah's emotions wavered between empathy for the woman in her arms and anger at the brother who'd always been her best friend. Right now, she wasn't sure which would win the day. The thought passed through her mind that it was probably God's doing that she hadn't a clue where her brother was.

"I don't know," she finally replied. "It'll be okay, Kat."

"How? How will it ever be okay?"

Sarah pulled Kat closer and closed her eyes. "I don't know how. I just know it will be."

Sarah looked on as Kat twirled the spaghetti on her plate endlessly. She focused her attention on Brie throughout dinner, listening attentively to her niece prattle on about school, friends, and afternoons at Nana's house. Kat had remained silent, occasionally offering Brie a half-hearted smile. The tension and sorrow that filled the room clenched Sarah's chest. One thing would never change: seeing Kat in pain hurt Sarah more than anything could. Kat needed to talk. Kat needed some space to be able to do that.

"What do you think about spending the night at Nana's?" Sarah asked Brie.

Kat's head snapped to attention.

"Really?" Brie asked.

Sarah nodded. "Why don't you go get some things together?"

Brie jumped up excitedly and ran from the room.

Sarah giggled. Brie melted her heart. She glanced over at Kat.

"Mom doesn't need to watch Brie," Kat said.

"No, but something tells me that you could use a little break."

"From Brie?" Kat asked.

Sarah sensed she needed to tread lightly. "I know that you want to keep her close."

"The last thing she needs is to think that I don't want her here."

"She doesn't think that. Don't look at me like that. You saw her just now. She doesn't think that, Kat. I get it. At least, I think I do. She's used to being at Mom's during the week. She's been with you for a few days now. It'll be good for both of you."

Kat's face fell into her hands. "I don't know what I'm doing."

"The best you can," Sarah replied.

Kat looked back up.

"You are," Sarah said.

"Whatever that means," Kat replied.

"Kat..."

"I'm so tired, Sarah."

"Which is why you need a break. I'll take Brie over to Mom's. You go upstairs and take a bath. Relax for a little while. I'll clean this up when I get back. Then we can talk."

"I'm not sure what to say."

"Well, we can talk, or we can watch *Scrooged.*"

Kat chuckled. "Aren't you over that obsession yet?"

"Nope."

"So, you came home to torture me?" Kat teased.

"I came home because I love you."

Kat's eyes filled with tears. "I love you too."

Sarah winked. "So, do we have a deal?"

Kat knew that Sarah was right. Brie had been asking when she could go to her nana's house. Neil's abrupt departure made Kat reluctant to be apart from her daughter. Deborah had offered to take Brie for a couple of days. Kat had declined. She already felt incredibly alone. Deborah had acquiesced. No matter what Kat knew, she could not seem to control how she felt.

"Kat, she'll be okay, and so will you. I promise."

"I just…"

"What is it?"

"I'm afraid to be alone," Kat confessed. Afraid didn't begin to describe what Kat felt. She'd been filling her nights with old television shows. She needed sound. She required distraction. Silence was her enemy. Once she allowed silence to fall, Kat was sure she would be sucked into an endless abyss or sorrow

Sarah reached across the table and took Kat's hand. "You're not alone."

Kat nodded when Sarah squeezed her hand. *I hope you're right.*

Sarah laughed as Brie ran up the stairs to find her grandpa. "She never stops."

"Not until she's ready to drop," Deborah agreed. "So? How did you get Kat to agree to this?"

"I didn't give her a choice."

"How is she?" Deborah asked.

"I don't know. She needs to talk. To tell you the truth, I think she needs to lose it. She'll never let herself do that with Brie there."

Deborah wasn't surprised at Sarah's astute observation. If Kat was going to let go, the most likely person she'd allow to catch her would be Sarah. "I can't believe he left her a note," Deborah groaned.

"Have you heard from him?" Sarah asked.

"Yesterday."

Sarah fought back her urge to scream.

"He wanted to know how they were doing," Deborah explained.

A caustic chuckle flew from Sarah's lips. "Stupid question."

"I know you're angry with him. I am too."

"Angry with him? What the hell, Mom? Angry? He walks out on Kat and Brie with a note? Who the hell does that? Jesus."

"I don't know what he was thinking."

"Probably about himself."

"Sarah."

"Don't," Sarah warned. "Don't ask me not to be pissed off."

"I'm not. He's hurting too."

Sarah shook her head. She didn't feel any empathy for her brother. "Just because things get hard doesn't mean you get to bail."

Deborah took a deep breath. "No?"

"No."

Deborah nodded.

"What?" Sarah asked. "You're not telling me that you're giving him a pass on this?"

"I'm not. Your brother isn't the only one who runs when it gets tough."

"What the hell is that supposed to mean?"

"He's not the only one who left when it got painful."

Sarah's mother had raised this point before. Sarah had chosen to live her life on the opposite coast after Kat and Neil became a couple. Gradually, she had spent less time visiting home. That had been her choice, and it had been because home had become too painful. Her mother wasn't wrong. But Sarah was not Kat's spouse. She was not anyone's parent.

"Hardly the same thing," Sarah said.

"Maybe not."

"There's no maybe about it. I would never walk out on my family with nothing more than a note."

"What about Beth?" Deborah challenged.

"Why are you making this about me?"

"Sarah, I'm only…"

"No. You're right. Beth and I didn't work. For the record, no one left a note behind, Mom. And, it wasn't my decision."

Deborah sighed. "I'm not attacking you, sweetheart. I just want you to remember that he's your brother."

Sarah shook her head. She could never stop loving Neil. She'd given him the room to love Kat. She'd stayed away while her heart splintered a little more each day in the distance she'd placed between them. Sarah had thought that Neil would cherish his family. She would never be able to understand how he could walk out on Kat without any discussion. She had forgiven him for breaking her heart. Sarah was not sure she could ever forgive him for breaking Kat's.

"That is something I will never be able to forget," Sarah replied. "I need to get back to Kat."

"Sarah?"

Sarah turned around.

"I don't want to see you hurt in all this."

"It's too late for that, Mom."

———◆•◆———

Kat filled the bathtub and slipped in beneath the bubbles. She let the hot water caress her skin. For a moment, it seemed to soothe her. She closed her eyes to savor the sensation. A few deep breaths and the silence suddenly became deafening. Her mind played the movie of her life. It blared in her ears so loudly that her chest began to pound. *How could he? How could he just leave?* Kat's sobs broke forth like a raging river, crushing the dam that had held them back for days. *How could he?*

———◆•◆———

Sarah walked through the front door. The heaviness that enveloped her the moment she closed it took her breath away. A faint sound drifted from above. Sarah recognized it immediately. *Kat*. Sarah took the stairs two at a time. She sucked in a ragged breath and rapped on the bathroom door.

"Kat?"

The only sound that greeted her voice were strangled cries from beyond the door.

"Kat, I'm coming in," Sarah warned. "Kat."

Kat forced her eyes open to meet Sarah's. Her body shivered in the cooling water as her tears continued to consume her.

"Kat." Sarah grabbed a towel and knelt beside the tub. "Come on." She reached for Kat's hand. Sarah nearly lost her balance when Kat's arms grabbed hold of her. "Kat," Sarah whispered. "Shhh. Come on, now. I'm right here."

Kat clung to Sarah. Her thoughts had gone blank, consumed by her emotions. The abyss had swallowed her whole. She would have drowned in it had Sarah not arrived.

The only word Sarah could discern through Kat's sobbing was, "Sarah."

"Kat," Sarah tried to steady her friend. She helped Kat stand and draped the towel around Kat's shoulders. "You're freezing. Come on, let's get you dried off and dressed, okay?"

"Sorry," Kat managed.

"Sorry? You don't have anything to be sorry for."

"You're all wet," Kat sniffled.

Sarah smiled warmly. *God, I love you so much, Kat*. She pulled the towel closed around Kat's body, willing her eyes to obey her commands. Kat grabbed hold of her again as another wave of sorrow encompassed her.

"Shh," Sarah kissed Kat's forehead. "Let it go."

Sarah's words gave Kat the permission she required. As her body slipped into Sarah's supportive embrace, Kat wondered if she would ever find the strength to hold herself upright again.

How could you, Neil? The question repeated in Sarah's mind. Kat was trembling with so much force that Sarah had no choice but to lower them both to the floor. She wrapped Kat in her arms and held her tenderly. "Just let it go," she repeated. "I'm right here."

Chapter Nine: Picking up the Pieces

at handed Sarah the letter that Neil had left. "Are you sure you want me to read this?"

Sarah took the letter and steadied herself. Several deep breaths, and she let her eyes fall on it.

Kat,

I know I probably should be talking to you. I don't know where to start. Things are cloudy. I think things between us have been cloudy for a long time. I know they have been for me. At first, I thought it was because I was on the road so much. Then I realized that might be the way we both like it. Do you remember when we used to talk all night long? I don't think we've spoken more than a couple of sentences to each other before bed in years. I remember when you would be waiting for me to come home. You don't wait anymore. The truth is, I don't long to get here. I don't think that's fair to you.

Gerry offered me a chance to travel on the circuit. It's what I've always wanted to do. I know you would have told me to do it. I think you would have. I can't do that and do us. I'm not even sure there is an us anymore. We're not Kat and Neil. I'm not sure who we are. I'm not sure who I am. I know that this is something I need to do, and I think there are things you need to do without me in the middle of it all.

I always thought we'd make it forever. Maybe forever is just too long. Before you even think it, there isn't anyone else. I hope that maybe one day there will be for both of us. I'm not sure I deserve that, but you do. You deserve to have someone you want to wait for. That someone isn't me. The road feels more like home to me. It has for longer than I want to admit. That's where I need to be. That's not where you and Brie need to go. I know that.

I hope one day you can forgive me. I do love you. I think you love me. I don't think it's what either of us hoped. I can't stay knowing that it will never be what we once thought it was.

Hug Brie for me. I'm taking off for Florida in the morning to meet with the team. When I get back, I will find someplace close enough to make it easy for Brie and for you. I guess that will give us both a little time.

I'm sorry, Kat. I wish it was all different.

Love,
Neil

Sarah folded the letter back up and placed it on the table beside the couch. She took a deep breath and let her eyes meet Kat's. What could she say? What should she say? Sarah struggled to suppress her anger. *How could you Neil?* "I'm sorry, Kat." That was the best she could come up with.

Kat remained silent for a few moments. "He's not wrong."

Kat's words stunned Sarah.

"I don't mean leaving with nothing more than a note. I mean that he's not wrong." Kat threw her head back and sighed. "God help me, he's not wrong. I haven't waited for him to come home for years. Sometimes…" Kat paused and visibly admonished herself.

"What? Sometimes what?"

Kat sighed heavily. "Sometimes I dreaded when he'd come back."

"Why?"

"I don't know. It's not like we fought. Of course, we argued sometimes. That was usually about bills or something stupid. I don't know, Sarah. Maybe I thought that was the way it is supposed to be, you know?"

"How is that?" Sarah asked.

"Just static," Kat answered. "No big highs and no scary lows, just living day to day."

Sarah wasn't certain how to respond. She'd been living her life that way for years. "I think I understand."

"It's not like it was unpleasant. It's just been…" Kat hesitated.

"Lonely?" Sarah guessed.

Kat nodded. "Yes."

"I'm sorry. I really am."

"I know. I am too. I don't understand how he could leave like that. Why wouldn't he talk to me? How could he just walk away with a note? I mean, Sarah we have a child. We have a life. He didn't even want to try to make things better."

"Do you think he could have?"

"I don't know. He could have talked to me."

Sarah didn't disagree. "I wish I could make this better for you."

"You do."

Sarah doubted that she had the ability to make anything better for Kat. She wasn't sure where to begin to help. All she could offer was a shoulder to cry on and company. Inadequate—that is how Sarah felt—again. The only thing managing to quell Sarah's anger at Neil was her concern for

Kat. Kat was vulnerable. The last thing that Sarah desired was to make anything worse.

"Sarah?"

"I wish I could—make it better," Sarah said.

"I told you, you do."

"I wish I could fix it somehow for you."

Kat smiled. *Oh, Sarah.* "You can't fix what you didn't break." Kat felt tears begin to sting her eyes. It had become a familiar sensation. One moment, Kat would feel that she had gained some perspective; the next, she would fall into a pit of despair. Her entire life had been upended by a note. What would she do? What could she do? What was she supposed to tell Brie? What about where she would live? Who was she now?

"Kat?"

"I'm so scared," Kat confessed.

"Scared of what?" Sarah asked.

"Who am I, Sarah? I mean, where do I go from here? What do I tell Brie? What if she blames me? What if she hates us both? I just…"

"Brie will be okay," Sarah said. She was confident that was the truth. "Look, I hate what he's done. I can't lie to you. Part of me wants to hunt him down and beat the shit out of him."

Kat chuckled through a few tears.

"He does love Brie. And, Kat? He does love you. I know he does."

"I don't understand how he could walk out that way."

"He's always had someone to take care of things for him."

"What do you mean?" Kat asked.

"I mean just what I said. He's always had someone there to take care of things when things got rough. If there was an issue with some kid at school or he wanted help with his homework—if it was someone to come home to that made sure he had what he needed—Neil's never been on his own, Kat. I'm not excusing what he did. It's change. He doesn't do change."

Kat considered Sarah's observation. "Marriage and fatherhood are pretty significant changes," she offered.

Sarah shrugged. "True. He moved from Mom and Dad's to a house around the block. He's had exactly one girlfriend his whole life and she ended up marrying him. I mean, Kat—other than for work, Neil has never traveled. There's always been someone to pick up the pieces for him."

Kat let go a heavy sigh. Sarah was right. "It hurts. The way he did it."

"I know."

"I feel so guilty."

"Guilty? Why would you feel guilty?" Sarah asked.

"Because that's what hurts," Kat said. "I can't believe he would walk out on Brie without talking to me—without helping me help her through this. Me? Oh, Sarah—he's not wrong. We've been living apart for a while in the same house. Maybe that hurts too—the fact that I didn't want to acknowledge it. Maybe if I'd tried a little harder or talked to him—I don't know anymore. I don't know how we ended up here. I always thought we'd live here, watch our kids play, and grow old together. That's the way it was supposed to happen. I thought that was settled. I never thought we would both be settling for something less than we wanted." Kat smiled. "I do love him."

"I know you do."

"I'm not sure we've been *in* love for a long time."

Kat's revelation surprised Sarah. Sorrow and regret were evident in Kat's eyes. As it always had, Kat's sadness twisted Sarah's insides. She reached over and pulled Kat into her arms.

"It will all work out," Sarah promised.

"I wish I could believe that."

"Well, I will believe it enough for both of you until you're ready."

Kat breathed Sarah in and closed her eyes. There had never been a place that Kat felt safer than beside the woman who held her now. Sarah had dried her tears countless times, and often found a way to turn them into laughter. Kat's grip tightened. Everyone seemed to leave. Eventually, it would be Sarah's turn again. That epiphany brought a fresh round of tears to Kat's eyes.

"Don't cry," Sarah whispered.

"I don't want you to leave," Kat choked.

"I'm not going anywhere."

"Can we stay here?"

Sarah guided them back on the sofa and held Kat. "As long as you need." She closed her eyes. "I'll stay as long as you need me."

That could be a very long time, Sarah.

Two Weeks Later

"Sarah!"

Sarah chuckled at the sound of her niece's blaring request for her presence. She poked her head around the corner. "You rang?"

Brie frowned.

Sarah held her laughter in check. Brie was standing on a kitchen chair wearing one of Kat's aprons that was six sizes too big for her. She had lined the kitchen counter with pots and pans. There was a can of tomatoes, a few other canned vegetables, and Kat's spice rack had been moved to a prominent place. She shook her head affectionately at her niece.

"We're supposed to make Mom dinner."

"I remember."

Brie put her hands on her hips.

Sarah laughed and held up her hands. "Okay, I get it. I'm a remedial helper."

Brie's nose wrinkled. "What's a 'readial' helper?"

"Remedial," Sarah corrected Brie. "It means I haven't done my job."

Brie nodded dramatically.

Oh, boy, I know that look. I'm in trouble. "So, what are we making?"

"S'ghetti."

"You want to make Mom spaghetti?"

"Yep, and Nana's sauce."

"I see."

"You know how."

Sarah chuckled again. "Who told you that?"

"Mom."

"I'll bet she did."

Brie held up a mixing spoon and pointed it at Sarah.

Sarah's heart melted. She loved Brie. Brie reminded Sarah of Kat more times than she could count. Brie could get

187

her to do anything, just like her mother had always been able to.

"So, sauce it is," Sarah agreed.

Brie smiled.

"But you have to help," Sarah said.

"I'm ready!"

"I see that." Sarah moved to fix Brie's apron that hung well below the chair Brie was standing on. "First things first. No falling off chairs."

Brie nodded.

Sarah inspected her handiwork. "That's better. Okay, Betty Crocker, let's get this show on the road."

"I'm not Betty Cocker!"

Sarah burst out in laughter. "Crocker," she said. "And, I guess not. You're too young."

"Yeah. You can be her. You're old like Mom."

Sarah kept laughing. "I guess I am."

———◆·◆———

"Aunt Sarah?"

Sarah stopped walking and stepped into Brie's bedroom. "What's up, String Bean?"

Brie fiddled with her blanket.

"Brie?"

"Where's Daddy?"

Sarah sighed and moved to sit on the edge of Brie's bed. "Daddy is working."

"Yeah, but he always calls."

"I'll bet he's just really busy."

Brie looked up at Sarah pleadingly.

"Aw, String Bean. He'll be back."

"Why does Mom keep crying?"

Now, what do I say? Sarah smiled and put her hand on Brie's leg. "Mom is okay," she promised. "She wants you to be happy."

"Daddy made her sad."

"Well," Sarah took a breath. "Sometimes, we all get a little sad. Sometimes, people have to go away from us for a while. Sometimes, they have things they need to do and places they want to see."

"But why can't we go?"

Excellent question. "I don't know, String Bean. I guess sometimes we just want to see different places. That's all. It doesn't mean we don't love each other."

"Like why you live in California?"

Sarah's heart plummeted in her chest. *If only you knew how true that is.* "Sort of."

"You still love Mom and Daddy."

"Yes, I do. And, I love you."

Brie smiled.

"And, I always come back, don't I?"

Brie nodded.

"So, see? Daddy will be back. Just because he isn't here all the time doesn't mean that he doesn't miss you and Mom."

"Do you?"

"Do I what?"

"Do you miss me and Mom?"

Sarah's eyes began to mist. "More than anything."

Brie's brow wrinkled in confusion.

"What is it?" Sarah asked.

"Then how come you don't stay?"

I wish it were that simple. "Well…"

"If you love somebody, you should stay. Then you don't have to come back."

Sarah's lips curled into a regretful smile. *You have a point, String Bean. How do you argue with that?* Sarah pulled the covers up around Brie. All the adult explanations she could give felt hollow. She leaned in and kissed Brie's forehead. "Don't worry so much," she said. "Daddy loves you. Mom loves you. Nana and Grandpa love you."

"You love me," Brie said happily.

"Very much," Sarah promised. She stood to leave.

"Auntie Sarah?"

"Yeah?"

"I love you too."

Sarah winked at Brie. "Goodnight, String Bean."

"'Night."

Sarah closed Brie's door slightly. Her hand lifted to cover her eyes. *What the hell am I doing?*

"Hey." Kat caught sight of Sarah and became instantly concerned. "Sarah? What's wrong?"

"Nothing." Sarah's forced smile did nothing to conceal her underlying turmoil.

"Uh-huh. Maybe you can tell me about nothing over a glass of wine on the front porch."

Sarah nodded. "I'll meet you there."

Kat watched Sarah as she descended the stairs. *What is going on with you?* She took a deep breath and stepped into her daughter's bedroom. "Hey there."

Brie looked up and smiled at her mother.

"I wanted to say goodnight."

"Mom?"

"Yes?"

"Are you mad at Daddy?"

Kat sat down beside her daughter. *Am I?* "No, sweetheart. I'm not mad at anyone."

"Do you miss him?"

Kat smiled. "I always miss the people I love when they go away."

"Like Auntie Sarah."

Kat's ears perked. "Of course, I miss Auntie Sarah when she goes home."

"Me too."

"I know you do. But Auntie Sarah always comes home. Daddy will be back to see you soon, sweetheart."

"I know. He has to work."

Kat nodded. *You had better start explaining some things, Katelyn.* "Yes, he does," Kat said. She took a deep breath. "But, I think when Daddy comes back he might decide to stay at Nana's for a while or something like that."

"How come?"

Kat sighed nervously. *How do you explain this to a six-year-old?* "Brie, you know that Daddy and I love you very much."

"Yeah."

"And, I love your Daddy but sometimes, well… Sometimes when people get older they find out they want different things."

"That's what Auntie Sarah said."

Kat was curious.

"About how come people go away sometimes, and how they still love you."

"Auntie Sarah's right. Just because someone doesn't live with you or even near you, that doesn't mean they don't love you."

"I know."

"You do?"

"Sure. Nana doesn't live with us."

"No."

"Auntie Sarah loves us, but she lives far away. And, you love her. You always cry when she leaves."

Kat bit her bottom lip gently. *I do.* "Auntie Sarah has been my best friend since I was just a little bit older than you."

"I know."

Kat snickered. *God help me in another six or seven years.* "I miss Auntie Sarah when she's home."

Brie shook her head. "You mean California."

"That's where Auntie Sarah lives," Kat reminded her daughter.

"Yeah, but she said this is home."

She did? "What did she say?"

Brie shrugged. Sarah had been spending afternoons with her for the last couple of weeks. She'd always reveled in her aunt's attention. She loved to hear Sarah's tales about growing up with her mother. Sarah made her laugh. More importantly, Sarah made her mother laugh.

The growing affection between Brie and Sarah hadn't escaped Kat's notice. Brie seemed to know where Sarah was at every moment. Kat was beginning to realize that the notion of Sarah leaving again was lingering in her daughter's mind, perhaps as much as her father's absence. She was curious about what Sarah had said. "Brie?"

Brie shrugged again. "She says that you can have lots of places you like to be, but you only get one home. That's where the people you love are."

Kat nodded. *Sarah.* "Sarah's right. Home is wherever the people you love are. And, that's why we always find our way back there."

"Then why would she leave?"

Good question. "I don't know, sweetheart. Adults do funny things sometimes."

Brie smiled. "Yep. Must be that old thing."

Kat laughed. "Must be." She leaned in and kissed Brie's cheek. "Goodnight. I love you."

"Love you too. Mom?"

"Yeah?"

"Maybe Auntie Sarah will stay."

Kat nodded. *Maybe.*

"Uh-oh." Kat walked out onto the porch.

"Why the uh-oh?" Sarah asked.

"You brought out a whole bottle of wine."

Sarah laughed. "You wanted wine."

"I was thinking a glass."

"Think bigger, Kit Kat."

Kat took a seat on the swing with Sarah. "Thank you."

"It's your wine," Sarah deadpanned.

"Not the wine, you fool." Kat chuckled. "Thank you for being here."

"You don't need to thank me."

"No? Maybe I should be apologizing instead."

"I'll pour the wine," Sarah tried to lighten a conversation she felt was about to take a serious turn.

Kat caught Sarah's hand. "Don't."

"Don't?"

"Don't avoid this again," Kat said.

Sarah stared at Kat. Kat hadn't changed. Kat had grown. Kat wasn't the curious girl that followed Sarah into caves and hid under the Masters' couch to watch horror movies. She was a thoughtful, beautiful, confident woman. Sarah was positive that Kat did not see herself that way, particularly the confident part of the equation. Kat's demeanor, while gentle, was poised and deliberate. Sarah wished she could allow Kat to see herself through Sarah's eyes.

"You've been avoiding talking to me for years," Kat said.

"Kat…"

"Don't. Let me say this. Please."

Sarah nodded.

"I'm sorry if I ever made you think that you didn't matter to me."

"What are you talking about?"

"I feel like Neil and I… Maybe we broke some unspoken oath between friends."

"Oh, Kat," Sarah sighed regretfully. "No. You didn't."

Kat nodded. "As much as I want you to stay here, I don't want to hold you back from going home."

"You aren't."

"Are you sure?"

Sarah took Kat's hand. "If anyone should apologize, it's me. I don't do touchy-feely all that well," Sarah admitted.

"You don't do vulnerable."

"There is that," Sarah admitted.

"You know, you can tell me anything."

How many times had Sarah heard that phrase? How many people had assured her that she could speak her truth without fear of judgment? If only that were true. It sounded good. It probably looked good on the paper of the romance novels her mother treasured. People meant it when they said it. Living up to that sentiment was a more difficult task. Sometimes, the truth that set one person free sent another to prison. She wished that the truth was as simple a thing as people liked to believe. It wasn't. Different people carried different truths within them. Truth could just as easily hurt as it could heal. The world was not as black and white as literature and law often depicted. Life was molded by love and hate, anger and hope, helpfulness and even retribution. Life was colored by a series of muted greys alongside brilliant blues, greens, and golds. Sarah had once told Kat that some people were meant to write the fairytales others lived. She left out the part she'd come to understand about fantastical stories. Fairytales did not all have happy endings. Children got shoved into ovens, and heroes fell to dragons. Truth. Freedom. Love. Loss. Happiness. Grief. Sarah had survived all of it—felt all of it. No, she couldn't tell Kat anything. At least, not now. Perhaps there had been a once upon a time many years ago. Perhaps, if Sarah had been able to summon the courage of a hero all those years ago, sitting under their tree, and spoken her *truth*, perhaps, the ending to both their stories would have been written differently. Once upon a time….

"I know you believe that," Sarah replied.

"You can," Kat countered.

"Oh, Kat, I wish that were true," Sarah said solemnly.

"You used to trust me."

"I do trust you. I trust you with my life," Sarah replied. "Some things change," Sarah said. "A lot of things change. And, some things never do. "

"What things?" Kat inquired.

"Home."

Kat took a deep breath and let her head fall onto Sarah's shoulder. Home.

Chapter Ten: On My Own Again
June 21, 2016

Sarah walked into the kitchen and her heart stopped. Kat was sitting with her face in her hands. "Kat?"

Kat looked up and shook her head.

"What's wrong?"

"He's home."

"Neil?"

Kat nodded again.

"When?"

"He stopped here early this morning when you were out."

Of course, he did. "He didn't call first?"

Kat shook her head.

"Are you okay?"

"I don't know," Kat admitted.

Sarah sat down at the table across from Kat. Her heart began to thrum in her chest. Her stomach ached. Her palms began to sweat. Neil was back. Sarah had fallen into a routine for the last month. She'd slept most nights on Kat's couch. A few times, she had fallen asleep holding Kat after one of Kat's momentary breakdowns. She'd been picking up Brie from school most days. Dinners had become a family affair. Family—that word had more than one definition. This was Neil's family. Sarah did her best to swallow her mounting sadness. *Reality check commence.*

"What did he say?" Sarah asked.

"Basically, what he said in the note. That, and a string of 'I'm sorry.' Nothing has changed," Kat said. "And, everything has changed. He's got a place already." Kat chuckled ruefully. "I think he might have had it for a while now."

Sarah listened without comment.

"He wants to talk to Brie. He doesn't want her to think that we're angry at each other." Kat licked her lips. "The problem is, I am angry with him. I know this is the right thing to do."

"It is," Sarah agreed.

"He wants us to have dinner together before he heads to his place."

Sarah needed to disguise her disappointment. She had planned a special dinner for Kat and Brie. It was Friday night. Brie loved Friday nights. She could stay up late. Sarah had bought everything to make pizzas. She'd taken a drive after dropping Brie off at school and bought a couple of DVDs for later that night—one for Brie and one that she knew Kat had been itching to watch. The entire situation felt eerily familiar.

"I'll clear out."

"Sarah…"

"It's okay. I'm sure Mom will be happy to put me to work."

Kat smiled weakly. "I'm sure."

Sarah pushed out her chair. "Call me if you need me."

Kat wasn't sure why, but she felt an overwhelming urge to grab hold of Sarah and beg her to stay. She'd seen that look in Sarah's eyes before. For the first time in her life, she understood what the darkened expression was telling her. *Oh, Sarah*. "I'll call you when he leaves."

Sarah nodded. She bent down and kissed Kat's cheek. "It'll be okay."

I hope you're right.

———————

Sarah was surprised when her phone buzzed. She looked down at the message from Kat.

Can you come over?

Sarah massaged her eyes.

I'll be right there.

"Sarah?" Deborah asked.

"Yeah."

"What's wrong?"

"Nothing, Mom. Kat just texted me."

Deborah sat down beside her daughter. "She probably could use a stiff drink."

Sarah appreciated her mother's levity. "Got any?"

"I do." Deborah walked across the room and opened a cabinet. "Brand new bottle of tequila. I seem to remember the two of you raiding my stash a time or two."

Sarah grinned. *A time or two.* "What makes you think it was us?"

Deborah smirked. "Remember that time you carried Kat upstairs, or rather tried to?"

Which time?

"You dropped the bottle on your way—right before you dropped Kat."

Sarah laughed. "I remember."

"Well, just don't go trying to carry her up those stairs tonight."

I don't think there's much chance of that.

Sarah accepted the bottle. "I promise we'll behave."

"Don't."

"Don't promise or don't behave?"

"I think Kat could use a night to let go."

"Probably. I'm not sure tonight's that night."

"Well, you have the means if it is."

Sarah held up the bottle. "I just hope they're okay."

"They will be. It's going to take some time. He should never have walked out that way."

Sarah nodded. She was nowhere near prepared to see her brother.

"Are you going to talk to him?" Deborah wondered.

"Not if I can help it."

"Sarah."

"Mom." Sarah shook her head. "I can't. Not yet. I don't want to say something I'll regret."

Deborah understood, and she had no argument to wage. It might be best if Sarah and Neil kept their distance for a week or two. Sarah had stepped in and helped Kat. She'd abandoned her life to pick up the mess Neil had left. She had every reason to be angry at Neil—every reason and every right. "I understand."

"Do you?"

"Yes."

"I will, Mom. I just want to be sure I can listen without punching him in the face."

Deborah chuckled. "Enjoy the tequila."

Sarah kissed her mother's cheek. "Thanks for the contribution."

"You're welcome."

Kat threw back a shot of tequila and wiped her mouth with the back of her hand.

"Easy there, sailor."

"I love your mom."

Sarah laughed. "Oh? You love my mom, or you just love her liquor cabinet?"

Kat swatted Sarah. "I needed this."

"Evidently."

"Hey, it beats crying in the bathtub."

"Just make sure you don't end up hunched over the toilet later."

"Ha-ha. I can hold my liquor."

"Uh-huh."

Kat narrowed her gaze. "You doubt me?"

"Me? Nope. Never."

"Hey, I remember when you drowned your sorrows in a bottle over Billy Donnelly."

Sarah rolled her eyes. "Billy Donnelly?"

"Yep. I saw you two kissing behind the science rooms. A couple of days later he was kissing Doreen and you were getting drunk with me."

"And, you thought that was because of Billy?"

Kat shrugged.

You really are clueless, Kat. "I was probably drinking to forget the way he nearly choked me."

"What?!"

"Yep. I don't know where he got the idea that he was supposed to stick his tongue all the way down my throat. That's probably what made me a lesbian."

Kat laughed. "You were a lesbian then?"

"I was always a lesbian, Kat."

Kat swallowed hard. Their banter had taken an unexpected turn. Sarah's voice was firm. Kat had unintentionally struck a nerve.

"Then why did you do it?"

"What?" Sarah asked.

"Kiss Billy. Date all those guys in high school."

"You asked me to."

"I never asked you to kiss Billy!"

Sarah sobered. She was in no mood to tread in these waters. Alcohol had a way of creating loose lips. "You were always trying to get me to date someone. Billy was just fall-out."

"I thought you wanted to date."

"I did," Sarah said. "I just didn't want to date the people you thought I should."

Kat regarded Sarah for a moment. She reached over and poured herself another shot of tequila, throwing it back in one swift motion. "Who *did* you want to date?"

She needs to lay off the tequila. Sarah reached over and moved the bottle of tequila aside.

"Well?" Kat urged an answer.

Sarah's lips grew taut. "You don't want me to answer that."

"Yes, I do," Kat challenged.

Sarah ignored her.

"Why won't you tell me?" Kat asked. "I thought we told each other everything."

Sarah licked her lips. A few shots of tequila had lowered her defenses. Part of her was tempted to answer Kat's question honestly with full-disclosure. *Well, Kat, you see, I fell in love with you when we were twelve, and I'm still in love with you. So, the only person I ever wanted to date was you. That's my problem, not yours.* She shook her head, grabbed the bottle of tequila and moved it to a cabinet.

"What did I say?" Kat wanted to know.

"Nothing. Let's talk about something else."

"Why didn't you tell me?" Kat wondered.

"Tell you?"

"If you knew you were a lesbian, why didn't you tell me that back then?"

I am going to throw up. "I didn't know that's what it was," Sarah replied as honestly as she could.

"I don't understand."

"I knew what I felt," Sarah said. "And, I knew that it didn't matter."

"Didn't matter? What are you talking about? What you feel has always mattered to me."

"Maybe," Sarah conceded. "That's not what I mean, Kat. No one that I wanted to love was going to love me." That was the truth. "Not the way I wanted them to—not here."

"Is that why you moved away?"

"Yeah, I guess it is."

Kat's eyes stayed with Sarah's. A million questions and admissions seemed to pass between them silently. Kat thought she should tear her gaze away. It was hopeless. Her heart skipped and thrummed in her chest. Her stomach flipped upside down, and her eyes watered. What had she missed all these years? What had she *chosen* to ignore all these years?

"I'm going to turn in," Sarah said.

Kat reached out and grabbed Sarah's hand. "Don't."

"Don't?"

"Go."

Sarah tugged at her bottom lip with her teeth. She needed a way to exit this conversation gracefully. She needed some space from Kat. Without warning, Sarah had been transported backward in time. Emotions swirled in her veins, wrapped in memories that she had thought she'd long ago banished. She tried to pull away from Kat's grasp.

"Sarah..."

She had never been able to deny Kat anything. She didn't want to. Now, she needed to. How many nights had she held Kat close while Kat recounted her date with some classmate? How many instances could she recall when she fell asleep with Kat under the stars after listening to Kat's romantic dreams about her future family? She wanted to grant Kat's request. Self-preservation won the argument tonight. Sarah loved Kat—still—always. She managed to gently free herself from Kat's grasp. "I need to get some sleep," Sarah said. Seeing the hurt that flickered in Kat's eyes, Sarah leaned in and kissed her on the forehead. "Get some sleep, Kat."

Kat watched as Sarah exited the kitchen. Sarah's back retreating in the distance summoned a new-found pain. Her eyes closed against the ache in her chest. "Oh, Sarah... Why won't you talk to me?"

Sarah was surprised when Neil showed up on the doorstep. She pressed down the urge to scream at him.

"Can we talk?" Neil requested.

Sarah shut the screen door and followed her brother to the driveway. "I don't know what you expect me to say."

"I want you to understand."

"Understand? What am I supposed to understand?" Sarah tried to keep any hint of malice out of her voice.

"I'm not trying to hurt anyone."

Sarah had no response.

"It was time," he told her. "Kat and me... We... Sarah, it isn't working."

"For you?" Sarah asked. "What about Kat and Brie?"

"I can't do it anymore."

Sarah let out a disgusted sigh.

"What do you want me to say, Sarah?"

"Say? What do I want you to say? That's it? You're just done? Done with your family?"

"I'm not done with my family," he replied as calmly as he could manage. "I *am* done with my marriage."

Sarah stared blankly at her brother for a moment. "Just like that? You just walk out on them? Too much for you all of a sudden?"

"Maybe it is," he admitted.

Sarah chuckled caustically. "What? Can't run off whenever you feel like it now? Is that it? Or is it that you're not the center of her attention?"

Kat leaned inside the kitchen door. She knew she was intruding. She should walk away. She couldn't. It felt as if her legs had been glued to the floor.

"I should think you'd be happy," Neil told his sister.

"Happy? Why the hell would I be happy?"

Neil smirked. "Oh, come on, Sarah. You don't think I know. Jesus, you've been in love with Kat since we were kids. You hated me for years. Admit it."

"Fuck you, Neil."

"Truth hurts, huh? You're pissed off because you'll never have her. Isn't that really what this is about? Why you're pissed? I'm walking away from the one thing you want more than anything, and she'll never want you. Perfect student, perfect kid—you had me beat everywhere except when it came to Kat."

"You're an asshole."

"Like I said, truth hurts. Kinda like love," he returned.

Sarah could feel her tears mounting. Neil's words were the lowest blow he could have dealt her. She'd hidden her feelings for years, buried them deep, always supporting the two people she loved the most. She did love Kat. She always had, and she always would—enough to stand quietly by and be her best friend.

"I don't know who you are," Sarah said. "You don't have a clue about me."

"Denial?"

"No. I love her. I'll always love her, enough to let her go where she needs to. I wouldn't treat a casual lover the way you've treated her."

"You? Take a lover? Come on," he said. "You've been pining for over twenty years. Do yourself a favor, move on, Sarah. Figure out why you're so determined to save her when she hardly knows you exist."

Sarah nodded. "Doesn't matter."

"Keep playing the fool," he said.

"Go to hell, Neil." Sarah choked on her tears. She shook her head and walked away. She had no idea where she might land—anywhere but here.

Kat closed her eyes. Her hands moved to cover her face as reality crashed down on her. *How could you, Neil?*

Sarah had no idea where she was heading. It shouldn't have surprised her that she ended up sitting under the gigantic oak tree that she and Kat had claimed as their own years earlier. She leaned against it and finally allowed her sadness, anger, fear, and regret to swallow her. And, as tears began to cascade down her cheeks, she entertained the possibility that all of it might swallow her whole. Maybe she should let it. She was tired—bone tired. Exhausted from a lifetime of loving someone who would never love her, not the same way. Neil wasn't wrong about that. Sarah had no choice. She hadn't made the choice to love Kat. One thing that Sarah did know, love was not a choice. Almost everything in life came down to choices. Love was one of the few exceptions. She'd loved, but she had never loved the person she believed she was meant to. Sarah chose to conceal her feelings for Kat. Oddly, it seemed Kat was the only person who hadn't recognized Sarah was in love with her. Sarah made the decision to distance herself from her family. That decision had been as much for her sanity as it had ever been to give Kat space. It hurt too much to be close. For the last few weeks, Sarah had enjoyed feeling the weight of unrequited love lift. Perhaps she had deluded herself. Neil was a permanent reality. She'd thought that something had shifted between her and Kat. She'd witnessed an unfamiliar sparkle in Kat's eyes the night before, or had she? *Fool. That's what you are, Masters—a love sick fool.*

Sarah closed her eyes and resigned herself to the truth. *Let her go, Sarah, just let her go. It's best for everyone.*

———•··•———

Kat woke up and wandered into the kitchen. The first thing she noticed was the envelope on the table. With a deep breath she took a seat and opened it.

Kat,

I wish I knew what to say. There are so many things I want to tell you. I'm not sure any of those things matter. We've lived separate lives for so long. I guess for a few minutes I thought maybe that could change. Lots of things have changed. Neil is home again. That made me realize that many things remain the same. One thing that has never changed and will never change is the fact that I love you. No matter what happens, I will always love you. I thought I'd let that go long ago. I thought I'd accepted what it meant to love you. I lost sight of that for a minute. You deserve to be happy—you and Brie. I want that for you more than anything. I do.

You will be. I know it. I love you, Kat.

Always yours,
Sarah.

Kat held her breath. *Sarah.* Another note. What was it with the Neil and Sarah and notes? She folded the paper back up and placed it inside the envelope. "Funny how everyone who loves me leaves."

———◆·◆———

The Next Day

"I don't want to argue, Neil."

Neil nodded. "I'm sorry, Kat. I am. It's just not the way it was anymore, and..."

"No, it isn't. You could have talked to me instead of walking out. Thirteen years, Neil. That's a long time. I gave you thirteen years of my life. You just walked away without a word."

"I didn't know what to say."

"The truth would've been a good place to start."

Neil rubbed his forehead. Kat was right, and he knew it. He couldn't face her. He'd tried more times than he cared to count. He would walk into the room to find Kat playing with Brie and he would chastise himself. He'd sit on the edge of their bed and watch as Kat slept peacefully, and he would hate himself for the pain he knew he was going to cause. He and Kat had built what appeared to be a wonderful life together to anyone looking in. And, in many ways they had. As he would watch his wife move about their home, he couldn't help but feel that something was missing. Neil had argued with himself, admonished himself—some days he couldn't stand to look at his reflection.

Kat had been the first girl he'd ever fallen for, other than Sharon Stone, and he didn't think that counted. While he loathed to admit it, Kat had been the first woman he had ever made love to. He'd had sex—once. She'd been patient with him, gentle and understanding, ignoring his clumsiness and easing his anxiety with her tenderness. She'd always been that way. She was still that way. Over time, he'd felt the gap growing between them. They smiled at each other in the morning. They laughed at their daughter's stories and delighted in her achievements and interests. When they made love, Kat was always attentive and demonstrative. But, those intimate moments had faded, not because of time constraints or everyday stresses, but because neither seemed inclined toward making love. A peck on the cheek and the lights were off, each to their side of the king-sized bed. That was one way Neil knew something had gone astray. But, it was far more than that. They seldom talked about anything other than Brie's adventures or the menial projects and bills that home ownership guaranteed. It left Neil wondering what had brought two people who had such drastically different interests and needs in life together in the first place. He'd puzzled over that question for nearly a year. He had hoped that the answer would hold the key to the compulsion he felt to move on from the life they had built together. His answer came unexpectedly one afternoon—Sarah.

Sarah hadn't made a visit home to the lake in over a year. It didn't seem to matter what invitations were extended or how many pleas were made, Sarah was determined to stay away. She had never missed a Christmas, but when December had rolled around the previous year, Sarah had told Deborah that her caseload was overwhelming and that she couldn't afford to take the time away. Sarah had never been absent for one of Brie's birthdays, but when March came upon them, she had made a brief call to Neil to extend her apologies. Her firm was growing and she needed to be present when she and her partner made the final decisions about who to bring on board. It was the afternoon she made that call that Neil got his answer.

Kat had expectedly asked to talk to Sarah. When Neil had told Sarah that Kat wanted to speak with her, he had noted the tension in Sarah's voice. But, when Kat picked up the phone in the kitchen and said hello, Sarah had immediately caved. She'd never been able to deny Kat a direct request. Neil had never listened in on one of their private conversations. That afternoon for some reason, he could not make his hand lower the receiver. He listened.

"Sarah?"

"Hey, Kit Kat," Sarah replied.

A long silence ensued. All that Neil was able to discern was Kat's sigh.

"How's the string bean?" Sarah finally asked.

Another long sigh preceded Kat's answer. "What did I do?" Kat asked Sarah.

"What are you taking about?"

"You're avoiding me like I have the plague."

"I'm not avoiding you," Sarah replied. "I'm just swamped."

"Too swamped to call? Too swamped to answer my calls?" Kat asked.

Neil covered the phone with his hand. He was positive the sharp intake of breath he had heard was his sister's.

"I'm just—it's nuts here, Kat. That's all."

"Are you okay?" Kat asked.

"Just tired."

"Sarah, please tell me what's wrong. You know, I'm here for you. Is it Debbie?"

"Debbie? Kat, Debbie and I haven't seen each other in almost six months."

"I thought this was it for you. You seemed so happy when you were home last Christmas."

"Yeah, well, that was a long time ago. And, anyway, you should never get involved with someone that has the same name as your mother. It's just creepy. Trust me."

"Find yourself calling out to Deborah?" Kat fell into their normal banter.

"Not really," Sarah replied more gruffly than she had intended.

"Sarah? Why don't you come home for your birthday?"

Neil waited for his sister's response. He heard her sigh heavily and knew what her answer would be.

"I wish I could. I haven't had much time for birthday parties lately."

"How about if I come there? You know, we could knock back some tequila and you could fall over on the dance floor a few times. Between Mom and Neil, I'm sure Brie would be entertained without me."

"Yeah, but entertained with what? Donuts, cookies, and cars?" Sarah joked. Kat chuckled. "I don't think it's really the best time," Sarah told Kat. "I'm working insane hours. When I get home, all I want to do is crash."

"What's her name?" Kat asked, trying to mask her hurt.

Neil was surprised at Sarah's response.

"The only her in my life right now is a woman named Claudia Gonzales. She's facing a nasty battle with her son-of-a-bitch, abusive husband over custody of their two kids. Well,

I suppose there's Claudia, Mary, and my administrative assistant Sean. Those shoes he insists on wearing scream *girl*."

Kat didn't find Sarah's attempt at levity amusing. "Well, if you change your mind…"

"I promise, I'll call. I gotta go. I have a meeting with Claudia and her social worker this afternoon."

"Saturday? Must be a special client."

"She's a good lady, Kat. She needs help."

Neil closed his eyes when he heard his wife's reply.

"She's lucky to have you then," Kat said.

"I guess we'll see. I'll talk to you soon. Kiss the string bean for me."

"Sarah?"

"Yeah?"

"I miss you," Kat confessed.

"I miss you too," Sarah replied honestly.

Neil was sure he heard them both begin to cry as the call disconnected. He waited until he was certain they had both left the line and hung up the receiver. He took a moment and made his way toward the kitchen. Kat had her face in her hands. He didn't need to see her expression to know the story it told. Kat was lonely. He was lonely. Sarah was lonely. Kat missed Sarah. He missed Kat. Sarah missed Kat. Hell, he missed Sarah, and he hated her for all of it at that moment. Something had brought them all together. Something had drawn him to Kat. Something had made Kat choose him. Sarah. It had always been Sarah. They'd all tried to live their lives apart from one another. It had been Sarah to step away—far away. Neil hated her for that. He hated himself for hating her. He didn't need Sarah's reasons or explanations. He'd known how Sarah felt long before the first time he had kissed Katelyn Summers. Sarah had always loved Kat. And, Sarah had always loved him. That's why she stayed away. Ironically, her absence lit the fire of his discontent.

Neil recalled that day as he looked across the small apartment at his soon to be ex-wife. "Truth isn't always a happy thing, Kat," he said.

"Neither is leaving without an explanation."

"Are we still talking about us?"

Kat took a deep breath and let it out slowly. "Right now? Yes, Neil, we are talking about us."

"Are you sure about that?"

Kat stilled herself before continuing. "I'm not here to pick a fight with you," she said. "I don't want to fight with you anymore," she told him. "That's not what either of us needs and it isn't good for Brie."

Neil sighed. "You're right—as usual. What is it? The custody? I told you, Kat. I want to be in Brie's life as much as I can, but I'm going to be on the road a lot. She's used to that. She needs to be where you are."

"She needs you too," Kat replied.

He nodded. "Thanks for saying that."

"Neil, I'm not just saying that. She adores you. You're a good father."

"Yeah, so good that I walked right out."

Kat sighed. She had no intention of lying to him. Neil's departure had rattled the entire family. His absence had been brief in the grand scheme of things, but it had undermined trust. And, it left both Kat and Brie confused, hurt, and insecure about his intentions. She considered how to reply honestly without reopening the rift that they had slowly begun to close.

"It hurt," she replied. Neil looked up in surprise. "You leaving like that. It hurt."

"I didn't mean to hurt you."

"Yes, you did," Kat disagreed. "On some level, Neil, you did. You didn't mean to hurt Brie. She just got caught in the crossfire. But, me? That's different. What did I do to make you so angry? I don't know what I…"

Neil groaned. "No, Kat, I was angry with me. Hell, I guess I was angry with all of us."

"All of us?"

"Yeah. You, me, and Sarah."

Kat nodded. "That explains what you said to her the other day."

"You heard us?"

She nodded.

"Shit. Kat, I didn't mean for you to hear that."

"No, I don't imagine that you did. Did you mean to say that to Sarah? I just want to understand, Neil. You decide to walk away from me, from our marriage without any conversation at all—Sarah drops everything to come pick up the pieces and you eviscerate her emotionally. Why?"

Neil hung his head. "Of course, she dropped everything. She's in love with you, Kat. How can you not know that?"

"I do know it. I suppose I've always known it on some level. I just didn't want to see it, I guess."

"Well, she's here now to clean up my mess, just like she always is," he commented.

"No, she's not."

"What are you taking about?"

"She's gone. Left me a note yesterday."

"Sarah left?" Neil was stunned.

Kat nodded.

"I can't believe she'd leave you now when…"

"Why not? You did."

"She's not me, Kat."

"Because she loves me, and you didn't?" Kat wondered.

"No. I love you. I'll always love you. For a long time, I was in love with you. But, Sarah... Sarah's always been in love with you. I don't think that the devil or God himself could change that."

"Funny how everyone who loves me seems to walk away."

"She left because of me," he said. "Again."

"What do you mean, again?" Kat wanted to know.

Neil had never told Kat about the night Sarah had seen them in Neil's truck on the dirt road that ran behind the lake. He'd told himself that he wanted to save Kat the embarrassment. After his confrontation with Sarah that week, he'd gotten thoroughly drunk. The memories of the many times he'd lashed out at his sister started playing like a film reel in his brain. He drank more hoping to turn it off. The more he drank, the more vivid his recollections became. It wasn't the first time he'd taken momentary satisfaction in causing his older sister pain. There had been more than a few over the years. The first time had been the day he had asked Kat out. The second time had been on that old dirt road.

"Neil? What do you mean—again?"

He sighed regretfully. "You're not going to like it."

"I think you owe me some explanation."

"Yeah, I guess, I do. Okay... Here goes... You want a drink?"

"No. Just tell me."

"Well, you'd better sit down in that case."

"Why? Is this revelation of yours apt to knock me out?"

"No, but it might give me a running start when you take your shot," he said.

Kat offered him a lopsided grin. She wondered if he had any idea how much he emulated his older sister at times. That is something Sarah would have said. "I can barely connect with a punching bag that's stationary. I think you're safe," she said.

"I guess we'll see," he said before taking a deep breath. "Do you remember that time Sarah came home to surprise you from college?"

"Which time?"

"Touché. The time she announced she was going to go to UCLA."

"Yeah, I remember. That threw me. I really thought that she was going to choose Harvard. I mean, that was always her goal. That was about the weirdest thing I ever saw her do," Kat recalled the visit. She noted that Neil had suddenly gone pale. "Neil?"

"See, the thing is, Kat… I heard her tell Dad that Harvard had rejected her application."

"What? Sarah's never gotten a rejection letter in her life."

Neil's heart dropped into his stomach. "She wasn't rejected."

"What are you talking about? All Sarah ever talked about was going to Harvard since we were in high school. You know her, she never quits on something she wants."

"Well, there is one thing," he said. Kat waited. "You."

"Neil…"

"I found a piece of her acceptance letter next to the fire pit in the backyard later that night. It must have blown out."

"Sarah burned her acceptance letter? Why?"

"Do you remember the night she came home at all?" Neil asked.

"Of course, I remember the night she came home! She showed up on your parents' doorstep soaking wet. She is so stubborn sometimes, walking three miles from the bus station in a thunderstorm."

"She didn't walk home from the bus station, Kat."

"Neil, what the hell are you talking about? We were on the front porch when she walked up the driveway with her backpack."

Neil nodded. "I remember."

"What aren't you telling me?" Kat demanded.

"Do you remember where we were when that rain storm started?"

"Why do you keep answering my questions with more questions?" Kat asked.

"Do you?"

Kat closed her eyes. "Of course, I remember, Neil. We drove out on that old dirt road behind the lake. I do remember those things, you know? A girl doesn't generally forget things like making love in a rainstorm."

"Neither does a guy," he told her. Kat's placid smile might have broken his heart at that moment if it hadn't already been shattered by the memory he was reliving. "Good to know," he said. "I should have told you this years ago."

"Told me what?"

"Sarah," he started and collapsed his face into his hands. "She was there, Kat."

"What do you mean she was there?"

"She saw us."

"Neil, come on. You were there with me when Sarah got home."

"Yeah, but she didn't walk from the bus station. She walked from the clearing by the road."

Kat's body began to tremble. "Are you telling me she watched us?"

He shook his head. "I doubt she stayed for the whole show," he replied. "She saw enough. I made sure of that."

Kat couldn't formulate a response. She stared at Neil blankly as her heart plummeted rapidly in her chest. "Why was she..."

Neil swallowed his fear and explained. "I think... I think she wanted to surprise you," he explained. "I think it was her first stop."

"I don't understand."

He nodded. "I went out there after I dropped you off that night. You know, to that spot you two always liked to go. She left a couple of things behind."

"What *things*?" Kat asked.

"A blanket and a bottle of champagne," he told Kat.

Kat's hands covered her face in disbelief, and she closed her eyes with regret. "Oh, Sarah."

Neil recognized the pained expression on his wife's face immediately. He imagined that it matched his closely. He saw something else when she opened her eyes—love. "I'm sorry, Kat."

"Why, Neil? If you knew she was there—why?"

"Because she loved you and I loved you," he said. "And, part of me knew even then that you loved her, maybe more than you could ever love me. I hated her for that."

Kat was stunned. "Neil, I never thought about Sarah that way."

"I know. Not then anyway. But, given the choice, Kat? Even back then? If Sarah had called, our plans would have been altered or put on hold. She was always the best at everything; you know? She was the better student. She was the star athlete. Shit. She basically shit glitter and gold."

Kat shook her head. "You wanted to hurt her? My God, Neil, is that what our entire relationship has been about, taking something from Sarah?"

"No. You know that it wasn't. I fell in love with you, Kat. Hard. Face first. And, I was terrified of losing you to her."

For the second time in minutes, Kat found herself speechless. She'd never entertained any idea about a romantic relationship with Sarah, not until Sarah arrived home a month ago. She suddenly felt as if she should defend herself against his perceived insinuations and it made her furious.

"I can't believe you. Are you telling me that she decided to move across the country because she saw us having sex?"

Neil closed his eyes as confirmation.

"She gave up Harvard because of that?"

"I, I…" he stuttered. "Yes, I think so. Things with me and Sarah—after that, they were never quite the same."

"Did she know that you saw her?"

"I don't know," he replied. "Maybe."

"Oh, God. Jesus…"

"I know. I was an asshole," he said.

"It wouldn't have changed our path, Neil. If she had never seen us, I mean. We both knew where things were headed."

"Maybe not," he agreed. "Then again, maybe if she'd been closer…"

"Maybe if she had been closer what?"

"Maybe you would have seen it sooner. Maybe I would have accepted it," he said. He didn't need to hear her reply. Kat's eyes confessed her heart without any need of words. "That's why you're here, isn't it?" Neil asked.

Kat sighed with resignation.

"So? Why are you *here*? Other than to remind me what a jerk I've been to my sister."

"To tell you the truth, I'm not even sure any more—about anything."

"Somehow, I don't believe that," Neil said.

Kat looked at him with surprise.

"Maybe it's not me you need to be talking to," he suggested.

"I'm not sure she'll take my call," Kat answered.

"So? Don't give her the choice."

"What?"

"Well, I'm home until Sunday. Go to California. Make her talk to you. You know Sarah. That's why she runs away. She can't deny you anything when she sees you. She never has been able to."

"Neil, I'm not sure I know what to say. I'm not sure I even know what I *want* to say."

"Well, maybe you should start with what you told me to do."

"What's that?"

"Tell her the truth."

"What if I don't know what that is anymore?"

Neil moved to sit beside his wife. He placed his arm around her and accepted Kat's head onto his shoulder. "You do. Tell her that you miss her. Ask her to come home, Kat. That's what you've wanted to do since the day she moved away." He heard her muffled cries begin and stroked her hair to calm her. "Aw, hell, it's what I wanted to do since the day she left too," he finally admitted. "Nothing was the same after she left. I felt guilty. I told myself I hated her; really, it was me that I couldn't stand."

"I love you, Neil."

"I love you too," he said. "But, I think we both know it's not what we thought it would be. We're so different, Kat. I'd been asking myself for a long time how it was we ever seemed to fit together so well. Then, I realized it was Sarah," he said.

Kat chuckled through a sob. She didn't need to examine the statement to know that it was true. Somehow, Sarah had always wound herself into the discussions and stories that she and Neil had shared. They always found themselves musing over what Sarah would say or something Sarah had done. For all his resentment and bravado, Kat had always known that Sarah was Neil's hero. In many ways, he tried to be his sister. More than that, he was constantly trying to impress her. Kat wondered if he'd ever realized that Sarah thought he had hung the moon.

"You know," she told him. "She thinks the sun rises and sets in you."

"I doubt that."

"That's always been your problem where Sarah is concerned," she said. "She does. She admires you more than you realize. She envies you too."

"Because I had you."

"Maybe," she admitted. "But, it's much deeper than that," Kat said. "Sarah—she has one speed, Neil—go. She always has. Capturing Sarah long enough to get her to sit still is like trying to catch lightning in a bottle. She craves that stillness, just to be quiet. She has a hard time permitting herself even a moment of it. That's the way you two differ the most, other than you being The Iron Giant, of course."

Neil laughed. "I don't feel much like iron these days."

"I don't think any of us do," she said. "You've always considered her the strong one. I don't think you ever considered the reality that she sees it differently."

Neil took a deep, cleansing breath and kissed Kat's temple. "It's okay with me, Kat."

"What's that?"

"That you love her. It's okay."

"I'm not sure that matters anymore."

"It matters. I can't tell you it's easy for me. But, I want you to be happy," he said. "I want Brie to be happy. Hell, I want Sarah to be happy."

"And what about you?" Kat asked.

"None of us have been happy since she left, not really. Something was always missing. Not just for you, Kat."

Kat nodded against him and molded herself to his body. She did love Neil. Her anger and her disappointment seemed to fade in the moment. He was right. Before Kat had entered their lives, Sarah and Neil had been inseparable. Kat had changed that in an instant. In some way, she understood that her love for Neil, his love for her, had always been rooted in the role Sarah played in both their lives. It was ironic; Sarah was the glue. Without her presence things had gradually begun to slip apart.

"Neil, I'm not sure Sarah wants me the way you are suggesting."

"She does. She's just spent so long trying to keep it from you, she doesn't know how to say it," he offered. Kat took a nervous breath and he pulled her closer. "It's my turn to step away," he said. "Not as far as she did, but far enough. At least, for now. We all need time to make the pieces fit back together."

"And, if they never do?" she asked.

Neil sighed. He had considered that possibility, but the notion had vanished as quickly as it had appeared. There was a new glue in their world. Someone who bonded them all in a unique way. "They will."

"And, what about Brie?"

Neil prompted Kat to look at him and he smiled lovingly. "Exactly." He saw Kat's confusion and moved to kiss her lips for what he was certain would be the last time. "There is one thing that trumps everything that's passed," he said.

Kat smiled at him. "Brie."

Neil nodded. "Go talk to my sister," he said. "It'll give me some time to corrupt our daughter with donuts and cars."

Kat laughed. "Are we going to be okay?"

"In time, Kat. Everything is changing again."

"Funny, it feels awfully familiar."

He chuckled. "I guess, it does. We've made it this far in our dysfunctional family. I'm sure we'll make it the rest of the way."

"You know; you need to talk to her too," Kat reminded him. He groaned. "Tell her what you told me," she suggested. "Don't run away again."

"Well, you've got us all there," he said. "I'm glad Brie takes after you."

"What do you mean?"

"Seems running is in the Masters' DNA. I hope that one skipped her."

Kat smiled. "Well, she seems to have missed both the dominant Iron Giant and the recessive short-stop chromosome. She's right in the middle. I hope she gets a blend of us all," Kat said. "I've been grounded my whole life as much as you or Sarah have ever felt the need to fly away. Hopefully, Brie got a bit of both of us."

Neil closed his eyes, content to share a quiet moment with Kat, knowing he'd never hold her this way again. "You want me to pick her up later?"

"Tomorrow," Kat said. "I think I just need to be here right now."

"It's really goodbye, isn't it?" he asked.

"No," she replied, feeling the gravity of their lives rooting her in place.

"I love you," he whispered. "Don't forget that."

"I won't. I don't regret it, Neil. You need to know that."

"Me neither. It sucks."

Kat laughed. Neil was right. It sucked. Breaking up was painful, even when a person knew it was the right path to take. She breathed in his scent one final time and closed her eyes. The moment she moved from his embrace, their world would shift again. This may not have been a goodbye, but it was the final step in letting go. Not just of their marriage or the love affair they once had reveled in, but of all their private doubts and long held secrets. It was strange, Kat thought as Neil held her; letting go was sometimes the only way you could hope to hold on.

Chapter Eleven: Truth Changes Everything
June 25, 2016

Sarah had been trying to concentrate all morning. She'd been reviewing notes on several of the cases she had handed over to her partners during her absence. Work had always served as the best diversion in her life. Concentrate on a problem, analyze it, plan how to combat it, and put the plan in motion; that is what Sarah excelled at. She'd been staring at the same page in the same file for over an hour. She was sure that she had read the first paragraph at least a thousand times. If anyone had asked her what the paragraph said she would have been at a total loss to recap it.

"Fuck," she groaned. "I have no focus."

Sarah collapsed her head forward and gently pounded it against the kitchen table. Maybe *that* would knock some sense into her or maybe she'd get lucky and it would serve to knock Kat from her thoughts. Sarah sighed. *Useless.* She sat back in her chair, closed her eyes and shook her head. Knock, knock. *Sarah—get a grip.* The faint sound of knocking in the distance stirred her from her private admonishment. She opened her eyes wondering if she had imagined the sound. A second later the gentle rapping repeated. Sarah took a deep breath and let it out forcefully. *Unless it's booze, I'm not buying anything.* She made her way to the front door of her condo and opened it, ready to scold whatever salesman awaited her. She froze for a moment in disbelief when her eyes met with Kat's.

"Kat?"

"Are you going to let me in?"

Sarah stepped back to let Kat enter. "Where's Brie?"

"With Neil."

Sarah stood dumbfounded. "Neil knows you're here?"

Kat took a deep breath. "I read your letter," Kat said. Sarah waited nervously. "Is it?" Kat asked.

Confusion played over Sarah's face. "Is it what?"

"Is it still the same?" Kat asked. Sarah made no reply and Kat took a step closer. "Sarah?"

Sarah closed her eyes. She could play the game she had for years and pretend that she had no idea what Kat was referring to. What was the point anymore? Everyone knew. She'd been playing the part of a love-struck fool for over twenty years. She was tired of evading the subject, skirting the truth, hiding the reality. She loved Kat. She'd always loved Kat. No matter how many things she changed in her life, that—that one thing had been immovable. She'd gone away to college. She'd buried herself in law school, even moved to the other side of the country. She'd stood beside Kat when Kat and Neil had married. She'd been the consummate best friend, the understanding big sister, the doting aunt. All the while, she'd been miserable. Why deny it any longer?

"Yes," she answered honestly. Kat nodded and waited for Sarah to continue. "That will never change," Sarah said.

Kat took another step closer. "Then why did you leave me that note?"

"Because everything else has. And, I can't watch it again. God knows, I want to. I can't. It hurts too much. Like I said, no matter how much everything changes, some things stay the same—even if I wish they wouldn't." Sarah looked at the floor.

"Sarah," Kat called for her friend's attention.

Sarah shook her head. "I can't anymore."

Kat lifted Sarah's face. "You can't what?"

"Love you."

"Do you? Love me?"

"Enough to know I should've stayed away in the first place."

"Oh? You love me, but you've never once told me."

"You knew."

"Maybe on some level I did. Maybe I wondered. But, you left. You had your life. When you came back—every time you came back, you were the poster child for success and happiness," Kat said.

"Sometimes you do what you have to."

"And, what about my feelings?"

"You loved Neil. You still love Neil."

Kat took a deep breath. "Oh, Sarah, I did. I do. But, he was never you."

For the first time in many years, Sarah felt a surge of anger toward Kat. She took a step away, needing some distance. "Not me? No, he's definitely not me. He was never me? What the hell is that supposed to mean?"

Kat's smile was laced with sorrow. She'd known. Of course, she'd known that Sarah loved her. No matter how much Sarah tried to conceal her feelings, anyone with eyes could've seen the admiration Sarah held for Kat. A couple of times, Kat's mother had suggested that Sarah's feelings ran deeper than friendship. Kat had always scoffed at the notion. It was absurd. But, it wasn't absurd. It was real, and it was staring Kat down like an old adversary.

Adversary—that's what Kat felt at this moment, as if she were facing her greatest adversary. How could she explain that to the woman standing before her? Sarah was not the issue. Sarah's love for Kat was not the daunting presence in the room. Kat had spent every night since overhearing Sarah and Neil on the back porch sleepless, rolling over a million memories, endless questions, and feeling a pull from deep within her soul telling her she'd been a fool. Kat closed her eyes. The one person she had always loved, the one person who had loved her through everything was looking at her through wounded eyes. She took a deep breath and opened her eyes to meet Sarah's.

"I wouldn't blame you if you hated me," Kat admitted.

The sentiment turned Sarah's stomach into knots. Hate Kat? Why on earth would she hate Kat? She hated herself—hated herself for being too weak to let go. Sarah couldn't look in the mirror without admonishing her reflection. Who wanted to love a fool? If Sarah Masters had played any role to perfection, it was the role of a love-struck fool. Neil had been right. She had taken many lovers, but she'd never let any get close, not even Beth. Five years living with a beautiful, intelligent woman who was willing to give her everything had been brought to its end by the simple truth: Sarah could love, but she had only fallen in love once. For Sarah, the idea of falling in love with anyone but Kat felt like the ultimate betrayal. Stupid, crazy, pathetic—stuck in a holding pattern for her entire life over a woman who would never love her.

Sarah sighed heavily as her momentary frustration gave way to regret for her harshness. "I don't hate you, Kat. I hate me."

"What?"

Sarah sighed again and collapsed onto the couch. "I do. Neil said something the other day. I've played a love-sick fool for over twenty years. And, sometimes I hated him for it. He was right. Fool is a perfect word for it—selfish fool."

Kat watched as Sarah put her face into her hands. She considered her best friend silently for a few moments. Her questions seemed to be immediately quelled by the evident pain that rolled off Sarah in waves. She moved to kneel in front of Sarah and peeled Sarah's hands from her face, holding them tightly.

Sarah looked at Kat and shook her head.

"There might be a fool in this room; it's not you," Kat said. Sarah's eyes closed. "Sarah," Kat called to her friend. "You're not a fool, unless you consider loving a fool foolish."

Sarah opened her eyes and chuckled despite the tension in the room. Kat always amused her. She couldn't contain the grin and the affectionate shake of her head that accompanied it. "You certainly do have a way with words."

Kat smiled. "I love you, Sarah."

Sadness filled Sarah's eyes. "I know you do."

"No, you're not hearing me. I love you."

"I did hear you. I do know, but it's not the same way that I love you and we both know it." There it was. Twenty-five years in the making, the truth was finally out in the stark light of day.

Kat nodded and tightened her grip on Sarah's hands. "Say it. Just once, tell me the truth—really tell me."

Sarah thought for a split second that she should lash out. Why should she have to say it? Profess it? Her anger abated as quickly as it had surfaced. She was exhausted. Maybe Kat had a point. Maybe she needed to say it so that she could finally let it go.

Sarah met Kat's gaze directly. She was surprised when she felt her lips curl into a genuine smile. Love was a strange thing. As she began to speak, she resigned herself to the truth. Sarah could let Kat go. Perhaps, she could even find joy in sharing her life with someone else, but Sarah would never love another soul as completely as she did Katelyn Summers—never.

With a deep breath, Sarah finally gave voice to the deepest part of her soul. "I love you, Kat. I've been in love with you ever since I can remember. That's just the way it's always been for me and I guess, if you want to know the truth, I think that's just the way it will always be."

Kat smiled, leaned forward and let her lips tenderly fall on Sarah's forehead. "I love you too," she promised.

Kat felt the wetness of Sarah's tears as they fell without restraint. She wiped them away gently. "You're still not hearing me," she said. She held Sarah's face in her hands. "I can't tell you that I knew it all those years ago. I don't think I ever considered it. I mean, Sarah—I was so caught up in all the things I was supposed to feel, I guess I just missed it."

"I was your best friend," Sarah offered. "I couldn't tell you, and when you and Neil... Well, I couldn't tell you after that."

Kat smiled broadly. "Oh, Sarah, you are priceless," she said. Sarah was bewildered. Kat guided Sarah's face closer. Sarah's lips were a whisper away. Kat traced over Sarah's lips with her thumb and moved to replace the tenderness of her touch with the sweetness of her kiss.

Sarah's head began to spin wildly. Kat's fingertips lovingly caressed her face as Kat allowed her kiss to linger.

"Kat?"

"Always talking," Kat whispered. "Must be the lawyer in you." She pulled back and smiled. "You always did love a good debate. Stop arguing with yourself, Counselor and listen to me. I love you every bit as much as you have ever loved me. No more notes. No more secrets. No more debates. I'm sorry it took me so long to see it."

"See what?"

Kat sighed. "I've spent so many years trying to create the perfect life, the perfect home. Something was always missing, not just at the big turns or the pivotal moments, in the everyday. Sometimes it was good. It was even great at moments, but it was never complete. It never felt quite like home after you left. Home was always right in front of me," Kat said. "It's been in every moment that you were there. I was so busy trying to create it, I didn't see it staring me in the eye."

"Kat... You know that..."

"I know that you have a million reasons why I can't love you. And, I don't blame you for not trusting what I'm saying. It doesn't make it any less true. I don't expect you to carry me off into the sunset. I do love you. I love you so much it hurts. And, what hurts the most is knowing I don't deserve you, but God knows I want to."

Sarah searched Kat's eyes in disbelief. She'd imagined a moment like this. She'd thought she would sweep Kat away, kiss her passionately, make love to her with abandon and live happily ever after. Now, she was frozen in place.

"Say something," Kat begged.

Sarah kissed Kat's forehead. There were so many words that still needed to be spoken, countless realities that Sarah knew they needed to face. She could feel the truth as it passed between them. They'd known each other nearly a lifetime. Sarah was certain that Kat meant every word she had said. She also understood that everything between them changed the moment they had each spoken their truth.

"Sarah, please," Kat begged.

"For once, I'm not sure what to say," Sarah replied. "I always imagined that if you were before me like this... That I would kiss you, hold you, and never let you go again."

"And, now?"

"I want to do that. I also know that we have a lot to talk about, a lot of things to consider, and…" Sarah took a breath. "We need to take it one moment at a time."

"You don't..."

Sarah smiled. "I do want you. I've waited most of my life to say those words to you and I never expected to hear them in return. I know what I want that to mean. I don't want to lose you."

"Lose me? Sarah, you could never lose me."

"I wish that were true. I want it to be. I want you— more than you could know. Just one day at a time. We've never tried this."

"This?" Kat smirked.

Sarah nodded. "Being something more than best friends."

"You mean being lovers."

"And, all that goes with that. At least, all that goes with it for me. I need to know this is it. Because, Kat, once I make love to you? For me, that will be it."

Kat smiled. "One day at a time. Can I ask you for one thing?"

"You can ask me for anything, you know that."

"Kiss me."

Sarah's heart thundered at the direct request. She put her hands on either side of Kat's face and slowly closed the distance between them. She felt her lips as they gently met Kat's. The kiss began tentatively, a cautious discovery. Sarah's eyes closed just as Kat's hands covered hers and tenderly stroked them in encouragement. Sarah answered the unspoken request and invited Kat to explore their connection. As the kiss deepened, Sarah's tears resurfaced, cascading over her cheeks in long trails, washing away years of sadness.

Kat pulled away slightly and kissed Sarah's lips one more time. "I do love you," she repeated her declaration. "And, it scares the hell out of me."

"I know it does," Sarah replied. "It scares me too."

Kat let her head fall onto Sarah's shoulder.

Sarah ran her fingers through the soft auburn curls that fell onto her chest. "One day at a time," she said.

"Sarah?"

"Yeah?"

"Tonight? Can you just hold me, please?"

Sarah kissed Kat's head as she had done many times over the years. She'd held Kat many times when Kat had cried after an argument with Neil, when their tickle fights had given way to a soft embrace, or when Kat had confided some teenage secret. Sarah pulled Kat up onto the couch and into her arms. "Better?"

Kat nodded against Sarah's chest. "I'm sorry, Sarah."

"No more apologies, okay?"

"Promise me you will always be my best friend no matter what happens," Kat whispered.

Sarah took a deep breath and let it out slowly. "Oh, Kat—I promise I will always love you. Nothing in the world could change that if it hasn't in all these years." She felt her shirt begin to grow wet. "Don't cry," Sarah soothed her best friend. "I hate it when you cry."

"I just don't want you to let me go."

Sarah held Kat tighter. "I won't, not without a fight."

Kat chuckled. That much she believed. She snuggled closer to Sarah, a familiar feeling of comfort encompassing her, this time accompanied by an unfamiliar sense of anticipation. She giggled nervously.

"What's funny?" Sarah wondered.

"Nothing. It just feels good to be close to you, only maybe a little too good."

Sarah laughed. "Welcome to my life."

Kat looked up at Sarah. "Was it always like this for you? I mean, all these years?"

Sarah smirked and blushed. "Yep."

"Oh, God, I think I would've died," Kat replied. Sarah's smile slipped into sad acknowledgement. Kat reached up and touched Sarah's cheek. "I'm so sorry."

Sarah shook her head. "No," she said. "I wouldn't have traded a minute—not one." Sarah brushed her lips against Kat's sweetly.

"You okay?" Kat asked.

"Yeah, I'm just not sure I will ever get used to being able to do that."

"Good. Don't," Kat replied. Sarah tipped her head in confusion. Kat laid her head back on Sarah's chest. "I don't think we should ever get used to it," she explained. "That way we will always know what it means."

Sarah closed her eyes. A myriad of emotions coursed through her all at once—contentment, fear, love, lust—gratefulness for the woman lying in her arms eclipsed them all. "I love you, Kat," she whispered. Kat's grip tightened around Sarah in reply. "One day at a time."

Deborah's hands continued to chop the vegetable on the cutting board. Her eyes remained fixed on her son. "Your father has a few beers in the refrigerator."

"Thanks."

"How are you?" Deborah asked.

"Okay."

"Are you?"

Neil grabbed a beer and popped it open. "How am I supposed to be?"

"I don't know that you are *supposed* to be anything."

"I'm okay, Mom."

"How do you feel about Kat going to California?"

"I told her to go."

"That's not what I asked you."

"I think it's a long overdue trip."

Deborah nodded.

Neil guzzled his beer.

"That won't make it stop hurting," Deborah advised.

"Probably not," he agreed. "Tastes good about now,"

Deborah offered her son a sympathetic smile. "What happened with you and your sister?"

"I fucked up."

"You mean the other day?"

"Not just the other day," he said. "A lot."

"With Kat?"

"No. I loved Kat. I mean, I *love* Kat."

"But?"

"Not the way Sarah does. Not anymore, anyway."

Deborah nodded.

He took another long pull from the beer bottle in his hand. "She beat me again."

"Beat you?" Deborah asked.

"Yeah. When push comes to shove, she always finishes first."

"Neil." Deborah set down the knife in her hand. "Please don't tell me that you see Kat's affection as some kind of competition with your sister."

"No," he said. "No. I thought I would be in love with her forever."

Deborah listened without comment.

"Maybe it's not me she fell in love with."

"Kat loves you."

"Yeah, I know," Neil said. "And, for a while, she was in love with me. I know. The thing is, Mom, Sarah was always there."

"You both miss Sarah."

"Yeah, but it's more than that."

"You think Kat is in love with Sarah?"

"You don't?"

Deborah took a seat at the table and sighed. "I'm not sure Kat knows what she feels right now."

"Yeah, she does," he disagreed.

Deborah shook her head.

"Just because Kat and I didn't work out doesn't mean things won't with Sarah," he said.

"Neil, what about you?"

He shrugged. "I'm glad I'll be on the road a lot." He chuckled. "I'm used to seeing them close, but…"

"I don't think Kat and Sarah will…"

Neil smiled. "You should be happy, Mom."

"Seeing my children in pain doesn't make me happy."

237

"We're okay," he said. "We will be. Maybe Sarah will finally forgive me."

"Forgive you? Neil, you don't need her forgiveness for marrying Kat."

"No? Maybe not for that. Trust me, Mom. She has reasons for hating me."

"Your sister doesn't hate you."

"That's what Kat said."

"Kat's right."

"Maybe it's me who hates me. I'm glad Kat went to see Sarah."

"And, what about you?"

"I don't know. I kind of like being on the road."

Neil's admission didn't surprise his mother. She suspected his love for traveling the NASCAR circuit had contributed to the demise of his marriage. There was more to his statement. She was sure of it. "Why?"

Neil laughed. "You know how Sarah used to tell all those stories about seeing the world?"

"I recall a few."

"I guess I always wanted that too. Maybe racetrack to racetrack isn't country to country. It is for me," he said. "Kind of funny, huh?"

"What's that?" Deborah asked him.

"All this time, she's the one who wanted to be home. I was the one who wanted to roam free." He smiled at his mother. "It hurts. It's hurt for a long time, Mom. All of us. Not just Sarah. Maybe it's time we all accepted where we belong."

Tears gathered in Deborah's eyes. She reached over and squeezed Neil's hand. *Maybe it is.* "I need to finish dinner." *Maybe it is, Neil.*

One Week Later

Sarah hovered in the kitchen doorway. Kat was sitting at the kitchen table sipping a cup of coffee. Sarah could see a myriad of emotions playing over Kat's expression. She'd always prided herself on the ability to read Kat. Now, she found herself wondering what was driving Kat's thoughts—fear, regret, or perhaps hopefulness. "Penny for your thoughts."

Kat looked up at Sarah and smiled. "Morning."

"I notice you left out the 'good' part of that statement."

Kat sighed. She had been up for hours. In fact, she had awoken in the middle of the night at the startling realization of what lay ahead. She was surprised that Sarah had not felt her grip tighten. Kat had fallen asleep in Sarah's embrace feeling contented and hopeful. At some point during her peaceful slumber, reality had triggered anxiety. Sarah's life existed here—three-thousand miles away from Kat. Kat could not envision moving to the west coast. Brie's family remained in Massachusetts. How could Kat expect Sarah to uproot her world? As much as Kat desired to ask, she felt it unfair to expect Sarah to change her entire life. She closed her eyes.

"Kat? Listen, I understand if this is just too far out of the…"

Kat's eyes flew open. Of course, Sarah would jump to the conclusion that she was having second thoughts. "Sarah, sit down."

Sarah swallowed hard and took a seat across from Kat.

"What happens now?" Kat asked.

"What do you mean?"

"Your life is here."

"My job is here."

"I think we both know it's more than that," Kat said. "What happens when I leave tomorrow?"

Sarah sat silently for a moment. She reached across the table and peeled Kat's hands from the coffee mug she was gripping tightly. "Kat," she began. "Look at me. Please?"

Kat looked up and bit her lip.

"I thought we agreed—one day at a time?"

"We did. Sarah, this is your life. I can't ask you to…"

"Yes, you can, but you don't have to."

"Sarah…"

Sarah tightened her hold on Kat's hands. "I'll be home at the end of next week."

Kat's eyes grew wide.

"Unless, you don't want me to come home."

"I want you to come home. I don't want you to…"

"Stop," Sarah said.

"I don't want to leave," Kat admitted.

"I don't want you to leave," Sarah said. "It's only a week."

"I hate it when you leave," Kat whispered.

Sarah smiled.

"It's because of me that you left at all," Kat said. "Now? I show up here and ask you to… I…"

"Hey." Sarah got up and made her way to Kat. She understood Kat's fears better than Kat might imagine. Sarah also knew a thing or two about regret. She could see a hint of regret in Kat's eyes. "Listen to me. No more about the past.

One day at a time means we go forward. Okay? We have all day today to spend together."

Kat reached out and caressed Sarah's cheek.

"Kat," Sarah pulled Kat close. Kat immediately began to sob. "Hey, come on. It's okay."

"It's all my fault."

"What's your fault?"

"You didn't go to Harvard because of me. You moved as far away as you could. And, now…"

"Stop," Sarah cooed. She pulled back and kissed Kat's forehead. "I moved because I loved you."

"I know."

"No," Sarah said. "I wanted you to be happy, Kat. Honestly, I did. It just made me feel like shit that seeing you happy made me feel, well, shitty."

Kat chuckled. "I'm so sorry."

"No more sorry. Now, come on, what do you want to do today?"

Kat finally offered Sarah a smile.

Sarah laughed. She could see the mischievous flicker in Kat's eyes. She easily understood Kat's feeling. Taking it slow with Kat would likely be the hardest thing Sarah Masters ever had to do. Kat's emotional display only served to convince Sarah that taking things at a snail's pace was the best chance she and Kat had of developing what existed between them into a successful relationship. She kissed Kat's lips gently. "I was thinking a drive up the coast. Maybe a walk on Santa Monica Pier and then dinner."

Kat nodded. "Safety in numbers, huh?"

Sarah winked. "Something like that."

"Sarah?"

"Yeah?"

"I love you."

Sarah was certain that some part of Kat feared Sarah's reluctance to seduce her equated to doubt. "I know. That's why there's safety in numbers." She winked again. "I love you too, Kat. Too much to screw it up again."

"You didn't screw anything up."

"Well, we will agree to disagree on that one," Sarah said. "What do you say? A day at the beach, a nice dinner with a view, and then…"

"We spend the rest of the night alone before I have to leave."

Sarah nodded. *This is not going to be easy.*

Three Weeks Later

Sarah sat on the front porch swing at her parents' home sipping a glass of lemonade. She breathed in the fresh air and savored it. The last three weeks had been the happiest Sarah had been since childhood. The first few days after she'd arrived had been laced with uncertainty for Sarah. She was confident that Kat loved her. She was not certain that Kat understood what that meant. Even now, Sarah remained concerned about Brie. How would Brie adjust to her Aunt Sarah becoming her mother's partner? That remained the one thought that plagued Sarah's mind and fed her insecurities. She and Kat had been cautious about outward displays of affection in front of anyone. The truth was, Sarah had not directly confronted her new reality with her parents.

242

"Beautiful day," Deborah Masters offered as she stepped out onto the porch.

"Sure is."

Deborah sat down on the swing beside her daughter. "Picking up Brie from school today?" she inquired.

"I had planned to, unless you had something that you wanted to do with her."

"No," Deborah replied. "I think she's grown to look forward to seeing you when she gets off the bus."

Sarah grinned.

"Sarah…"

Sarah took a deep breath. *Here it comes.* "Yeah?"

"Have you thought all of this through?"

"All of what?"

"You and Kat."

Sarah looked her mother directly in the eyes. "Mom, I've spent over twenty years thinking about Kat."

"I know that."

"Neil said something to you," Sarah guessed.

"I asked," Deborah clarified.

"What did he say?"

"He said that he thinks things are the way they should've been long ago."

Sarah nodded. "But you disagree."

"I didn't say that."

"But you do."

"Sarah, Kat has been through a lot these past few months."

"You don't think I know that?"

"I didn't say that."

"What *are* you saying, Mom?"

"Are you sure this is what you want?"

Sarah stared at her mother, dumbfounded by the question.

"I don't mean Kat."

"What do you mean?" Sarah challenged her mother.

"What about Brie?"

"Are you concerned about me being part of Brie's life?"

"No," Deborah laid the thought to rest. "I've never heard you talk about wanting a family."

"I've never considered having a family." Sarah smiled when her mother's brow furrowed in concern. "I didn't say I never *thought* about it."

"There's a difference?"

"Yes." Sarah sighed. "Beth wanted that."

"And you didn't?"

"It wouldn't have been right for me to have a family with Beth."

"Because you loved Kat."

"Yes," Sarah admitted. "Mom…" Sarah started and then stopped.

"What?"

"Tell me the truth. Do you disapprove? Of me being with Kat, I mean?"

The look on Sarah's face made Deborah's heart ache. Her heart had ached for Sarah for years. She'd hoped and prayed that Sarah would find someone to share her life with. She'd never entertained the idea that ultimately that person might be Kat. She let out a soft sigh and smiled at her daughter.

"No," she told Sarah. "I've watched you hurt for so long," she said. "All of you have been hurt. That's the hardest part of being a parent—not being able to protect your children from pain."

Sarah thought for moment. "I think I can understand that—more than I ever could have before. You're right, we have all been hurt. We've all hurt each other without ever meaning to. But, you might be forgetting something."

Deborah was curious.

"We've also loved each other—all of us. That hasn't changed even if the way that might look has."

Deborah nodded. Sarah had always had a unique way of looking at the world. She did know that Sarah loved Kat. Sarah loved Neil. Sarah loved them both so much that she had kept silent most of her life about her feelings. Deborah looked at Sarah now and realized that it wasn't only Sarah who had been devastated by her need to walk away, it had been Kat too. On some level, it had also broken a part of Neil. Sarah was right.

"It's not easy, sweetheart."

"What's that?" Sarah asked.

"Loving someone and living with them—it's not as easy as it sounds."

Sarah laughed. "I don't think it's easy at all, Mom."

"Sarah?"

"Yeah?"

Deborah hesitated.

"What is it, Mom?"

"Your entire life is in California."

Sarah smiled. Kat had said something similar before she had left California. "No," she disagreed. "I have a job in California. I have friends. I have memories. That's never been where my life was."

Deborah put her arm around Sarah and squeezed. "She is lucky to have you."

Sarah's tears threatened to spill over. "No, Mom, it's the other way around. It always has been."

Deborah smiled. *Oh, Sarah, if only you could see what the rest of us see. She most certainly is lucky—we all are.*

<hr />

"Auntie Sarah?"

Sarah looked up from the book she was reading and smiled at her niece.

"Where's Mom?"

Sarah closed the book in her hands and set it down. She directed Brie to come sit with her. Kat and Neil had a late afternoon meeting with the attorney that was handling their divorce. Sarah had no intention of traversing that subject with her niece. It wasn't only awkward, Sarah didn't feel it was her place. She and Neil had gradually begun to find their footing again. The fact was, Neil was hurting, and Sarah was too. Her brother's decision to leave Kat without any word at all still perplexed Sarah. He loved Kat. Sarah didn't doubt that. Sometimes, as much as she loved Neil, Sarah thought he could be incredibly impulsive and selfish.

Seeing the pain in Kat's eyes when Sarah had first arrived back home had nearly destroyed Sarah. She'd witnessed sadness in her best friend before—never the way it enveloped Kat that day. The sight broke Sarah more than any hurtful words Neil had ever hurled at her. She loved Neil. Nothing could change that, but she was still angry. And, Sarah would never deny that she was also struggling with a guilty conscience.

As the days and weeks wore on, Sarah found it increasingly difficult to keep a physical distance from Kat. Kat had no intention of making it easier which both amused Sarah and frustrated her. She'd spent nearly a lifetime fantasizing about loving Kat—in every way possible. For Sarah, making love to Kat would seal forever. Sarah was positive that once she held Kat as a lover, she would never be able to take another.

Chapter Twelve: Once Upon a Time

"Auntie Sarah?"

"Yeah, String Bean?"

"Are you leaving again?"

Sarah pulled Brie onto her lap. "For a few days."

"Daddy is going with you?"

"Yep."

"Can I go with you?"

Sarah smiled at her niece. "You have school."

"I want to go with you and Daddy."

"Daddy and I will be back. Who would take care of Mom if you went with us?"

"Nana," Brie replied.

Sarah laughed. "And, who would take care of Nana?"

"Grampy and Mom."

"I see. You've done some thinking about this, huh?" Sarah asked. Brie nodded. "Brie, I promise, Daddy and I will both be back before you know it. You won't even have time to miss us."

"Til you go back again," Brie mumbled.

Sarah looked at the little girl on her lap. Brie reminded her so much of Kat sometimes it took her breath away. She'd seen the same expression in Kat's eyes every time she would leave to go back to school or back to the life she'd made in

California. Kat would look at her pleadingly and then cast her eyes into her lap, just as Brie did now. Sarah pulled Brie a bit closer and smiled when Brie moved to tuck her head beneath Sarah's chin.

Sarah had always loved Brie. Brie was a part of the two people that meant the most to Sarah for nearly her whole life. Over the last few months, that love had grown in ways that Sarah had never imagined possible. Brie wasn't just a part of Kat and Neil anymore; she was a fixture in Sarah's everyday life.

Having children had never been on Sarah's radar. Being a cool, distant aunt was safe. There was no way that Sarah could've screwed that up. And, if there was one thing that Sarah wanted to succeed at, it was having a positive influence on the small person in her lap. She hadn't given much thought to how the presence of a six-year-old would affect her life with Kat. Over the years, Sarah had concocted some creative daydreams about what life with Kat would be like. None of those fantasies had ever included parenthood. More than she ever had, Sarah now understood one of the reasons Kat had been drawn to Neil. Family had always figured in Kat's plans.

While Sarah dreamed of whisking Kat away into a passion-filled, romantic life, Kat had always dreamed of living here by the lake with 2.5 kids and a dog named Whisper. Kat had always hoped to have a few kids. She'd talked about it many times to Sarah. Sarah imagined that Kat's desire for Brie to have siblings stemmed from Kat's only child syndrome. She wondered if recent revelations regarding sibling rivalry and envy might have cured that desire. The grass was always greener on the other side of the fence. Kat had envied the companionship she witnessed between Sarah and Neil. Sarah often wished for the solace she imagined Kat enjoyed growing up.

"I'm not leaving once I get back," Sarah assured Brie. Brie moved and looked up into Sarah's eyes. Sarah smiled and winked at her. "I'll be here *all* the time. You'll be sick of me soon enough," she teased.

Brie shook her head. "No, I won't."

The emotion and self-assuredness in Brie's declaration surprised Sarah. She was learning a little more each day that kids had as much to teach adults as adults could ever hope to teach their children. Sarah found Brie's perspective on life fascinating and humbling. At times, the innocent observations of a six-year-old seemed to Sarah to hold more insight and truth than the knowledge and wisdom her most respected professors and mentors had ever imparted.

Sarah hugged Brie. "I hope you're sure, because I'd miss you if I had to stay there again."

"Mom would miss you. She doesn't like it when you go away."

Sarah closed her eyes. "No more going away, Brie. I promise, okay?" Brie sat back up and smiled deviously. "What's going on in that brain?" Sarah asked with a tap on Brie's forehead. Brie shrugged, but Sarah noticed the mischievous sparkle in her eyes. "Uh-huh. Come on, you're up to something. I know that look."

Brie's eyes brightened. "That means you can teach me to waterski."

Sarah arched an amused brow at her niece. "Oh? Why not Mom or Dad?"

Brie shook her head. "Daddy shows off too much, and Mom has to drive the boat," she explained.

Sarah laughed. "Can't argue with that," she said.

Brie hopped off her lap. "Can you make bananas?"

"Do I look like a tree?" Sarah joked.

Brie giggled. "No! Pancakes. You're silly."

"You didn't say pancakes. You said bananas."

Brie frowned. "You and Mom call them bananas."

Sarah nodded. She couldn't argue with that either. The first thing Sarah had ever learned to cook had been banana pancakes. She had proudly displayed her culinary skills for Kat the first time Kat had slept over her house in the sixth grade. Ever since, whenever the two shared a morning breakfast, Kat would request bananas. Sarah sometimes entertained the notion that Kat might have some latent monkey DNA.

"How about blueberry instead," Sarah suggested.

Brie wrinkled her nose. Sarah held back a fit of laughter. Over the years, Sarah had tried to suggest substitutions to Kat—strawberry, blueberry, chocolate chip. The answer was always the same. "With banana," Kat would reply.

Brie huffed and nodded her head. "Okay—with banana," she said as she turned on her heels and headed to the kitchen. "Auntie Sarah's making bananas," she told her mother as they passed in the doorway.

"Is she?" Kat asked, turning to a Sarah.

Sarah shrugged. "This whole house is bananas," she commented.

Kat crossed the room and claimed the space her daughter had just vacated on Sarah's lap. She leaned in a placed a gentle kiss on Sarah's lips.

"What was that for?" Sarah asked.

"Because I love bananas," Kat replied.

Sarah laughed. "You're nuts, Kit Kat."

"You haven't called me that in forever."

Sarah ran her thumb tenderly across Kat's cheek. "You've always been my Kit Kat."

Kat smiled. An emotional storm was brewing in Sarah. She could see it. "It's not that long," she said knowingly.

"Still too long," Sarah replied.

"Sarah," Kat whispered.

"Come on," Sarah pushed Kat from her lap. "I have bananas to make."

Kat grabbed Sarah's hand and held her steady. "Sarah," she said. "This is not another goodbye."

Sarah sighed.

"We will miss you, though."

"Not as much as I will miss you."

Kat smiled. "Not true. I always miss you when you're away. I always have."

"You only want me here so you can have bananas every morning," Sarah attempted to shift the conversation.

Kat sighed. Sometimes Sarah frustrated her. She'd seen the shadows of regret and fear in Sarah's eyes the last two days. In some ways, it made Kat feel more secure. In the past, every time Sarah would drive away, board a train, or walk through the doors to the airport, Kat would feel as if a part of her were disappearing. Phone calls, emails, messages—those were nice, but they were a pathetic attempt at replacing Sarah's presence—Sarah's pranks, Sarah's humming as she flipped the "bananas" in the pan—Sarah's smile. Kat had been so consumed in the void that Sarah's absence had left, she had not taken the time to consider how leaving had torn Sarah's heart apart. Even knowing that she was coming home, that this separation was a temporary necessity, Sarah was struggling.

"Sarah…"

Sarah closed her eyes when Kat's hands tenderly took hold of her face. "She thinks I will leave again," Sarah said.

"Brie?" Kat asked.

Sarah nodded.

"She loves you."

Sarah opened her eyes and met Kat's compassionate gaze. "I don't ever want to disappoint her. Not like I disappointed you."

Kat leaned in and brushed her lips across Sarah's. "Now, you really are talking bananas," she said. "You have never disappointed me," Kat promised.

"Yes, I have."

"No. We both followed the path we thought we were meant to. You need to let this go now," Kat said firmly. "It might have taken us in some unexpected directions, but it led us straight back here. That's what matters," Kat said.

Sarah gazed adoringly at Kat.

"What?" Kat asked.

"You."

Kat sighed. "I love you, Sarah."

"I know."

"Humble to a fault," Kat teased.

"When it comes to you, yes, I am," Sarah replied seriously. "I should just hire someone to…"

Kat grinned. "No, you need to go face that down," she said. "You've made your life there for the last twelve years."

"I lived there. I don't know how much of a life it was."

"It was. Stop denying that. You have memories there, Sarah."

"It's a law firm, Kat—cases and caseloads. Meetings and clients…"

253

"Beth?" Kat offered. Sarah's eyes closed at hearing Kat speak the name. "Sarah," Kat said gently.

"Beth and I haven't been together for a long time."

"I know, but once upon a time you loved her."

"She was never you."

"I know that too," Kat said, surprising Sarah. "Well, I do know that. But, Sarah, you loved her. I know you did. And, God knows she loved you. Just because you weren't meant to be together doesn't change the reality. Have you ever told her?"

"Told her what?"

"The truth?"

Sarah groaned. "She told me."

Kat nodded. "Maybe you should tell her."

"Why? What would it matter now? That has been over…"

"Maybe. But, if there is one thing I have learned these last few months, it's that until you speak it, you can't really let it go."

Sarah groaned again.

"You know that I'm right, Counselor."

"Beth has a new life. I doubt she feels the need to re-visit our past."

"I wasn't talking about what Beth needs. You still talk to her, don't you?"

"Occasionally."

Kat smiled. Beth and Sarah's mother were still close. And, she knew that until Beth had met her wife, Deborah had always held a glimmer of hope that Sarah and Beth might reconcile. It had taken more than a year after Beth had left for the two to rekindle a friendship. Kat found it ironic. In many ways, she and Beth's role in Sarah's life had reversed. Kat was the lover and Beth was the best friend. Kat also suspected that part of Sarah's anxiety regarding this trip was potentially facing Beth with the truth.

"She'll understand," Kat said. "And, so do I."

Sarah's expression gave away her trepidation.

"It is okay that you have loved someone else, Sarah."

"Kat, I have never been in love with anyone but you."

"Not the same way. You have loved, Sarah, just like I have. Why do you think that having loved Beth is some kind of betrayal?"

"Because for me it is."

Kat shook her head. "Do you think that my loving Neil was a betrayal?"

"No, I don't. I get it. More now than I ever did before."

Kat wrapped her arms around Sarah's neck. "Don't get me wrong, I am selfishly glad that you and Beth didn't run off into the sunset."

"Is that so?"

"Yeah, I don't much like sharing your bananas."

Sarah smirked. "Are we still talking about breakfast?"

Kat winked. "We're talking about all of it."

"Is that right?"

"It is, but I know that loving her in some way brought you back here to me. I can't explain it. I just think that's true."

Sarah sighed and kissed Kat on the forehead. Kat's intuition was correct, not so much about Sarah finding her way back to Kat but preparing Sarah for what that entailed. Kat was right. Sarah's relationship with Beth—the best of it and the missteps had given Sarah a different perspective on relationships—preserving them, growing them, destroying them too. Beth had forced Sarah to consider what commitment meant. It wasn't all romance and roses. It wasn't all angst and yearning. Sharing life with someone was not all about passion and need. The long haul incorporated all those things. It required friendship, understanding, patience, and acceptance as well. Beth had tried to build that foundation with Sarah. Beth had pushed, and Sarah had pulled until it finally cracked. Two things had held Sarah back: fear of it falling apart and fear of losing Kat forever. In the end, fear had been Sarah's greatest enemy.

Sarah was anxious about traveling back to California. Kat was also correct in her assumption that Sarah was apprehensive about facing Beth. It was silly, and Sarah knew it. She and Beth had slowly developed a strong friendship. Beth was happy with her life. She'd married a college professor the previous year and they were expecting their first child together. Beth would be equally happy for Sarah. But, Sarah also knew that even after time and healing, her love for Kat would be akin to revisiting a ghost from that past for Beth, one that had caused Beth enormous pain. Sarah regretted causing that pain. She had loved Beth. A part of her always would. That was not where she belonged. She had always felt the pull back home. Even when Sarah had tried to convince herself that she would never return to Massachusetts, deep within her something always whispered that she would. There had only ever been one person that Sarah had the heart to give everything to. That person was standing in her arms.

"Sarah?"

"You're right."

"Really?" Kat gloated.

"Okay, don't rub it in."

"I am curious," Kat confessed.

"That I admitted you're right?"

"No, why you think I'm right."

"Sarah!" Brie yelled from the kitchen. "Are you coming?"

"Bananas," Sarah replied.

"Come again?"

Sarah gestured toward the kitchen. "She's waiting for her bananas."

"She'll survive a few more minutes. I've waited years."

Sarah chuckled. "I meant that *she* is waiting for *me* to make her bananas."

"Lost me, Counselor."

Sarah nodded. "This might take longer than a few minutes."

"Try me," Kat suggested. "I catch on quickly."

"Yes, you always have," Sarah agreed. "Kat, you always wanted kids."

"Yes?"

"I never gave it a passing thought—for me, I mean."

"Oh… Sarah, are you…"

"Until Brie was born and Beth brought it up."

"You and Beth talked about having kids?"

"No, Beth talked about having kids after Brie was born. She brought it up when we got home after Christmas."

Kat was confused. "You two broke up a week later. How did you go from talking about families to separate residences in a week?" she asked. Sarah sighed.

"You didn't want to."

"No."

Kat blew out a heavy breath. "I see."

"No, you don't. I told you, I never thought about being a mom, Kat. To tell you the truth, I never thought I'd be very good at it."

"What? What are you talking about?"

"I didn't. When Beth brought it up… Well, all I could think about was how happy you looked holding Brie. That's not something I could have given you. And, it wasn't something I wanted to have with Beth. Maybe that's how we both knew it wouldn't work—even if I wanted it to."

"Why didn't you try?"

"Because, Kat, when I came home that week I realized that you were it for me. Watching you and Neil—you had the life you'd always imagined. Believe it or not, I was happy for you. I think in some way it's also when I realized that the life I always wanted was with you. I couldn't pretend to build that with someone else. It wouldn't have been fair. It wouldn't have been fair to Beth. Kids? Well…"

"And, now?"

"And, now it scares the shit out of me. But, Brie has you and Neil. I hope I can help. I mean, I hope that I can be the best Aunt Sarah she has."

"You're her only aunt. And, you are a lot more than that to her, Sarah."

"I know. She's a lot more than that to me," Sarah admitted. "She's part of you. See, the thing is, I loved Beth enough to share a lot of myself with her. I didn't love her the way I needed to—not to be a family. A couple? Yeah. A family? There's only one place I could do that. And, there's only one person I'd have the courage to try that with."

"I think I understand. I also think that you need to talk to Beth. You and Neil have a love of notes. It doesn't matter that you're not together anymore. She's your friend. Near as I can tell, she is about your best friend."

"You're my best friend."

Kat smiled. "And, I always will be. She deserves more than a note—more than a phone call. And, so do you. Just tell her the truth. Don't leave behind the pieces of you that mean something there unresolved. Look at us, Sarah. Look at all the things we didn't say—all of us—you, me, and Neil. I'm not saying it would have changed anything. But, I will never leave things that matter that much unsaid again. Not with Neil and never with you."

"You're pretty smart, you know?"

"Yeah, it's hard to be me."

"Mom!" Brie called.

"Bananas," Sarah shook her head.

Kat grabbed Sarah's hand and pulled her toward the kitchen. She stopped just before they reached the doorway. "Let it go so you can come home."

Sarah nodded. "I hate leaving."

"I know you do. Sometimes you have to let go before you can hold on."

"Speaking from experience?"

Kat smiled.

"Auntie Sarah!" Brie's face appeared in the doorway. "I thought we were having bananas?" she looked at her mother and her aunt.

Sarah laughed. "You and your mother are part monkey, I swear it," she said. "Come on."

"Monkey?" Kat asked as she followed behind.

"Yep."

"Because we like your bananas?" Kat asked. Sarah flashed a flirtatious grin over her shoulder at Kat. Kat rolled her eyes. "In that case, you must be a chocoholic."

"Why is that?" Sarah wanted to know as she began pulling things from the cupboards.

"Well, you are obsessed with Kit Kats."

Sarah turned on her heels in astonishment. Kat tipped her head in challenge.

"I like Kit Kats," Brie commented innocently. "Hey! Can you make Kit Kat bananas?"

Sarah blushed, and Kat erupted in laughter.

"Instead of chocolate chips," Brie explained her reasoning.

Sarah was seldom at a loss. Kat couldn't stop laughing. "Maybe we will have to try that one day," Kat offered. Sarah glared at her for a second, took a deep breath, and returned to her task.

"Mom?" Brie stepped in front of Kat.

"Yes?"

"Can Auntie Sarah stay here when she comes back instead of at Nana's so much?"

Kat smiled. "Auntie Sarah can stay here any time she wants to."

Brie nodded happily and skipped back to Sarah. "See? She misses you when you leave," Brie whispered. Sarah smiled. "So, you can stay here!"

Kat raised her eyebrow at Sarah.

"We'll see, String Bean," Sarah said. "You might get sick of seeing me so much."

"Nah," Brie dismissed the thought. "Just don't make that stuff on a shingle again," she said. She turned and started to skip away.

Kat hid her face in her hands. Sarah and Neil had both tried to convince Brie that chipped beef on toast was a delicacy. They'd attempted that same snow job on Kat for the last twenty-two years. Shit on a shingle was just that—shit on a shingle. Apparently, Brie had inherited her taste buds from the Summers side of the family.

"Where are you going?" Sarah called after Brie.

"Gonna see if there's any Kit Kats in Mom's secret candy stash!"

Sarah shook her head. "She's yours."

Kat shrugged. "Guess we have some things to talk about when you get back, huh?"

"We'll get there, Kat. One day at a time, remember?"

"Yeah, I do. I just don't know how many more of them I want to endure without you here."

Sarah set aside her task and walked over to Kat. "I'm not going to screw this up," she said.

Kat let her head fall onto Sarah's shoulder. They had agreed that slow and steady would win the race. This was not a sprint and they both knew it. This was the marathon. Kat knew that Sarah was right. She couldn't help but feel they were hanging on at the last mile marker with no end in sight. It seemed crazy when Kat took a moment to analyze it. After all the time that had passed, all the upheaval, all the changes, and the emotions that she, Sarah, and Neil had suffered through, taking time should have been easy. Somehow, for Kat, all of that made it infinitely more difficult. She felt as if she had woken up from a crazy dream. Suddenly, Kat had clarity. Her life was meant to be spent beside Sarah.

Sarah had pointed out that Kat had been through an enormous amount of upheaval in a short time. She had shared her life with Neil for the last thirteen years. She'd been married to him for seven, had raised Brie with him for six; ending that part of her life deserved a period of healing. Starting a new relationship with Sarah was part of that, but Sarah wanted Kat to give herself time to adjust. And, Sarah understood that she and Kat were not the only two people who would need to adjust to the new dynamic between them. There was Neil, who she was surprised seemed supportive. Kat's mother would likely prove a challenge. Sarah's parents had already guessed that something had changed. Sarah could tell her mother had concerns for them all, but she was confident that her parents would not only accept, but support whatever Kat and Sarah decided was best for them. And then there was Brie. Brie was a bright child. Six was not sixteen. Sarah wasn't sure what Brie understood and what she didn't understand. She did know that eventually Brie would have questions. She and Kat had become more demonstrative and open as the days passed. Sarah had expressed all her concerns to Kat. She wanted to be cautious and compassionate. Time, Sarah had argued was an asset in this case.

Kat agreed—to a point; a point that was growing finer by the minute. She was tired of worrying about how everyone else would react. Nothing was going to change the course that she and Sarah were on. There wasn't going to be any going back. The only direction they could take was forward. And, the more time that passed, the more determined Kat became to walk that path openly and soon.

Kat and Sarah had been spending as much time together as they could. Sarah had been engaged in making plans to start a new legal practice locally. Kat was teaching during the day. Normally, Brie spent an hour or two with Deborah after school. Now, most days Sarah met Brie at school and they walked back to Kat's house together. Sarah helped Brie with her reading and her spelling. Kat would arrive home at four-thirty to find the pair creating some unique cuisine for their dinner. Sarah seemed to enjoy teaching Brie, and Brie delighted in teasing her aunt. Every so often, Sarah let Brie get creative in the kitchen. The results, while not always a culinary delight, amused Kat endlessly—grilled peanut butter sandwiches with French fries in the mix, macaroni and cheese with chicken nuggets mixed in, complete with a side of ketchup, cheeseburgers with tater tots on top—okay, Kat had to admit that one had been pretty good. It didn't matter to Kat what was placed in front of her. Watching Brie follow Sarah around while Sarah gently teased and instructed her made Kat's heart sing.

After dinner, the threesome would play a game or take a walk. When Brie crawled into bed, Sarah and Kat would make their way to cuddle on the couch. They spent long hours talking and even longer hours in silence, soaking in their new reality. They hadn't made love. Sarah insisted that they wait until they could be together the next morning. Kat's desire to be with Sarah was growing by the moment. She was sure that Sarah shared her frustration. Tender kisses and caresses were becoming more difficult to contain. Earlier that week, Sarah's lips had strayed to Kat's neck and Kat nearly ended the suffering for them both. She longed to be in Sarah's arms—no longer a friend seeking comfort, but a lover craving connection.

"Sarah…"

"Kat, we'll get there."

Kat took a deep breath, looked Sarah squarely in the eye, and nodded. "I understand not living here," she said. "But, when you come back this waiting is over."

Sarah's body quivered in response. Kat's words were not playful. Sarah nodded. Nothing about the road they had traveled nor the relationship they shared fit any stereotype Sarah knew. There had been no textbook written on what to do when you loved your brother's wife. And, Sarah was sure, no one offered a class on how to handle a situation like hers—your brother leaving the love of your life. That woman finding refuge in your arms, and you contemplating when you could finally marry her. No—not typical—complicated, convoluted, and terrifying. Kat knew Sarah better than anyone. Kat was right. It was time to move forward. Kat had been right about everything she had said. Sarah needed to let go of the past, and she needed to embrace the future. She smiled and kissed Kat on the forehead.

"Pretty determined," Sarah observed.

"I need you, Sarah. I need all of you."

"And, Brie?"

"I'll talk to her," Kat promised.

Sarah released a nervous sigh.

"She'll be fine. She's six," Kat said.

"I hope so."

Kat offered Sarah a grin. "Trying to get out of it?"

Sarah cupped Kat's cheek. "Never."

"Good."

"Let me finish breakfast," Sarah suggested. "Before your daughter finds some ancient Tootsie Rolls and decides we should add them to the mix."

"Since when do you not like Tootsie Rolls?" Kat asked.

"I like them just fine. I like your teeth better."

Kat laughed. She watched fondly as Sarah returned to making their breakfast. The morning had turned more emotional than Kat had expected. Oddly, it left her feeling more peaceful than anxious. She had meant everything she told Sarah. Kat was ready to move on. She'd realized she had been existing in her marriage to Neil for more than a few years. She had no regrets about the track her life had taken. Neil had been a caring husband and he was an attentive father. Sharing their lifetime together would be tied up in the two people they both loved the most—Brie and Sarah. It might not make sense to people looking in. It made perfect sense to Kat. She didn't need to ask to know that Neil and Sarah felt the same way. Knowing they were all on the same page gave her the confidence everything would work out. Brie would take her cues from the three of them. And, when it came right down to it, the only people that mattered had already accepted the truth.

***

"Why did we decide to do this?" Neil asked.

"Drive across the country together?"

Neil laughed. "I only did it because you offered to pay for all the food I wanted."

"Shocking."

Neil kept his eyes on the road as he cautiously began to wade into a deeper topic. "Sarah?"

"Don't tell me you're hungry again?"

"No." He chuckled. "I'm sorry."

"For eating my salary?" Sarah asked.

"For being an asshole."

Sarah swallowed hard.

"I'm serious. You didn't deserve what I said to you. You didn't deserve that show I put on either."

"It's ancient history."

"Not really," he disagreed.

"Neil, it's over."

"Maybe."

"It is."

"This is why I wanted to drive together."

"Why is that?" Sarah asked.

"So, you couldn't escape."

"Don't go there."

"Come on, Sarah. Don't you think it's time we cleared the air?"

Sarah did not have any desire to clear the air. "I came prepared." She pointed to the air freshener draped over the mirror."

"Why do you always do that?"

"What? Your farts stink more now."

Neil laughed despite his frustration. "Yours aren't exactly rose petals."

"No. More like violets."

"Right. I'm serious."

"So, am I, and not just about your farts. Let it go, Neil. It was a long time ago."

"Maybe it is for you. I've relived that day over and over again."

Sarah looked out her window. She'd relived the same day countless times, at some of the most inopportune moments. "Why did you keep going?" she finally asked the question that had been on her mind for years.

"It hurt you."

Sarah closed her eyes as a wave of pain flooded her soul. "Why?"

"I don't know," he confessed, happy to have the road ahead to focus on. "I don't know. All I know is that the minute you walked away, I felt like shit."

"It would've happened anyway."

"Yeah, it would've. I could have pretended not to see you."

"You could have."

"I'm sorry," he said. "And, I'm sorry for what I said when I came home. The truth is I was angry at you."

"For what?"

"I always thought that one day you would fall out of love with Kat. I thought when you met Beth… And, then at the wedding, I knew that was never going to happen. Back then, at least, I thought I would always be in love with Kat. Turns out you bested me there too."

"Jesus, Neil." Sarah took a moment to consider a reply. "Do you know how many times I wished that I didn't love Kat?"

"Yeah, I can imagine."

"When Beth left me, I hated myself."

"Is that why you've never had another girlfriend?"

"I couldn't do that again," Sarah said. "I was never going to stop loving Kat."

"I know."

"I never tried to come between you," Sarah said.

Neil glanced over and smiled. "You are a bigger person than me, Sis."

"No," Sarah disagreed. "Just a different person."

"Listen," he said. "I know she wants to be with you. It sucks."

"I'm sorry."

"Nah, I left. It was the right thing to do. Not the way I did it. I just had to get out of there."

"I get it."

"You do?"

Sarah nodded. "More than you think."

"Anyway, I don't want you to hold back with her because of me."

Sarah sighed.

"What?"

"I'm worried about Brie," Sarah said.

Neil reached over and patted his sister's knee. "I wouldn't worry too much about Brie."

"Why not?"

"She's a lot like you, Sarah. She'll be okay."

"She's a lot like you and Kat," Sarah said.

"Yeah, she is. We've made it this far. Just don't tell her where that cave is."

Sarah laughed through a few tears. "Deal, as long as you promise never to unearth Buddy."

"Buddy? I tossed him in the garbage years ago."

"You did?"

"Yeah. I just liked making you think he was hanging around in a box somewhere, ready to spring at any minute."

"Asshole."

Neil laughed. "Guilty."

"Hey, Neil?"

'Yeah?"

"I love you. If you ever tell anyone I admitted that, I'll kick your ass."

"I love you too, even if you are a jerk."

Chapter Thirteen: All the Way Home

"Mom!" Brie called out.

Kat followed the sound of Brie's excited cry to the front door. She sighed happily at the sight of the woman approaching the front porch.

"Auntie Sarah's home!" Brie opened the front door and jumped through.

Kat stepped out onto the porch and smiled as Sarah ambled up the driveway.

Brie flew off the front steps and bolted for her aunt. "Sarah!"

"Hey, String Bean. Did you miss me?" Sarah asked, crouching down to hug her niece.

"Mom made pie."

Sarah grinned and then looked up at Kat standing on the porch. The sight stole the air from her lungs. She'd never missed Kat as much in her life. "Pie, huh?" Sarah asked, her attention squarely on Kat. She took a deep breath, stood up straight and lifted Brie onto her hip.

Kat smiled at Sarah as Sarah closed the distance between them.

"God, you got heavy!" Sarah teased Brie as she set her on the porch.

Brie giggled.

"Why don't you get some plates out?" Kat suggested to her daughter.

"Okay!" Brie skipped back through the front door.

Sarah's voice nearly failed her. The only word she managed was, "Hi."

Kat's heart ached to hold Sarah. Seeing Sarah standing before her meant more to Kat than any moment she could recall. Sarah was *home*. She smiled. "Hi."

Sarah searched Kat's eyes. Kat's eyes twinkled with a golden hue that Sarah had come to understand reflected deep emotion. She moved a step closer and took Kat's face in her hands. "I missed you."

Kat closed her eyes when Sarah's lips met hers. She clasped Sarah's waist to steady herself. "I missed you," she whispered.

Sarah's forehead fell softly against Kat's. She felt Kat's arms wrap around her waist and pull her closer. "I'm home, Kat."

Kat pulled back to look in Sarah's eyes. "Yes, you are."

"Sarah!" Brie's voice called. She stepped into the doorway and rolled her eyes. "Are you guys kissing again?" Brie rolled her eyes.

Sarah's cheeks flushed with embarrassment. Kat laughed. She kept her eyes locked with Sarah's when she addressed her daughter. "Yes, we are," she said. Kat placed a sweet kiss on Sarah's lips and turned to face Brie. "And, you're next!" Kat wigged her eyebrows.

Brie took off in a sprint with Kat on her heels. "Mom!" Brie cried with delight.

Sarah stepped through the screen door. Kat was lightly tickling Brie on the couch. Brie's laughter lifted through the air. Sarah looked on fondly. Home. *I'm home.*

"Penny for your thoughts?" Kat asked.

"I'm not sure they're worth that much."

Kat shifted in Sarah's embrace and looked at her. "Are you okay?"

Sarah was better than okay. She was also terrified. She had enjoyed the day with Kat and Brie. They immediately fell back into their usual routine. She knew Kat was curious about her trip to California. She also sensed that Kat had no intention of allowing them to sleep apart for one more night.

"You haven't said much about the trip," Kat commented.

"You mean I haven't said anything about my conversation with Beth," Sarah replied.

"Do you want to talk about it?"

Sarah nodded and closed her eyes. "She was amazing." When Sarah opened her eyes, she was surprised to see Kat smiling. "What?"

"She loves you," Kat said.

"In her way."

"Well, it might not matter what I think, but…"

"It always matters to me what you think," Sarah said.

"I think," Kat said, "that if you truly love someone, you will always love them. Life changes. There's no way to stop that. Beth loved you, Sarah. Anyone would have to be blind not to notice that."

"I know," Sarah admitted.

"And, maybe you realize how much you did love her," Kat guessed.

"I guess maybe I did realize that."

"And, that's bothering you?" Kat asked.

"No," Sarah said assuredly. "She wasn't surprised—about us, I mean. She was happy for me. I know that she was. It hurt her. I know that too."

"What did she say?" Kat asked.

"She said that she worried I might never be happy because she didn't think I would ever give myself a chance."

Kat nodded. "With someone else."

"Yeah, but also with you," Sarah explained. She took a deep breath. "The night that Beth left me, she said something right before she walked out the door."

Kat was curious.

"I'll never forget it. She stopped, turned around and looked me directly in the eye. She said, 'If you love her, Sarah, if you love Kat that much, you owe it to yourself to let her know. You owe it to her.' Then, she picked up her bag, opened the door, and walked through it."

Kat reached over and squeezed Sarah's hand.

"I swear to you, Kat—I swear, I thought my heart was broken beyond repair long before that. The second that door shut?" Sarah closed her eyes again and shook her head. "Those words, watching her back as she walked out that door—I swear, my heart shattered into a million pieces. I realized that I had been so consumed in my pain, I never stopped to realize how much I hurt everyone else."

"Sarah."

Sarah opened her eyes. Kat wiped a few tears from Sarah's cheeks.

"Beth is happy," Sarah said. "And, she was happy for me—for us."

"That surprised you?" Kat wondered.

"I don't know. She said that we both landed where we were supposed to. And, the truth is, I'm not sure we would have if we had never loved each other."

Kat smiled.

"What?" Sarah asked.

"You finally realize that loving Beth was never a betrayal of me?"

Sarah chuckled. "I suppose I have."

Kat edged forward. She stroked Sarah's cheek. "I'm glad that you talked to her."

"She asked me to be the baby's godmother," Sarah said.

"Smart choice."

"I hope so."

"Sarah, you're amazing with kids."

"I hope I do okay with them both."

Kat stood up and held out her hand. "Come on."

Sarah accepted Kat's hand. She felt the gentle squeeze of reassurance that Kat offered. "Kat, I…"

"Sarah, no more running."

Sarah nodded. Her heart had begun to thrum in her chest like the roar of a race car engine. Kat sensed Sarah's uneasiness and squeezed her hand again gently. Sarah followed Kat, praying her knees could support her weight to the top of the stairs. She hesitated when Kat opened the bedroom door. Kat tugged gently on her hand. Sarah nearly fainted when Kat moved past her and shut the door.

Kat stepped into Sarah's arms and brushed Sarah's hair aside. "I love you," she said.

"I love you," Sarah replied.

Kat placed a tender kiss on Sarah's lips. "Sarah," she whispered. She placed her hand on Sarah's chest and felt the ferocious pounding of Sarah's heart. "If all you do is hold me, that will be enough—at least, for tonight."

Sarah closed her eyes. "I don't know if I can do that."

"Sarah…"

Sarah chuckled nervously and opened her eyes again. "Just hold you, I mean."

"You've done it a million times. It's just me."

Sarah's lips found Kat's. She let the kiss deepen gradually. It was hardly the first time she had tasted Kat's lips. As Kat's searching continued to softly tempt Sarah, Sarah realized that this moment differed from all those that had passed before it. She pushed Kat away gently.

"Sarah?"

Sarah shook her head in amazement. "I don't want to leave."

"Then don't."

"No, I don't mean tonight. I mean ever."

"Then don't."

Sarah sucked in a ragged breath. "If I stay… Kat, I don't think I will be able to leave again."

"I don't want you to leave," Kat said. "I want you here. I want you here when I wake up in the morning. I want to feel you next to me when I fall asleep at night. I want to sit with you on that front porch when Brie brings her first boyfriend home. I want to dance with you at her wedding."

"You mean like fifty years from now?" Sarah joked.

Kat smiled, but remained focused. Emotional conversations sometimes challenged Sarah. As much as Sarah reveled in mastering a challenge, the one challenge she still avoided facing was laying her emotions bare—even to Kat. Kat cupped Sarah's face in her hands. "That's the point. You've been my best friend for nearly my entire life," she continued.

"I want you to be my partner for the rest of it—in everything, in every part. And, I don't want to wait any longer to start. I don't want to wake up one more day without you."

Sarah studied the brown eyes before her. *Kat.* A million memories flooded her thoughts in a single second. Images rushed by, each one highlighted by the warmth and love reflected in the brown eyes searching her blue. Sarah's hand fell to the bottom of Kat's T-shirt. Kat smiled, giving silent permission for Sarah to continue. Sarah lifted Kat's shirt over her head in one fluid motion. She willed her eyes to remain riveted to Kat's even as her fingertips sought to explore the softness of Kat's skin.

Kat's eyes danced as they watched Sarah's expression change from apprehension to anticipation. Sarah's fingers tentatively explored the outline of Kat's bra. Kat reached behind her back and released the clasp. She forced herself not to laugh at the gasp that escaped Sarah's mouth. She tossed the article aside and noted that Sarah's hand began to tremble against her. She reached out and directed Sarah's hand over her breast.

Sarah's heart resumed its frenetic pace. It hammered so hard that she wondered if it might explode. Kat was softer than Sarah had dared imagine, and she had done a lot of imagining over the years. She watched her hand as it explored the curves of Kat's breasts. Her hand began to quiver, and Kat covered it with hers.

"Sarah," Kat called. Tenderly, she lifted her hand to caress Sarah's cheek. A million emotions painted the blue irises imploring her for safety and assurance. She wiped a tear from the corner of Sarah's eye. "I'm not leaving either," she promised.

"I never want to disappoint you," Sarah confessed.

Kat always found Sarah's vulnerability endearing. "You have never disappointed me," she said. "Not once."

Kat began to unbutton the shirt Sarah wore, steadily holding Sarah's gaze. Her hands pushed the shirt gently off Sarah's shoulders. Kat smiled at Sarah's sharp intake of breath when the shirt fell to the floor. In a million years, Kat would never have imagined that she would take the lead in this scenario. Looking at Sarah, it made perfect sense. Sarah had always led Kat through adventures. Kat had always kept Sarah steady. This *was* their dance. Sarah was creative and impulsive. Kat was intuitive and careful. They balanced each other. Kat shook her head softly. How had she missed it all those years? She'd loved Sarah Masters for a lifetime. Funny—the way something could be staring you in the face and you somehow failed to recognize it. She took a deep breath and said a silent prayer of thanks for the woman standing before her.

Kat freed Sarah of her clothing. She spoke no words. No words needed to be spoken. Holding Sarah's gaze, Kat removed her jeans and tossed them aside. She stepped into Sarah's embrace and kissed her lovingly. Kat's hands traveled sensually over the back of Sarah's neck, content to enjoy the connection of their kiss.

Sarah lost herself in Kat's tender caress. She guided them softly to the bed and laid Kat back onto it. She stared down at Kat in awe. Kat was the most beautiful person Sarah had ever known. She'd learned what love was from the woman in her arms. Sarah had never needed to examine the past to understand when she had fallen in love with Katelyn Summers. Love happened the moment she saw a twelve-year-old girl sitting on the sidewalk holding her scraped knee. Kat's eyes glistened with the same wonder and curiosity that captured Sarah's heart all those years ago. She placed a sweet kiss on Kat's lips. "I love you," Sarah said. "I've always loved you, and I always will."

Sarah's tenderness never ceased to amaze Kat. Behind the comedienne, the adventurer, and the achiever that most people saw in Sarah Masters, lay the kindest, softest heart Kat could imagine. Sarah never did anything half-way. Loving was no exception. Kat closed her eyes and gave over to Sarah's touch. She'd never desired the touch of another person the way she did Sarah's now. "Touch me," she told Sarah.

Sarah's lips moved down Kat's neck to her shoulder, tasting and teasing Kat's flesh in a painfully slow descent. She had waited a lifetime for this moment—to feel Kat in her arms, to speak her truth to Kat without any words clouding it.

Kat's hands traveled up and down Sarah's back gently. Quietly urging Sarah to continue. She lost her breath when Sarah's lips circled her nipple. Kat thought she had experienced making love. Perhaps, she had. As Sarah's tongue explored her body, Kat realized that making love was a rare experience. It differed with each person. Making love with the person you were meant to find, the person you were meant to love, that experience was incomparable to anything in the world. The racing of her heart was familiar. She could recall the tingling on her skin that signified anticipation. But amid those familiar sensations an indescribable fullness arose within her. Sarah's touch was not only arousing, it was all-encompassing. Sarah was running through her—part of her.

Sarah glanced up at Kat. Kat's eyes were closed. She wondered what images might be playing in Kat's mind. Her fingertip replaced the exploration her lips had enjoyed. She could touch Kat forever and never grow tired. If she died here in Kat's arms, Sarah would leave the world feeling complete. Something had always been missing for Sarah. She'd accomplished every goal she had ever set. She'd traveled the world. She'd loved, and she had been loved. Somehow, there seemed to be one missing piece in the puzzle of her life that she could never find. Kat's eyes opened and met Sarah's. Sarah smiled as the final piece clicked into place.

Kat watched in rapt fascination as Sarah's kiss meandered over her stomach. She swore she could hear the blood rushing through her veins. Sarah's hands caressed the softness of Kat's sides as she continued her descent. Kat ran her fingers through Sarah's hair in encouragement. She bit her lip when Sarah reached her destination. The warmth of Sarah's tongue bathed Kat's center in a loving caress. Kat's head fell back onto the pillow. She gripped the sheets, desperately seeking anything to ground her.

Sarah took hold of Kat's right hand with her left and held it. She felt Kat's thumb stroke the back of her hand, imploring her to continue and reminding Sarah that she desired this moment equally. Sarah heard Kat's breathing transcend into a series of soft moans. The sound fueled her need to feel Kat let go.

"Sarah." Kat's strained voice choked on the name.

Sarah answered the plea by entering Kat gently. Kat's hips lifted to meet her. Sarah fought the urge to relieve the ache that had taken up residence in her core. She could feel her body moving in time with Kat's, desperately wanting to feel Kat fall into her—desperately desiring to fall into Kat.

Kat felt the warmth of Sarah's arousal brush against her leg and sucked in a ragged breath. It heightened her need to touch Sarah. A dance—this was meant to be a dance. Kat gripped Sarah's hand and tugged lightly. "Sarah," she pleaded.

Sarah pulled away slightly and looked at Kat.

"I need to feel you," Kat said. Sarah's confusion brought a smile to Kat's lips. She reached out and guided Sarah up to face her.

"Kat?"

"I need to feel you," Kat repeated. Sarah was still puzzled. Kat giggled. *Sarah.* "I want to touch you," she explained. Sarah's mouth fell open. Kat brought their lips together. "Please," Kat urged.

Sarah would never deny Kat anything. She held Kat's gaze as Kat's hand wandered to her breast.

Kat's heart pounded wildly. She had imagined that she would feel some trepidation in touching Sarah. Being close to Sarah was the most natural sensation in the world. She didn't need instruction. She understood the woman next to her unlike anyone else. Her hand journeyed lower, enjoying the dips and curves of Sarah's body along the way. She looked in Sarah's eyes. "My God," Kat whispered when her touch met with the soft warmth of Sarah's need.

Sarah struggled to keep her eyes open. *Dear God. She's going to kill me.* Sarah lowered her touch to Kat's center. Kat's lips found hers immediately, silencing both their cries.

Kat moved in time with Sarah. The need to remain connected to Sarah consumed her. She gentled her kiss when Sarah's shuddering began. The sensation of Sarah quivering against her sent Kat soaring and she could no longer resist the urge to make her pleasure known.

"Sarah!" Kat cried out.

Kat's cry was Sarah's undoing. Her body thrashed against her will and fell into Kat's. Kat refused to release her. "Kat… Jesus…. What are you…"

Kat had no conscious thought as she flipped Sarah beneath her. She'd never desired anything or anyone the way she craved Sarah. Without reservation or invitation, Kat lowered herself to taste Sarah.

Sarah was stunned into silence. A momentary inclination to resist was banished the second Kat's mouth began to explore her.

Kat's hands held Sarah's hips as if they were a lifeline. The notion that making love to Sarah could be more arousing than Sarah's touch seemed inconceivable. Then again, inconceivable became reality when it came to loving Sarah Masters. That had always been the case. Making love proved no exception. Nothing on earth moved Kat the way giving to Sarah could. Sometimes, Sarah resisted accepting love from others. Kat's entire body hummed at the realization that Sarah had given over to her completely. She pulled Sarah closer until she felt Sarah's body quake violently. Sarah tried to pull away. Kat held her firmly until she felt the waves of pleasure in Sarah's body give way to gentle ripples.

Kat kissed her way back up Sarah's body until their eyes met again. "Thank you."

Sarah shook her head. "What?"

"Thank you for letting me love you," Kat said. Her tears broke forth, cascading down her cheeks in long streams. "I do, Sarah. I love you so much."

"I know," Sarah said. She wiped away Kat's tears and kissed her lips reverently. "I know," she promised. She pulled Kat into her arms and held her close.

"Sarah?"

"Hmm?"

Kat's fingertips traced circles on Sarah's chest. "I missed you so much. I didn't know how much. I don't know why it took me so long to realize it."

Sarah pulled Kat closer, and kissed the top of Kat's head. "You never have to miss me again."

Kat sighed and closed her eyes, praying that she would never wake up alone again. A day without Sarah seemed too long. Inevitably, she knew that the day would come. "I love you," she promised.

Two Years Later
Halloween

"This feels vaguely familiar," Sarah commented to her reflection in the mirror.

"What's that?"

"Why?" Sarah asked. "What is your obsession with orange. And, do *not* tell me this is Autumn Leaf or some ridiculous thing like that."

"No, honey, this one is pumpkin."

"Why do I love you?" Sarah asked.

Kat shrugged. "I think you make a lovely pumpkin."

"You would." Sarah looked at Kat looking at her in the mirror. "I'd tell you to hold me because I'm afraid, but I don't think your arms will wrap around me."

Kat laughed.

"Why do you get to be the ghost?" Sarah asked.

"When *you* make the costumes, you can choose the role."

"Oh, I see how it is."

"Good."

Sarah shook her head. "Where is the string bean?"

"Downstairs with Daddy."

"And, why doesn't my brother have to dress up as a squash?"

"Stop complaining, He didn't."

"Because he's dressed as a NASCAR driver! It's like his wet dream!'

Kat spun Sarah around, and kissed her. "You look adorable."

"You are so lucky I love you."

"Mm."

"And, I'm not wearing orange next weekend."

"Is something happening next weekend that I should know about?" Kat teased.

"Yeah, a pumpkin and ghost are getting married. It's a twisted version of *Into the Woods*, called *Beyond the Garden*."

Kat shook her head. "Want to back out?"

"No way. I've been chasing that ghost for a lifetime."

"You do love your *Ghostbusters*," Kat teased.

"Never gonna let that go, are you?"

"Not likely."

"Mom!"

"Oh, looks like you need to float downstairs," Sarah said.

"Need a hand?" Kat asked.

"No, I can waddle on my own," Sarah promised.

"You are very talented that way," Kat agreed.

Sarah looked at herself in the mirror one last time. "The things you do for love."

———◆•◆———

A Week Later

Simple. Sarah was grateful that Kat agreed to a simple exchange of vows. She imagined it would've seemed strange to most people. Neil would stand by her side when she promised her future to Kat. Brie would stand with Kat. It made perfect sense to all of them. Questions often had open-ended answers. Sarah learned that the hard way. The answer to a question often changed. Life was never static. Love was anything but stolid. Life and love flowed together, then apart, and together again. Both came into existence without your permission, and both required work. Sarah spent many hours examining life and love, how they came to be, how they ebbed and flowed like a river. She hadn't chosen to be born. She hadn't made the choice to fall in love with Kat. In all her searching for answers, Sarah inevitably found more questions to pose. Her constant quest for answers was a living lawyer joke waiting for delivery. Long before Sarah considered her career choice, she would lie awake and ponder why life happened, how love came to be and what it all meant. "How did that work out for you?" she chuckled.

"I'm almost afraid to ask what that question is about?"

Sarah turned and smiled at Kat. "Ask me later."

"Are you ready?"

"For what?"

"Cute." Kat held out her hand. "Mom and Dad are downstairs."

"Kat?"

"Yeah?"

"Thanks."

"For?"

"Not making me wear orange again."

Kat rolled her eyes. "Let's go."

———◆◆◆———

Neil leaned in and whispered in Sarah's ear. "You okay?"

"I might throw up."

"I remember that feeling."

"I hope I remember what I wrote," she told him.

"Sarah, you argue cases daily."

"So not the same thing."

Kat squeezed Sarah's hand.

The Justice of the Peace addressed Kat and Sarah. "Are you ready?"

Kat smiled. Sarah nodded.

"Katelyn?" She directed Kat to speak.

Kat looked at Sarah and smiled brightly. "Well, here we are," she said. "I can't believe it took us so long to get here," she admitted. "I do know I'm glad we found our way. I'm not sure it's possible to sum up what I feel. I know this much, I love you more with each day that passes. You've been part of the most wonderful, and even the most difficult moments of my life, Sarah. The day we met, I knew you would be. I can't explain that. I remember that all I wanted to do was go home. Here I was in this strange place. I didn't know anyone. I wanted to run away. I even plotted a way to do it." Kat chuckled at the memory. "First, I had to figure out how I was going to get to the train station. I took out my bike."

Sarah listened. Kat had never told her this story.

"I was going to find my way. That was my plan until I crashed. I looked up into this pair of sparkling blue eyes. In that moment, I knew I was already home."

Tears trailed over Sarah's cheeks. She made no effort to conceal them or beat them in to submission. All these years later, Kat was telling her that she felt the same thing Sarah had from the moment they met.

"I wish I could tell you that I knew what that meant back then. I didn't. You always looked at the world with wide eyes and wonderment. My field of view was a bit narrower. You can call it short-sightedness. I do."

Sarah shook her head. *No.*

"Now, I know that I l loved you from that first moment. You were always my safe harbor, Sarah. You have also always been the person who challenges me to dream, to look beyond what is right in front of me. More than that, to look inside myself. When I do? Do you know what I see?"

Sarah shook her head again.

"You. I see you." Kat took a deep breath. "And, for the rest of our lives that is what I intend to remind you—you are the biggest part of me, Sarah. You're not just my past or my future. You're my life."

Sarah heard the direction for her to speak.

"Kat," Sarah paused to still a rising tide of emotion. "You know, there isn't any adventure that compares to loving you. All the schemes, all the crazy places I led you when we were kids, and all the stories I told you while we sat under that tree, they were all about you. You were the adventure. You are the adventure. I didn't care where we went. I'm your safe harbor? Kat, you've saved me over and over again. I remember the day we met as clearly as if it were yesterday. I lost my heart that day. I never asked for it back. I never *wanted* it back. It wasn't always the *safest* place to be. I don't think that loving someone is about being sheltered. Loving you... Loving you isn't a choice. I don't know if that's destiny or not. I do know that if I were given a choice, I would choose you over and over and over again. I wouldn't change a moment of our past—not one. That might surprise some people. It's the truth. I can't imagine our life without Brie. I wouldn't want to. To be honest, I'm not sure how you've put up with me all these years."

Kat giggled.

"I've gotten you into more than a few pickles. I'll assume that dressing me as squashes is your payback."

"Maybe," Kat whispered.

Sarah faltered. Kat squeezed her hand.

"I love you so much," Sarah said simply. "More than anything. I think you can love many people. I think you can find endless places that hold your interest and where you might want to linger and explore. You only get one home— only one. That's you. God knows, I took a lot of wrong turns on my way. The only turn I needed to make was a U-turn, back here, all the way home to you. You've always been home for me. And, I promise, I will give everything I have and all that I am to be that for you and Brie."

Kat wiped away Sarah's tears. She heard the Justice of the Peace make her proclamation. She didn't need any papers or ceremonies to solidify her commitment to Sarah. Sarah? Sarah might not have needed it either. Sarah deserved it. Kat stopped Sarah before Sarah kissed her.

"You," Kat began, "have always been my home, Sarah. Always." Her lips found Sarah's.

Brie jumped up and down.

"Someone's a little exited," Kat commented.

"Bananas!" Brie cheered.

"What?" Sarah laughed.

"There's bananas on the cake!" Brie pointed to the kitchen.

"What is she talking about?" Sarah asked Kat.

"You'll see."

Brie pulled Sarah and Kat into the kitchen.

Sarah shook her head. "Only you, Kat."

Kat grinned triumphantly. The small wedding cake that sat on the table was adorned by a sprinkling of sliced banana, a few Kit Kats, and at its center sat a toy bicycle lying on its side.

"I helped!" Brie exclaimed.

"I'll bet you did." Sarah kissed Brie's head.

"The bike was Mom's idea."

Sarah laughed. "You really are something else, Kit Kat."

"What might that something else be?" Kat asked.

Sarah's hand pressed to Kat's cheek. "Everything," she said. *Home, Kat, you're home.*